I0633204

MARKED

POPULATIONS CRUMBLE: RESURGENCE, BOOK ONE

K. A. GANDY

THIGPEN-
GANDY
PUBLISHING

THIGPEN-GANDY PUBLISHING INC.

Copyright © 2023 by K. A. Gandy.

All rights reserved.

No portion of this book may be reproduced in any form without written permission from the publisher or author, except as permitted by U.S. copyright law.

This is a work of fiction. Names, characters, business, events and incidents are the products of the author's imagination. Any resemblance to actual persons, living or dead, or actual events is purely coincidental.

CONTENTS

CHAPTER ONE

THE MAN IN BLACK

DEMY

The man in black found me yesterday. I was able to slip away for the night, but he's getting closer. It's awful timing, him cropping up *right now*—as I'm only two blocks from the bus stop—but I just caught a glimpse of his hood again. For the last six years, whenever one of them catches my trail, I lie low until they lose my tracks, and then hop the next bus or train out of town and hit the farthest tri-state I can afford the fare to.

Simple. Clean. Safe.

Unfortunately, that's not an option right now. I *have* to be at the bus stop at three p.m. The shuttle only comes once a quarter, and I'm not going to make it another three months. I look down at my banged-up watch and see there are only fifteen minutes left. Making a split-second decision, I take a hard left into the alley in front of me, and duck into the side entrance of a smoke-filled bar. As soon as the door shuts behind me, I dash into the bathroom—a single stall, thankfully—and slide the bolt home.

I don't know what's changed since I turned eighteen, but I haven't made it a full month since without one of them finding me,

1

and it's freaking frustrating. What's changed? I have no idea. But after five months, I'm out of cash and out of options. I can't keep a job long enough to build up my cash cushion without getting busted again.

Which is why I finally pulled my last-resort card and contacted the New Life Center about getting matched.

Yes, I technically have six months left before the deadline to meet my genetic match and start popping out babies, but I don't have six more months of running in me. And I refuse to be caught.

My throat tightens involuntarily at the sudden memory that assaults me, and I lean back against the bathroom door, breathing in and out for a moment. If I don't, I'll get pulled into the nightmare, and I desperately can't afford that if I'm going to keep myself safe.

In through the nose, out through the mouth. Once more, then twice. My pulse slows, and my hands shake a little less where they're pressed against the door. *You're okay, Demy.*

I look down at the watch again, the peeling face reading 2:51. Nine minutes. A fist pounding the door at my back makes me jump away, and I spin to face the solid oak, lifting my hands into a fighting stance.

"Hey! I need to pee!" a drunk girl slurs on the other side, and I slowly let my hands drift back to my sides.

"I'm going to be a minute," I call back quietly.

"Hurry it up, would you? I've had—*hiccup*—a lot of beer, and I gotta *go.*"

I roll my eyes at her drunken urgency, but look around for a plan B. Her calling attention to this bathroom is the exact last thing that I need. I spot a high, small window about two feet below the ceiling. It should lead back to the alley, and then it's a five-minute walk to the bus stop. Two minutes, if I have to run for it.

My fingers drum restlessly against my thigh, and the back of my neck starts to itch as the pounding starts back up on the door again. The man in black has surely realized he's lost me by now. The only question is whether he's made it into the bar and is scanning the crowd for me, or he's kept walking, and is still circling back.

"Come *on*, lady! I don't even hear you flushing in there. What's the hold—" She stops abruptly, and I leap toward the window, attempting to wrench it open.

The pounding stops and her voice doesn't come back, but that just drives me harder to get my fingernails between the window frame and the casing it's seated in. She didn't just go away. Someone stopped her. The only downside of holing up in a bathroom is there's no way to see who's on the other side of that door.

Years' worth of untouched grime and gunk have built up in the window's track, effectively gluing it shut. No matter how hard I shove the little metal handle, it won't spin. I use my elbow while standing on my tiptoes, and bash as hard as I can against the frame, but it doesn't budge. Muttering a string of curses under my breath, I take a quick inventory of the bathroom, looking for anything that might get me out of here without unlocking that door or missing the bus.

My eyes land on a square towel bar, sunken into the ancient, crumbling bracket. Bracing one foot against the wall, I grab the end and pull with everything I've got.

The bar starts to bend, and then pulls free with a loud pop. The silence outside the door abruptly ends, the handle jiggling as someone on the other side tries to force it open.

With renewed vigor, I wedge the towel bar into the window, twisting as I shove, in the hopes that something gives. The frame creaks, the bar in my hands tries to bend, but a sliver of light appears around the window frame, and it creaks outward with painstaking slowness. As soon as there's enough room for my fingers, I abandon the towel bar and spin the handle as fast as I can to crank it all the way open.

I hear the lock *snick* behind me as I drop through the window, landing painfully on my shoulder and almost losing my flimsy duffel bag as I execute a messy roll away and stagger to my feet. I don't wait to see who's behind me, taking off at a dead run for the corner where the alley meets the road, thoughts of subtlety long gone.

The running jolts my shoulder, so I hang onto it as I sprint, trying to brace it against the jarring impact traveling up my body from the pavement. It doesn't work, but I don't stop. I can't stop.

Two minutes. I just need to last two minutes, and for the bus to be on time. I dodge and twist between people on the sidewalk, and nearly lose my footing as I slam into one who stepped the wrong way.

"Hey, watch it!" he hollers, but I don't respond. I see the road sign I need up ahead, and my entire being is focused on it. That's the road the bus stop is on, and that's the only chance I have for safety.

My lungs burn as I round the corner, darting in front of a sleek black car whose driver honks in annoyance. Footsteps pound the pavement behind me, and I push my muscles that last bit further as the bus comes into view.

It's there, and there is only one girl standing outside it, with a man in a suit holding a tablet to check her in. I grit my teeth as I let go of my aching shoulder, and pump both arms. Wind slices through my short hair as I cover the last bit of distance. The man reaches out and shakes the girl's hand, before gesturing up the stairs and into the bus.

They hear me coming and turn, wide-eyed as I skid to a stop, nearly bowling the poor girl over. The man reaches out a hand to steady me, but at my flinch he drops it without making contact.

"In a hurry there, are we?" he jokes, and gives a patronizing smile to the other girl, who's staring wide-eyed at me. I'm sure I'm a mess—sleeping on bathroom floors in bus stations will do that to a person—but I do my best to ignore her.

"I'm Demy Carlisle, here to check in. Quickly, please." I suck in a lungful of air, and do my best not to look back the direction I came from.

"Demy Carlisle, nice to meet you! Let me see, we have a Leilani, Camille, and Demelza—"

"Yes, that's me," I urge. "I'm Demelza. Can I go up now?"

His eyebrows shoot up, and he taps the tablet a few times before passing it to me. "You can, though I admit it's unusual for the girls to be so . . . eager."

"Uh huh." I quickly skim the page, scrawl a messy signature at the bottom without reading a word of it, and shove it back into his hands. It's been less than a minute, and that will have to be good enough. I charge up the stairs, and don't stop until I hit the back row of recliners. I take the window seat facing the street sign I'd turned at; within seconds I spot the man in black rounding the corner, nothing visible of his face, hidden deep in the recesses of a hood. The loose black robe hides any identifying details—a fact I learned was important the first time I tried to report my pursuers to the tri-state police. They'd hunt for the man in a robe, but every single time he'd disappeared—or he'd take off the robe, and leave them nothing to go on.

He runs a few more steps, then stops. To my surprise, for the first time since I've been pursued, the man lowers his hood, revealing his clean-shaven face, and an angry-looking red brand of some kind peeks out from his robe's collar on the side of his neck. Dead eyes stare in my direction, frowning over at the shuttle bus.

I'd like to blame the goosebumps that ripple over my arms on the cool wave of air conditioning surrounding me, but it has a lot more to do with those menacing eyes, which seem to connect with mine through the tinted shuttle windows. The man slowly backs away around the corner, and I blow out a shaky breath before resting my head against the back cushion of the recliner.

I got away, but now he knows exactly where I'm heading. Running my eyes over the ridiculously lavish interior of the bus, I spot a lone security guard, seated behind the driver.

Now I guess I wait and see if they're willing to risk snatching me from the New Life Center, surrounded by their attendants, guards, and cameras.

Well, not the only question.

I still don't know why they're following me, or why they killed my parents. Maybe with a reprieve from being hunted, I'll finally be able to figure it out.

CHAPTER TWO

GLAMOROUS

DEMY

I keep to myself in the back, and watch carefully from my recliner as two other girls enter the bus, but the man chasing me
never comes back. I still don't relax, though. He could be back any
minute; as long as we're parked here, I'm a sitting duck.

It's not until I hear the hiss of brakes being released and we pull
away from the curb that I allow my shoulders to un-knot and start
paying attention to the other two girls on this bus. One I saw at
check-in. She's got thick, dark hair almost to her waist, and deep
copper-toned skin. Her eyes were wide when I leapt past her into
the bus, but once she boarded she sat quietly as well, in one of the
middle seats. The other girl is a pint-sized redhead, who barely
comes up to my armpit. She strode onto the bus like she owned
the dang thing, and took the entire first row with her several small
bags.

The suited man stands once we are on the main road, and gives
us all a welcoming smile.

"Hello, everyone. My name is Jones, and I'll be your attendant
on this journey, as well as a helper once we arrive at the New Life

Center. Things have changed in the past year and a half, and we're all trying to adapt to the new normal here in the NAA. Overall, I think you'll find the changes to be positive, with King Patrick and Queen Sadie paying a lot of attention to the details of this program, and how to make it better. If you're unaware—though it's unlikely, unless you've completely avoided all news for the past few years—"

That'd be me.

"We have an informational video to catch you up to speed. We have a long journey ahead of us, so please settle in, and let us know if you need anything at all; we're here to support you during this exciting new phase of your life."

Jones gives us all a smile, and sits down in a special seat up front with the driver, which faces back towards the three of us instead of forward to the road. I expected there to be a single large screen upfront, but am surprised when a blinking blue light catches my attention to my left. There is a large tablet lying on top of an armoire, blinking with a silver play button. I hadn't even noticed the tiny, carved armoire next to my seat when I climbed aboard, but sure enough I not only have an oversized plush recliner, I also have a small cabinet with more things than I could ever think to want. One by one, I pull out each drawer, finding hair ties, palettes of makeup, headphones, and at the very bottom, a teeny-tiny fridge with bottled waters and fruit.

I snatch a piece of fruit—my first food since yesterday—and the headphones. Three bites into my banana, I take a deep breath through my nose and press play on the tablet.

A beautiful young woman with her deep chestnut hair pulled back from her face, and a delicate, silvery floral circlet on her head appears on the screen. She gives the camera a warm smile, and when she speaks, her light country accent surprises me.

"Hello, and welcome. My name is Sadie, and I wanted to give you some more information about the program you're embarking on, and check in with you about how you're feeling. I recently found myself sitting exactly where you are today, and the experience has changed my life forever." She bites her lip and drops her hand to her belly, and I realize she was pregnant when this was filmed.

"For me, it turned into a beautiful love match. However, we now know that not everyone had that same experience. That is why Patrick and I are working to change that. There are some key things you need to know. But first, I want to tell you that no matter how you feel today, it is going to be okay."

There is a firm conviction on her face that I want to admire, but I also distrust it. The idea of her being able to just declare everything *okay* is ludicrous to me. My life has never been okay, not for going on six years. Although, I have to admit that fresh food, a comfy recliner, and a mountain of unexpected luxuries could mean my life is taking a turn for the better. The cost is my freedom, though, and I'm not going to forget what I'm giving up. I shake my head and force myself to pay attention to what she's saying.

"—which is why we've put a team of women in place to handle all issues you may come across. I want to make it very clear: this is *your* life, *your* body, and *your* future. Does humanity need more babies to be born? Absolutely. Are we willing to put your safety at risk to accomplish that? No. *Absolutely not.* So please, do not hesitate to reach out at any time. There will be an icon on each of your provided devices with the ability to contact someone on my response team twenty-four seven. You are not alone in this, and we are here for you, and any concerns you may have." She gives a decided nod, and starts pointing to the side of the screen like

9

a weather woman, where a small help icon displays for a second before disappearing.

"Now, we've tried to make things as easy as possible, while also providing you more options. Depending on your intake paperwork choices, you will either be assigned to your top three genetic matches automatically, or you can choose your top three matches *and* up to three additional men of your choosing from the Bachelor Book. Here's the icon for that, and you'll get a full walkthrough once this video is done."

Crap. I really should have read all that stuff I signed before getting on the bus. A little icon with two elegantly entwined Bs pops up next to her finger and rotates slowly for a few seconds before winking out.

"Next up, you'll have a fertility exam, and a monitoring band. These can feel intrusive, and we are working with the scientists on our team to make this as painless as possible. Within the next three years we hope to have less invasive tracking methods than the wristband. Unfortunately, I haven't been able to change this one yet. Again, though, everyone you deal with is expected to be polite and professional. If that is *not* your experience at any time, notify your cohort's assigned helper, or contact my team. We will handle it from there. You are a valued member of our society, and at no time should you feel otherwise. It is my sincerest hope that each and every one of you find not only someone to have a child with, but more than that, to build a family with."

My throat tightens at her sincere expression, frozen in place as the video ends. *Family.* It has been so, so long since my parents were killed; so long since I've had any sort of stability or comfort in life. This was always going to be a big change, but I didn't expect to get an emotional gut punch first thing out of the gate. The tablet closes the video and spins up a home page full of other apps, but I click it off and set it aside. I'm pretty sure that in my haste to get on this bus and away from the man in black, I signed away the choice to have three picks of my own brought out for me, so there's not much point in obsessing over the *Bachelor Book*. What an obnoxious name.

I stand and stretch, and realize the other two girls at the front are also done with their video, and out of their seats talking. *Should I go up there? Attempt to be friendly?* I waver and consider hiding in the bathroom which I can see a few steps away, but the pocket-sized redhead makes the decision for me, waving and motioning like a wild thing that I should come up.

"Hey, girl," she drawls as I approach, and tries to give my hand a squeeze, but I tuck it into my jeans pocket. She smoothly reroutes her own hand back to her hip, but cocks an eyebrow at my evasive maneuver. "We were just gettin' acquainted. I'm Cammie, this is Leilani."

"Demy," I say with a nod.

"That's an interesting name," Leilani says, giving me a small smile. She's so calm the feeling practically radiates from her. The polar opposite of the fiery redhead, who's a crackling ball of energy, and . . . now she's bouncing on her feet.

"So, how many guys are you planning to invite? I think I'm going for all three, right up front. I'm going with a combination strategy." She ticks off on her fingers as she talks. "Best looking, but *also* highest fertility rating. I assume we'll be able to narrow it down. I don't want a guy I don't find attractive, but I also want to get a bun in the oven the old-fashioned way, you know what I mean?" Cammie gives us a lascivious wink. "Fertility assistance sounds like

11

a drag. Anyways—I haven't started looking yet because I'm just too *amped*. This is big, really big."

I'm blown away by how easily she's taking all this. I might have signed up a few months before the deadline for my own reasons, but nothing about this feels like a walk in the park to me. We're about to marry strangers and lose all of our personal freedoms for the next three years for the sole purpose of popping out babies. This is heavy stuff, and she's grinning and talking about getting buns in the oven *the old fashioned way?* I know the population is in decline, but this is our lives.

"It's a bit frightening, too," Leilani says. "I did give myself the option to add men, but I'm not sure if I'll take it. My cousin went into the program five years ago, and she still hasn't conceived despite being on her second match. Sticking with my highest genetic matches is probably my only chance." She frowns down at the hem of her brightly-colored tunic top, and Cammie swoops in with a hug—enveloping the taller girl without reservation.

"Now listen here, I don't want any trash talking or putting ourselves down between us three, okay? There aren't any guarantees, but being all down about it won't make it better. Let's keep positive and stick together. Deal? We can do this as a team. It'll be better for everyone. Besides, I'm going to need someone to rehash dates with, and you two are officially my people, ready or not."

"Deal," Leilani agrees. They both turn wide eyes on me, and I feel the sudden need to agree. *Peer pressure apparently still applies when you're nineteen freaking years old.*

"Yeah. Sounds good." I force a smile, and it feels awkward on my face. It could be a lot worse; they could be stuck-up narcissists, or perpetually smelling like broccoli, like that one bus boy. I can take a little extra enthusiasm, as opposed to that.

"Perfect," Cammie practically purrs. "Now, let's get to know each other. Where are you both from?"

Dread pools in the pit of my stomach. I've leapt onto this bus—literally—and have no plan for how to handle the most basic of get-to-know-you questions? What am I going to tell the guys I have to date?

Sorry, old chap, just here to avoid the creepy stalker group who's been chasing me since they murdered my parents six years ago. Ha-ha, hair toss! Think, Demy, think!

"My family is from the Calivada Islands, so things are a lot different there. It's always hot and humid, so I was hoping to try somewhere a bit different."

"Wise. Better for the hair, too. You want to make a good first impression on your matches. The guys have a choice now, too," Cammie adds.

Leilani looks down, hiding under a curtain of shining black hair at the reminder that she might not be chosen.

I give Cammie a pointed look, then look over at Leilani.

She realizes her mistake almost immediately. "But honey, you're a stunner. We're going to get you in a ballgown to show off those hips, and they're going to be trailing you like lovesick little puppies! Just you watch."

Leilani peeks up, and I see the end of an eye roll at Cammie's hype. I have no idea how to diffuse the awkwardness, having missed the phase where teenage girls *bonded* over boys and beauty products. Instead, I just change the focus.

"Where are you from, Cammie?"

"Oh, well, I thought that was obvious! New Texas, born and bred." She gives a little shoulder wiggle, and I'm beginning to see that motion is a constant for her.

13

"Cool."

They both stare at me, and once again I realize I'm supposed to talk. "I'm from Wiscigan, originally, but I've moved around a lot the last few years, mostly in Missiana and Chitucky." I offer a shoulder shrug, as if this is completely boring and honest, rather than a bald-faced lie.

"Huh, never been to either place. Interesting. So, we're from all over!" Cammie smiles wide as the bus makes a turn and sends us all tilting towards the left row of recliners. "Whoops-a-daisy! Better get back to our seats. I don't want to show up banged-up and bruised. Can't damage the goods, after all." She spins and wiggles her fingers over her shoulder at Leilani and I as she sashays back to the front of the bus.

"Boy, she is something," Leilani whispers.

"Yes, she is," I agree before carefully making my way back to my own seat, her words echoing in my mind. *The goods.* That's all we are now, goods to be traded until we pop out babies for the government.

It's going to be a long couple of months, if the first hour is any indication.

CHAPTER THREE

WADING IN

DEMY

The bus drives through the night, stopping once at a rapid-charging station, where Jones goes out and gets us each a gourmet, three-course meal. I eat every single crumb while listening to Leilani and Cammie trade growing-up stories, and to my surprise, I don't mind it. The few short conversations the three of us girls have as the night wears on are actually pleasant, once I relax a little. It's the best night I've had in a long time, and to my surprise, when I lay the recliner back to a completely flat, plush bed and pull up the provided blanket to my chin, I fall asleep in minutes.

I'm startled from a deep sleep early in the morning. I jolt and hinge upright, snatching my arm back from whoever's touching me, and my chest is still heaving when everything clicks into place. No one is attacking me. Judging by Leilani's startled expression, I've far overreacted to a gentle hand on my forearm.

15

Humiliation floods me, and I bite my bottom lip between my teeth and try to think of a reasonable excuse for my crazed, overly defensive behavior. At the front of the bus, I see Cammie staring, her wide, shocked eyes bouncing back and forth between the two of us. "I'm so sorry, I—I—"

"It's okay," Leilani cuts me off with a reassuring smile and her usual quiet calm voice. "Next time, I'll be sure not to touch you. I just wanted to let you know we've arrived, and they're unloading our luggage now. Jones said that the intake process is lengthy, so, I thought you'd like to use the bathroom before we get off the bus." She gives me a polite smile and a nod, then turns and walks gracefully back to her seat.

"Thank you," I whisper to her retreating back. It feels wrong to say nothing, even if it doesn't begin to cover my ludicrous reaction to a simple touch.

Dating is going to go great, at this rate. With a heavy sigh, I turn sideways and hop from my still-extended chair, and make quick work of freshening up. Despite my speed, I am still the last one on the bus when I come out. A little pang in my chest that the other girls hadn't waited for me takes me by surprise, but I push it down. We've *just* met, and I'm acting weird.

They probably want some space, and I can't say that I blame them. I gather my few belongings—including the headphones, which are so squishy and fit my ears just right—and walk briskly from the bus. When I trot down the steps and turn to look for where I'm supposed to go, I have to bite my lip again at what I see: Cammie and Leilani, each holding the handles of a few bags, waiting for me.

"There you are, Sleepin' Beauty! Do you have any other bags? The driver said it was just ours under there." Cammie gives me a bright smile, and it's like my freak-out never happened.

I could sob with relief, but instead I just shake my head. "Nope, I travel light." I pat my duffel bag for effect.

Her jaw drops, and she glances down at the three suitcases—sparkly pink, every one—cylindrical pillow, shoulder bag, and purse clustered around her feet.

"I can grab a couple of yours." I trot over and take two of the handles, so she can get the rest.

"Thank you, and don't think we're going to let this fly. It sounds like our first group date needs to be shopping!" she trills excitedly, and I resist the urge to wince.

Shopping with no money officially just became the top of my avoid-at-all-costs list.

Leilani snorts, the sound surprisingly indelicate compared to every other thing about her. "I'd bet my entire last Island Milkshake paycheck that you don't have room in those bags for one more stitch of clothing."

"Hey! Shots fired. We're a girl-squad now; you're supposed to be on my side," Cammie jokes as we follow Jones up a nicely-manicured sidewalk. "Besides, the first thing I'll shop for is a new suitcase. Problem solved."

Now it's my turn to snort. Nothing keeps Cammie down, and she is already growing on me.

We haven't walked down the sidewalk a minute away from the bus with our bags when a swarm of men and women in crisp navy uniforms descend upon us.

Our luggage is whisked away by the horde of attendants, and a woman with a clipboard stops to speak with Jones, pointing towards a path off to the right, covered by a wisteria-laden arbor. She wears her blonde-streaked hair pulled back in a ridiculously tight bun, and I quickly grow bored waiting for the conversation to end. Instead, I look around, taking in my surroundings.

The lawn slopes gently upward away from the woods behind us and is covered in dense green grass. There are no buildings visible from here, but the lush landscape and strategically placed islands of vibrant plants could be hiding a lot. The sidewalk where we're standing is lined with tall, bluish, crisp-smelling bushes that loom at least six feet over my head, and I'm five-eight.

The woman turns and takes us in, arching a thickly-furred eyebrow in our direction. "Take them by the dining room first, since you didn't stop for breakfast," she chides, then strides away, hips swinging in a tight blue pencil-skirt suit.

The path the woman with the clipboard pointed to has an arbor with fat purple blooms hanging like grapes along the length of it, and my stomach growls hopefully at the thought of more food.

Jones chuckles abashedly and turns to the three of us. "That was Director Churtle. She's something else. But, she's absolutely right! Let's get you three something to eat from the main hall, and then we can begin the intake process." He nods once when we stay silent—as if we are going to argue with food before medical exams—and then leads us into the floral-scented tunnel.

It curves lazily back and forth, and finally I begin to catch glimpses of buildings, nestled amongst small hills over what seems to be an expansive property. The arbor ends, and we come up to a series of short, picket fences covered in vines dotted with sweet-smelling white flowers.

Jones leads us up to a white-columned red brick building, two stories high with a wraparound porch on each. Ivy creeps up the sides of it, clinging and giving it a softer effect. When we walk up the front steps and through the oversized double doors, I'm blown away by how luxurious and gorgeous the interior is. There's some sort of wood paneling on the bottom of the walls which makes it look high-class, and fancy gilded wallpaper on the top of the walls, which by the way, are super high. Crystal chandeliers dot the length of the foyer, and deep mahogany furniture is situated at perfect intervals reflecting the glow from each of their glossy surfaces.

I have never been anywhere so fancy in the whole of my life, and I'm afraid to breathe in case I break something and they tell me I'm supposed to replace it. Discomfort creeps up the back of my neck like an inchworm, and I want to be *anywhere else*, bad.

The rest of my group has gone on ahead, completely unaware of my inner loathing of the posh interior. I rush to keep up, and stumble over a wrinkle in a patterned rug underfoot. Mentally cursing, I catch myself against a table, causing the legs to *screech* across the gray stone floors. The sound makes everyone stop and turn, and I can't help the scowl on my face as I straighten and try to look like I'm not an utter klutz as I close the distance.

"Everything okay, Demelza?" Jones asks, the sound of my full name as grating as mahogany-on-stone a few seconds ago.

"Yep, perfect. This place is wicked fancy," I mumble by way of explanation, drawing a chuckle out of him.

"It's beautiful, isn't it? Historically it was based on some local mansions built back in eighteen ninety-five. Director Churtle is an absolute stickler when it comes to both historical accuracy, *and* property care."

Joy. They really would kill me if I broke something. *No pressure, Demy.*

Cammie drops back from Jones a few steps, grabbing both mine and Leilani's arms to slow us, as well. She whispers loudly once we were far enough back, "Raise your hands if that just made you *super* afraid to touch anything in this gaudy mausoleum. How can something that cost so much look so *ugly*?" She squints up accusingly at the wallpaper.

I choke on a laugh, and she slaps my back a few times before wiggling her fingers up at Jones, who is once again stopped and looking back, this time with a hint of exasperation peeking through.

"Sorry, Jones, we're coming," she says breezily, then shoots us both a smirk and speeds up to catch him. "So, you were saying it was built in eighteen ninety-five?"

"No, no—It was only built forty-five years ago. It was based, however, on a beautiful private residence . . ." He continues chatting with Cammie as we reach the end of the foyer, and pulls open one side of a large double door, peering through.

"Ahh, looks like they're ready for us. Ladies, please take a seat." He steps back and holds the door for us. I'm the last one through, and the first thing that hits me is the glorious smell of sugar and carbs.

"Oooh, I smell French toast!" Leilani quickly picks a seat at a round table in the middle of the massive dining room, and uniformed waiters pull out three chairs for us. As soon as we're seated, we're presented with printed menus listing every breakfast delight a girl could want, and quite a few I'd never heard of.

Although, if they didn't serve it at a greasy spoon or a train station, I probably haven't heard of it. So, maybe that wasn't a high bar.

Cammie orders something I've never heard of and can't pronounce; Leilani asks for French toast—extra whipped cream and powdered sugar—and then the head waiter stares at me expectantly.

Anxious about sticking out like a sore thumb again so soon, I look down and order the only thing that looks diner-worthy.

"Scrambled eggs, please."

"Certainly, ma'am. Would you like the full complement of breakfast sides?"

"Uhm, sure?"

"Right away," he says with a smile, and strides off to the kitchen to make breakfast dreams come true.

I don't have time to think too hard about how I'm constantly sticking out, though, because the same waiters who pulled out our chairs are back. Each one is carrying a glistening, iced pitcher. They arrange them on the table and pull stemmed crystal glasses from behind their backs.

"Ladies, can we offer you freshly pressed orange, apple, or pomegranate juices? We also have water, coffee, and hot tea available."

The other girls choose a fancy juice, but I stick with water, not looking to make a fool out of myself with even more unfamiliar things. I fiddle with the hem of the cream tablecloth dangling in my lap as we make small talk until the breakfast dishes are served.

Leilani's French toast looks divine; whatever alien egg dish Cammie ordered—literally, it jiggles like it has a mind of its own—looks disgusting; and I'm brought *three full plates* of food. My jaw drops as it takes two waiters to deliver just my food. My eggs are piled high on the middle plate along with steaming potatoes sliced into delicate disks, a bean dish of some kind, and three different kinds of meat. There is also a cold plate, with fresh cut fruit in fancy designs as well as yogurt, and a bagel with smear and thinly sliced salmon. The third plate is all bread and pastries, and Cammie groans at the mere sight of it.

"Please tell me you hate cheese Danishes. Pretty, pretty please!" She makes a grabby hand motion towards the pastry plate, and I pass her the whole thing. She plucks two from the plate, and I gesture for Leilani to take some too. She grabs a turnover, and then takes the first bite of her French toast.

"Oh my god, it's worth getting married just to eat this breakfast. It's *bananas foster* French toast. And there's some sort of cream cheese wizardry happening, and I will die if I don't have this every single morning." She moans loudly as she chews her second bite.

My eggs are delicious and perfectly fluffy, but not quite so moan-inducing. When I finish them, I do try a small, square pastry from the other plate, and it's delicious. Apples and cinnamon, with some other spice I can't pinpoint. I'm covered in bits of pastry flakes when it's gone, but I have no regrets.

Jones appears at the side of our table like a genie as soon as we've all pushed our plates away, and claps his hands together loudly.

"Ladies! Are we ready to begin the intake process?"

"No, I need to process this food baby before I can think about a real baby," Leilani says.

Cammie and I laugh, and it appears to take a great deal of effort for Jones to keep the smile on his face. Poor Jones.

"Nonetheless, the medical staff is ready for you. If you'll follow me, we can get this bit of unpleasantry behind us."

Joy. Who doesn't love a little unpleasantry after a good breakfast?

We leave the remnants of our feast behind, and follow Jones back down the beautifully landscaped paths to another, smaller building. It's more utilitarian than the main hall from the outside, with no porch or trailing ivy, but it does have elegant double glass sliding doors. The strong scent of disinfectant wars with loud, floral potpourri as soon as we step inside. If we're here for more than five minutes, it's going to give me a headache.

It's a pretty standard waiting room, with a nurse in pink scrubs sitting behind a desk, a little starched white cap perched on top of her head. She rises to greet us before we even sit down.

"Ladies! We're so glad you've made it safe and sound. I'm nurse Diane, and if you'll meet me at the door, we'll get this show on the road." The look she sends Jones speaks of sarcasm, but you'd never know it from her sugary tone. "I've got your fertility trackers, here, which you'll be wearing around the clock from here on out. These monitor your temperature, heart rate, and a dozen other medical details which add up to give us a picture of your fertility at any moment in time. Right now, it's only gathering trends and helping us monitor your health. But once you've chosen your bachelors, it will use this data to predict when you're most likely to conceive."

"This is it, ladies," Cammie says, her tone grave. "Just remember, when it's stirrup time, lie back and think of all the hot bachelors coming to meet you."

"*Gross*, Cammie. Just no." Leilani elbows her indignantly as we line up to receive our tracker wristbands.

I say nothing, wondering with mortification what she means by *stirrups*. Those went on saddles, right? I lost my parents before puberty really kicked in and had only been to the doctor once in the past few years, when I'd gotten the flu and felt like death warmed over.

What might be involved in a gynecological exam, I had no freaking clue. I'd been quite happy in my ignorance up until now. When nurse Diane passes me my band, a feeling of dread fills me, as if I'm slipping on a pair of handcuffs, rather than a slim, white device.

At least this round of humiliation will be private, I think as the three of us walked through the side door, leaving Jones to wait for us.

CHAPTER FOUR

THE GLORIOUS, INFAMOUS NELL

DEMY

When our *lengthy* and highly unpleasant medical exams are over, each of us is led back to a decked-out two-story dormitory building. It houses twelve women, so it's way too big for just the three of us. The pale pink walls are lined with photos of pregnant women, or newborn babies wearing absurd outfits. One of them is a penguin, another is dressed as a cupcake. And all the women are wearing a rainbow of gowns snapping in the breeze.

The bedrooms are upstairs, with the living areas below, so we make our way up and choose the right side to make our temporary home. We each pick a bedroom at the very end, so our part of the dormitory doesn't seem too empty, at least. Cammie and Leilani are neighbors, and I'm across the hallway. The tiny bit of extra privacy works for me, while they seem happy to be attached at the hip. I like them, but I haven't lived in close quarters with anyone for so long, I'm still . . . unsettled by constant company.

Their bags have been placed helpfully at the top of the stairs, and we each agree to two hours of alone time to recoup some energy before reconvening downstairs for food.

The rooms are nice, and mine has a view of the rolling hills stretching away from the back of the dormitory, plus a tiny, private balcony. I run my hand along the wrought-iron railing, my stomach a jumble of emotions after the long day and a half.

I'm safe from the men hunting me for now, but the intrusive medical exam earlier in the day has underlined exactly what I've signed up for. I'm a glorified egg basket, just waiting to be fertilized. It isn't flattering, and suddenly, the price for safety feels *steep*.

I let my hips press against the railing, the decorative spiraling metal biting in uncomfortably. I like the feeling, though, as it grounds me. I'm used to discomfort; what I'm not used to is living as a pampered princess. Eating rich, complicated food and being watched twenty-four seven by ever-present staff and monitoring devices.

That's not even considering the guards. So far they've been careful to be unobtrusive, but I still know they're there. *Hovering*. In fact, there are three of them clustered near the back corner of our building, pointing and talking about something I can't see out front. One of them stands out, a blond mountain of muscle a full head taller than the other two, wearing a tight black t-shirt that shows off an extensive tattoo collection covering both of his forearms, and peeking up from the neck of his t-shirt. He seems to be the boss, because as soon as he stops talking, one of the other men jogs off in the direction he'd pointed.

A soft knock at my bedroom door pulls my attention away from our omnipresent guards.

"Demy?" Leilani calls through my door. "Can you come out? There's someone downstairs for us to meet."

With a sigh, I push my hips away from the cold railing, and walk to answer the door. "Hey, Leilani. Who is it?"

"I don't know, a notification just popped up in our rooms." She peeks around my shoulder, and points at the oversized television hanging on my wall. "You didn't turn your tv on, so you didn't get the message."

"Huh. Well, let's go then." Cammie is already waiting for us, checking her coppery locks in a tiny compact mirror. She snaps it shut decisively and gives us both a grin.

"Do you think one of the guys got here early? I already picked two of my three." She does an excited little shoulder shimmy at the thought, but I want to run back to my room. I'm not ready to meet my guys, and I *really* hope we'll get a little more time.

I still haven't even opened the app. But if people are already showing up, I need to get on that. I trail behind Cammie and Leilani to the top of the grand staircase, and we only make it halfway down before a chipper, feminine voice calls out.

"Whassup, my ladies?!"

My head snaps up from the woven stair runner, and I see another blonde girl waiting in the middle of the foyer.

Cammie and Leilani both call out excited greetings, and I belatedly add a "Hello" to the mix.

We make it down into the foyer, and she's bouncing on the balls of her feet like a boxer. Though as a boxer I can't imagine she'd do much. She's maybe a hundred fifteen pounds soaking wet, short, and delicate-looking in a slouchy green t-shirt, ripped jeans, and scuffed-up tennis shoes.

"My name's Nell, and I'm joining you three for this round of matches! Have you guys met your dudes yet?"

"Uh, no? We just did all the medical exams this morning. The schedule in our e-planners says we have a week of training classes before the introductions," Cammie answers, mirroring Nell's peppy tone.

A week before any guys show up? Oh, thank God. I've got to snap out of it, and start paying attention to more than day-to-day survival. Other people have run my life long enough; it's time I take the reins.

"Okay, so the fun is just beginning, nice!"

"Uhm, have you done this before or something?" Leilani asks.

"Oh, yeah. Couple years ago, now. But, uh, things didn't work out." She shrugs one shoulder blithely but doesn't offer any other explanation. There's tension in her jaw, and it's clear she doesn't want to talk about it. "So, this is round two for me. Sucks I couldn't have gotten here *after* the boring classes, though." Nell rolls her eyes dramatically.

"So, what was it like?" I blurt the question, suddenly needing to know everything, while simultaneously afraid to hear what she has to say.

"Which part? The matching? The honeymoons? The breakup?"

"The matching—let's start with that," Leilani cuts in, anxiety ratcheting her voice up to a higher register than usual, and for a moment, there's a tangible sense of camaraderie between us. We're all going through this roller coaster of unease and unknown.

"Ahh. Well, if we're going to start at the beginning, we need sustenance. Follow me." Nell spins on her heel and struts to the left, into a room we haven't explored yet.

We follow her like baby ducklings, and she flicks on the overhead lights to reveal a gorgeous, sprawling kitchen with shiny over-sized appliances everywhere my eyes land. It's all deep mahogany cabinets and sparkling stone countertops with a giant red seam running down the middle of them. She walks to the fridge and pulls it open like she owns the place, while I stop at an island that's longer than I am tall, and run my fingertips over the cool, smooth stone. I've never stepped foot in a kitchen this fancy, and it's hard to believe it's here just for us, as if having access to a full kitchen and waitstaff in the dining room isn't *more* than sufficient.

"Who wants breakfast for dinner?" Nell calls over her shoulder, already pulling out thick packs of bacon, eggs, and milk.

"Me!" Leilani answers first.

"That was a rhetorical question, because breakfast is the only thing I know how to cook." She kicks the fridge door shut with the toe of her banged-up tennis shoe, and nods towards a cabinet off to the side. "Can one of you grab some pancake mix out of there? The bowls and stuff are usually in one of the bottom corner cabinets. She then points at the opposite end of the kitchen with the toe of her shoe like a ballerina.

I come around the counter and dig in the cabinet she pointed to, and sure enough there is a tidy stack of bowls nested together, each one a different shade of red. Not being much of a cook, I pull out the whole stack so she can pick which one she wants.

"Medium sized bowl, instructions are on the back of the box," She gives the instructions breezily and passes me a red whisk and the box of pancake mix Leilani retrieved. I read the back of the box while she sets Cammie to cracking eggs, and Leilani on drink duty.

Within minutes, we've gone from strangers to a well-oiled cooking crew, and then, as soon as the last strip of bacon hits the hot skillet, Nell starts talking again.

"So, three years ago, give or take, I entered the matching program at sixteen. I lucked out, and met the nicest human on the face of the planet on our bus. Sadie, my best friend. Anyways, we were a much bigger group than this go around. There were ten of us, I think?" She mumbles names off under her breath and nods.

"Yeah, ten. Anyways, the medical exams sucked. Then, for a whole week we did the classes—most of it's basic biology, reproduction, infant care, program basics, and some history of the realm type stuff—do any of you read fantasy? No? *Boring.* Anyways, they tell you the history so you know *why* you're packed off to be society's favorite brood mare. Then there was the app, the Bachelor Book. Back then, you could look, but you didn't know who you were assigned to, or how many, until the night you met."

"Seriously? You just showed up and got a group of complete strangers?" Cammie cuts in, incredulity thick in her voice.

"Yep, and the ones with the group were lucky. One of the girls in our group got a single guy, and he was the *worst.*" She shudders visibly at the memory.

"So, she couldn't pick backup guys?" Leilani asks. I just whisk milk into pancake mix, and try not to focus too hard. *At least I get a heads up about what's coming. Knowledge is power. This isn't like the last six years of running. I chose this, and I can choose my match.*

"Nope. Not then. The new leadership is working on that. Did y'all see a message . . . ?" Nell asked.

"Yeah." Leilani nods. "We watched it on the bus. There's, like, a help line, and we can pick up to three of our own guys. Which is *nerve-wracking* because how do you know who you want to marry

30

and spend three plus years with from a picture and a profile?" She slaps a cup onto the counter with a loud smack, and I flinch away from the sudden, sharp noise.

"Listen," Nell puts a hand on Leilani's arm. "It *is* a lot. I'm not going to sugar coat it. It can be overwhelming, and the more guys, the more difficult it can be to figure out who is the right one."

"So how *did* you decide last time? Chemistry? Career? Looks? Location?" Cammie asks, eyebrows scrunched down in frustration.

"Nah, that's all going to lead you astray. I mean, location *is* somewhat important. Not every guy can move, and we are expected to move in that case. My bestie dealt with that, but for the right one, you'll work it out together. That's how it *should* be—partners, working together. But you're right. You can't tell how they're going to feel or act until you meet them in the flesh." She pauses, and turns to grab the no-longer-lumpy pancake batter from me, and starts scooping it onto a second skillet while she talks.

"All of that is fine, but the real test is your gut. Do you feel safe with them? Do you have real conversations, or are you just making polite chit-chat? Because polite talk is fine on an hour date, but three years of your life? Living together? That's a whole 'nother story." She matter-of-factly flips a pancake, the splat and sizzle as it hits the warm pan punctuating the sentiment.

"This is going to be harder than I thought," Cammie says, her voice barely above a whisper.

"Ahh, it won't be bad. You lean on your friends, and you do group dates if you're unsure of someone. You don't have to go from strangers to one-on-one hot and heavy. You can warm up a bit."

"So, tell us about your last guy. Was he good? Did you follow your gut, or did you take the risk on a dreamboat?" Leilani asks.

Nell snorts, flipping bacon and thinking a moment before she answers. It's a bit awkward just standing and twiddling my thumbs, but Leilani presses a glass of orange juice into my hands.

When she finally speaks, it's slower, more measured than her exuberant talk so far. "I picked a good one. He was my other half, and we were really good together."

"So, why are you splitting up?" I ask. If he's the one, what's she doing here waiting on some other schmuck who won't compare? I don't know much about love and relationships, but finding your other half seems like the ideal. I'm not holding my breath for that—when in my life have I ever had *ideal*? Never—but, to walk away from it? Something inside me balks at the idea.

"Ahh, you guys haven't done your classes yet. Well, if you're together three full years, and there's no baby . . . you're split. You have to go back into the pool and try again with a new match."

Cammie's jaw drops. "Wait, say *what* now?"

Nell chuckles, the sound high and bright as she shovels the first round of pancakes and bacon onto plates. "You'll see. The rules are changing, and if it doesn't work out with this higher match, I can go back to him and request RA."

"What's that?" I ask, taking a tentative sip of my juice.

"Oh, Reproductive Assistance. If you guys choose a match below fifty percent compatibility as *the one*, you'll probably get sent straight to RA at your honeymoon location."

"I think I need to sit down," Leilani murmurs, and crosses around the oversized island to perch on a bar stool. She sits and bites her lower lip, wearing her upset plainly on her lovely face.

"Listen, this is all worst case scenario stuff. Don't stress until it's happening. If you freak over every single *maybe* in this program, you'll never make it out the other side sane. Trust me on that. You just need to roll with your own situation. They're giving you your three *best* matches, automatically. If you pick one of them, you've got a good shot of popping out a kid in three years, truly. The birth rate was actually steady this year, for the first time in living memory. The program works. And if you really love the guy, you can get RA and yeah, it's no fun from what I've heard, but, you do it three times, get three kids, you can be done."

"The idea of having three children is overwhelming. I'm not sure I'm mature enough to have *one* yet," Cammie muttered.

"I mean, I've been at this nearly four years, and I'm still kidless. So, again, take it one step at a time. You aren't worried about a kid yet. Right now, you're just worried about picking the right guy. That's it—no more, no less. You're going to meet some men in a week, and hopefully one of them is mouth-wateringly hot *and* has a great personality. It's the holy grail." She flips the last pancake onto the top of the pile, and makes a little twirly gesture with the spatula before dropping it to the counter. "Now, enough man-talk. Let's eat some carbs and forget everything else for a while."

"Hear, hear!" Leilani agrees with a smile, but I can see the troubled look hiding there, deep in her eyes. I have no doubt she sees the same worry reflected in mine.

CHAPTER FIVE

TRAINING DAY

DEMY

When the sun rises the next morning, I haul myself out of the bed, and wander my room to see what's inside. I hadn't been able to sleep the night before. The bed was too soft, the sheets smelled like flowers, and no matter how hard I hauled on the curtains, a carriage light from outside was shining directly onto my pillow.

We'd stayed up late, swapping stories and getting to know each other better. I didn't say much, but it was interesting learning about how different all of our lives were. They all seem so normal, and by the end of the night, I was feeling isolated again. I was odd, my life on the run strange and not something I could—or *wanted* to—share. So, here I am avoiding breakfast and taking a long, hot shower.

Once I'm clean, dry, and pruney from the extended shower, I wander out in my towel to get dressed. I pull on a soft, flimsy tank, and a pair of short shorts. Most of my clothes are thin, and well-worn from years of constant use and washing in bathroom sinks.

I'm pulling open all the drawers in my desk, when a soft wind chime sound fills the room, and my television lights up. I freeze, but as far as I can tell I haven't hit anything. Turning around, I spy a mid-sized tablet perched on the bedside table. It's lit up, and when I tap the surface, the music stops.

Training begins in one hour.

Great. Nell didn't go into the specifics, but from what she mentioned yesterday, it is going to be a real bore. At least it's only a week. I lay the tablet back down and wander over to the closet door. I can at least tuck my bag in here and lay out my shirts and shorts before I head downstairs. My stomach rumbles, reminding me that it would very much like to continue eating on a regular schedule. That has been the one consistent perk of this place so far—the food is plentiful, delicious, and always available.

When I swing it open, my breath catches in my throat. It's full. Slap full, every *inch* of space filled, with more clothes than I've ever seen outside a store window. I step into the walk-in closet—which by itself is bigger than most of the places I've ever stayed. How bougie!—and the subtle scent of rich fabrics washes over me. There's a floor-to-ceiling cubby with the most beautiful, shiny, high-heeled shoes I've ever seen. They're organized like a rainbow, deep reds at the top melding into oranges and yellows, all the way through the spectrum and down into dusky purple. The bottom rack is full of flats and tennis shoes, and I pick up a pair of matte black flats and see that they're my exact size—eight and a half. Out of curiosity, I slip my toes into one, and they immediately sink into a glorious, cushioned comfort like I've never experienced. I grab the other one and put it on, and I may never take them off.

Moving on to the racks of clothing, I gently run my fingertips over some of the fabrics, and they slide smooth and silky under my caresses. I gently push one of the hangers to the side so I can see the dress hanging on it, and a lump rises in my throat at the sight. The dress—no, gown; it's definitely too fancy to be called a dress—is floor-length, deep blue satin with a cinched-in waist and fitted hips, where it then flares out at the knees into a gorgeous, poofy cascade of fabric. It's so shiny it reminds me of a waterfall. I can say with absolute certainty that this single gown cost more than all the clothes I own put together, and this closet is packed full. I let the gown go, and the hanger slides smoothly back into place as soon as I drop my hand back to my side.

Spinning slowly, I see an entire wall of fancy gowns, another section at the end of the closet full of day dresses and sparkling tops, the final wall is pants, skirts, and even a small section of blue jeans. I cross to those, and quickly flip through, noting that even the denim is thick and springy and *new*, the polar opposite of my threadbare shorts and single pair of jeans. There is another cubby that's full of various accessories, but I'm too overwhelmed by the clothes to dig any deeper. My bag of ratty clothes abandoned in the doorway, I slowly back out of the closet, taking nothing but the cloud-like flats already on my feet.

I am weirdly numb as I cross the room and sink onto the side of the mattress. When I was on the run, I never thought about anything beyond the next few hours, or the next day. Survival had consumed my every thought—whether that was a no-questions-asked job working in a kitchen, or which bus departure time could get me the furthest for the cash I had in my pocket, I'd never had the mental bandwidth to think beyond my immediate needs.

Now, surrounded by the overabundance of luxury and *ease*, it suddenly hit how deeply poor I'd been since my parents' deaths.

I mean, I've been hungry at times, and don't have a real home. But it was easy enough to tell myself that I couldn't have a home because I was on the run, not because I was too poor to afford one. I used the local gyms as a "home base" and pretended that was what all the gym rats did. The few times I've been able to find jobs with room and board included, they were the absolute basics—some of them didn't even have working door locks. And I've spent many a night curled up in the corner of a big bathroom stall, sleeping with my head cushioned on my duffel bag, or huddled up in the back corner of a gym locker room. Now that I have some distance and have spent time around the other women my age, that façade is crumbling fast. Their life stories sound like fairy tales, and it's starting to sink in just how messed up my life has been the past five and a half years.

Another dose of reality hits me in a wave, and I catch my breath. I'm about to get matched with three men—three strangers—and what am I going to tell them? I don't have a steady job, or a home address, or any money to speak of. Are they going to be disappointed? I mean, to heck with them if they judge me for being poor—they can go right back where they came from if they'll judge someone for the size of their bank account—but how could I build a life with someone, without sharing those details?

Even if I dress up like a fancy pinup in all of these clothes, that's not the reality of my situation; it's all fake. And eventually, this little fairy tale is going to come to a grinding halt . . . unless I figure out why these black-cloaked men are chasing me. But how am I going to find out what I need to know? It's something to work on, but as a wife, what do I have to offer someone in the meantime?

Nothing; I have *nothing*. The truth turns into a hot, tangled ball of sorrow and shame that feels like an anchor in my stomach.

The tablet next to me chimes again, warning me that I've only got thirty minutes until the training classes start. I force a few deep breaths in and out through my nose and stand up. I've got a week at least before I have to meet my matches. That will at least give me some time to figure out how to explain my messed up life to three complete strangers. *Three strangers I haven't been brave enough to open the app and look at yet.*

Leilani and Cammie are chattering away as we follow Jones through the twisting garden paths to the training center, a nervous edge to their tones. Nell walks silently at my side, an oversized turquoise tote bag tucked under her arm, and a thoughtful look on her face. Her silence suits me, and I'm glad she's not the type to press me to talk and fill the void.

The training center is in the same building as the dining hall, but at the opposite end. Jones leads us there, whistling lightly with his hands in his pockets, as if it's any other Tuesday. I suppose for him, it is. The room he leads us to is bright and open, with a wall of windows at the back, framed by heavy red drapes. The chairs, however, are facing away from the lush landscaping. They're in a semi-circle, aimed towards a large screen and podium at the opposite side of the room. A prim-looking brunette who looks to be in her late forties stands behind the podium. She's got an easy smile, and greets us warmly as we file in.

"Good morning, ladies! I know it can be hard, being in a new place, but we all hope you're settling in. We've got a lot to learn this week! How did you all sleep last night?"

We all fire back variations of *fine, thanks,* and she nods effusively. "Great, I'm glad to hear it. I'm Susan, and I'll be your instructor this week for your motherhood courses. One of you has attended before, according to my notes. Is that correct?"

Nell waves. "Me, but I've got some other reading material here. You just do your thing, and don't worry about me. I'm along for the ride."

"O-kay, then." Susan's smile falters a bit, but she recovers quickly and moves on. "This morning we'll be jumping right into reproduction basics, and then after lunch we'll start tackling some of the laws and provisions the North American Alliance has made for the compulsory marriage program, and your professions as mothers moving forward. You have rights, and we're going to make sure they're clear and covered this week." She tucks a lock of brown hair behind her ear, and continues.

"It's assumed you're all familiar with the history of this program and why it was created by the NAA, but I like to include a run-down anyways, before we get to the meat of our lessons. Hundreds of years ago, scientists created a gene therapy which was meant to be a safe and effective alternative for birth control, and essentially turn off your ability to reproduce. At the time, it was seen as a leap forward for men and women who were done expanding their families, or who were medically unable to use standard birth control medications. That technology, however, was modified by a group of extremists, and turned into the Sterilization Vector, which decimated the population within two generations of them poisoning our water with it."

Whoa. They were tampering with genes? Well, *now* I get why that's illegal.

"The population has been in steep decline ever since, leading to the creation of tri-states, instead of the larger, more populous states of the past. It's also resulted in changes to our transportation, government organizations, and, most obviously, family planning. As I'm sure you all were taught in high school, all methods of birth control are illegal, and to prevent the spread of disease any sexual liaisons outside of your selected and assigned spouse carry severe penalties."

I decide on the spot that I never want to be in a position to find out what one of those *penalties* entails.

She clears her throat, and scans the four of us, waiting for questions. When none appear, she claps twice. "Okay, then. Let's dive right in. First thing's first, reproductive anatomy."

"Oh, boy," Leilani says with a sigh, and scrunches down in her chair on my right.

A diagram of the female reproductive tract appears on the large screen, and we're all staring at a four-foot-high uterus. *Oh boy, indeed.*

The day passes in a blur of what I can only classify as *way too freaking much information*, and by nightfall, my brain is still a muddle. The four of us ate dinner together—which was relatively quiet, all of us processing—and parted ways early. I check the clock and see it's only eight thirty. I briefly consider showering and trying to go to sleep early, but there's a restless itch under my skin that I can't seem to shake.

Making a snap decision, I wander into the closet, pull buttery soft, pale pink exercise clothes from a shelf, and slip them on instead of pajamas. I then choose a pair of pink tennis shoes—comfy, but not *as* good as the cloud-like flats I'd worn all day—and in minutes, I'm shutting my bedroom door behind me.

Jones mentioned earlier in the day that there is an exercise room, and with a few quick taps on my fertility tracker, I have a blinking arrow directing me towards it, past the main building with the dining hall. As I walk through the quiet evening, the cool air caressing my skin, I can finally suck in a deep breath.

This whole experience has been so . . . *much*. Too much change, too much information, too much company. I usually spend so much time alone, every waking minute here feels overstimulating, and overwhelming. With just the quiet *tshh tshh* of my tennis shoes kissing the paved walkway, I can think.

Only four more days of classes, and I'll be meeting my matches. Tomorrow is the deadline to choose additional matches, and I still haven't opened the Bachelor Book app, as if hiding my head in the sand is going to make it any less real what's about to happen. *It isn't, Demy. It's time to pull up your big-girl panties, and open the freaking app.*

I considered it, when I was in my room staring at the walls like they were going to close in on me, but the anxious urge to move sent me out here into the night air. The path curves under my feet again, and I see another, smaller building peeking out from behind an over-tall hedgerow. It's simpler, with only two columns out front and no ivy climbing up the brick. I can see bright, modern overhead lights through the plate-glass windows lining the front and highlighting a pristine exercise facility.

The door opens with a soft *shush*, and the night sounds fade away to the steady, low hum of air conditioning. There are screens dotting the walls, but they're all blank, and it suits me just fine. I take a deep breath, letting the familiar scents of old sweat and cleaning chemicals soothe me. It's the fanciest gym I've ever set foot in, but no matter where I wander, the local gym has always been my safe space. I could get a hot shower, and nobody questioned my lack of new, clean clothes. Everybody wore ratty t-shirts most of the time. I *fit*. The gym has been the closest thing I've had to home for six long years, and finding one here made my heart swell with joy.

My freedom is rapidly coming to an end—I'm about to give my body and my future away to a man that I didn't know—but for now, I can push all of that aside and lose myself in the familiar routines and rhythms of exercise.

Scanning the room, I decide to start with a simple warmup on one of the rowing machines tucked into the far corner of the room. I click my feet into the stirrups with a satisfying snap, grab the handle, and pull.

Within moments, my focus has narrowed to the repetitive motion, allowing the world and all of my problems to slip away, drowned by the whirr of the rope, the spin of the machine, and the air rushing in and out, in and out of my lungs.

When I'm completely sweated out, I stop pulling, my simple warmup having turned into a full-body, drenched-in-sweat workout. My legs shake as I pull my feet from the stirrups, and that anxious itch is finally gone.

In its place, there's resolve. I'm going back to my room to shower, get settled against the headboard of my big, fancy bed and an obscenely large pile of rich-lady pillows, and then I'm going to look at each of my matches. Tonight. No more delays.

The walk back passes in a tired blur, and I'm so zoned in on my plan that as I walk through the foyer of our dormitory I almost miss Cammie sitting alone in the front room. She's hunched over with her elbows on her knees, red hair falling around her in a sheet, her face in her hands. I pause, utterly unsure of what to do in this situation. Should I say something, or should I give her privacy?

Hesitantly, I speak up. "Cammie? Everything okay?"

She jolts upright, her face red and puffy, and I am hit with an instant shot of guilt. She did *not* want company. So, I backpedal.

"I'm sorry, I didn't mean to interrupt your alone time. I'm just headed up to shower, I won't bother you." I force a smile and turn to bolt up the stairs, but her shaking voice stops me.

"Wait! It's okay . . . I could actually use some company."

Frozen, I turn back towards her. "Uhm, yeah. Sure. I can be company." I smile again, and this time it isn't so difficult.

She returns a watery one of her own as I sink into an armchair across from her. Cammie pulls her knees up to her chest, and wraps both arms around them, like she's trying to hug herself into feeling better, and we sit in silence for a few long moments.

I have no experience with other girls my own age, and no idea how to offer her comfort, or get her talking again—with Cammie, it seems like she's fine as long as her mouth is moving, so this silence is disconcerting. Just as I'm about to offer to leave again, she speaks.

Her voice is low, and unusually subdued. "I thought I was ready for this. For a relationship. *Motherhood.* I thought I knew what this would be like—come, dress up, make a few new friends and then meet some hot guys. You know, that doesn't sound so bad,

43

even if it's mandatory." She sniffles, pausing. "But, everything is so . . . *clinical*. I didn't expect that, and it took me by surprise. When you're a little girl, you dream of the fairytale, you know? A handsome knight to sweep you off your feet. Not three years of scheduled sex, constant monitoring, and then a mandatory divorce if you don't get pregnant fast enough."

I snort involuntarily. Apparently, we were two very different little girls, with very different dreams—I always wanted to be an officer in the NAA Police force. But, to each her own. Plus, she's not wrong about the details. Getting whisked off to a honeymoon resort had sounded *great*, until the other shoe dropped.

"Okay, snort all you want. But I'm serious. Did any of us dream of being handed a dude, and told '*go procreate with this one, and get it over with already?*' No, we did not. And it's just . . . it sucks. Where's the romance, man?"

I bite my lip, unsure what to say. I hadn't come here for romance; I'd come for safety, and a bit of breathing room. But still, I know what she means.

"The guys aren't here yet, Cammie. And there's nothing that says you have to jump straight into the procreation part. Tell them what you want, after you meet them. If you want romance, ask for romance. I mean, I know nothing about men. But, if you're going to marry a guy, he should care a little bit about making you happy, right?"

She looks thoughtful, bobbling her head back and forth on her shoulders. "I hadn't thought of it that way. Do you think that would work?"

"What kind of fun do we have going on in here?" Nell's sing-song voice precedes her from the hallway. She rounds the corner into the sitting room with her hair in a top knot, a lidless carton of ice cream in one hand, a giant medical textbook tucked under the same arm, and four giant soup spoons clutched in her other fist. Leilani walks in behind her, a second flavor of ice cream and a wad of napkins her only loot.

"Apparently less fun than you two are having," I say with a chuckle. "We were just talking about the differences between what we expected and the reality that was class today."

Nell practically cackles, she laughs so loud. "They sure know how to make sex *un*-sexy, don't they? Don't worry, it won't be as bad as all that." She winks and passes each of us a spoon. "Just focus on picking a good guy, and the rest will work itself out."

Leilani sinks into the chair next to mine and offers me the carton of strawberry ice cream. I take a big, heaping spoonful out, slowly nibbling around the edges.

"Is it really that simple? Because it feels harder than that," Cammie whispers, clutching her empty spoon.

"I mean, there are no guarantees, but, yeah, it can be that simple." Nell shrugs and takes a bite from her vanilla carton. "My last match was a great guy, and I have no regrets about being married to him. We clicked; you know? Even when we first met, something about him was just *right*. You guys get more choices this time around than I did, so the odds are even better you'll be able to find a guy you like. Last time, a whole bunch of us only got one match."

"What? Just one?" Leilani's horrified question matched my feelings perfectly.

"Just one. But things are already getting better. So, really, don't worry so much. Meet your matches first, then throw the funeral if they all suck." Nell takes another scoop of ice cream before pressing the carton into Cammie's grip. She woodenly digs her spoon in, worrying her bottom lip with her teeth the entire time.

"It seems like something's still bothering you, Cammie. What is it?" I ask.

She drops her eyes to the parquet flooring, and whispers, "I'm scared. It doesn't feel how I thought it would, and I'm scared. Of everything."

"Me, too," Leilani admits, clutching the tub of ice cream to her chest.

That surprises me, given how detached I am about the entire matching-and-marriage process. After being on the run for so long, this place feels cushy and safe. That is probably just another sign of how messed up my life has been so far. *Depressing.*

"What if none of my matches like me? They can choose to leave now, too. The way it was before, it was entirely up to us. That was kind of the only bad change," Leilani continues.

"Listen," Nell interjects. "I get that this all feels overwhelming and scary. I do. But I promise, it's going to be okay. The people in charge now care, and we have a way to report back if something goes wrong. And the guys? They're going to love you. You're all three smart, beautiful, kick-butt women. What's not to love? Also, remember, just because they *can* leave doesn't mean they want to go back into the pool—they may never get another match. And these guys all chose to be matched, because they want to raise their own kids, instead of just being donors."

"That's true, I hadn't thought of any of that." Leilani looks pensive, her eyebrows drawn down tight.

"Hey, we're a girl squad. We're in this together, and we're going to stick together. We have problems, we help each other." Nell makes pointed eye contact with each of us, and we all nod in agreement. "This is your time to find out who's the one for you, but that doesn't mean it has to be unromantic and full of pressure. Take it one

46

day, one date at a time. If you don't like something, *speak up*. You deserve to get what you want, even if this is a weird way to go about it." She waves her spoon around the room to underline her point.

We spend the next hour passing ice cream cartons around the circle and talking about what we hope for in a match, until the cartons go soggy, and we start yawning in earnest. Cammie goes around the circle and gives us all bone-cracking hugs, and then we split off to our separate bedrooms. By the time my shower is done, I'm exhausted and sore, but a lot less lonely. I've never had a girl squad before. It's better than I expected.

CHAPTER SIX

THE BACHELOR BOOK

DEMY

I'm once again awake before my alarm, but I don't waste any time. I'm up and ready for the day in under fifteen minutes—probably because I'm still too scared to go past the comfortable clothes portion of my closet into the land of shiny fabrics—so I grab the tablet and sit down at the desk to look at my matches. Two deep breaths in and out through my nose, and I click the little app with the intertwined BB icon.

It opens with a spiraling flourish on the screen, and then I'm staring at miniature photographs of men's faces. I run my finger down the side of the tablet, and there are hundreds of portraits. Smiling men, serious men, handsome men, quirky men, men of every color, height, and body type. Some of the photos are casual, appearing to be taken themselves, and others are professionally lit and posed for the perfect angles. I stop scrolling, the feeling of overwhelm trying to sink its claws into my throat. I shove it down.

This isn't life or death—if I can handle that, I can handle this. It's just details.

The first page must be everyone in the database, but where are the men I'm going to be meeting in just a few days?

Going back to the top, I realize there's a little red bubble notification that I've completely missed. I tap the bubble and see there are three messages.

New match assigned: Beckett

New match assigned: Fletcher

New match assigned: Jax

Okay. So, those are my three. I chew my bottom lip for a minute before clicking the top message for Beckett. His picture loads first, and I suck in a breath. Everything about the photo screams money. He's got dark, slicked-back hair, a strong jaw, perfect teeth, and a three-piece suit on with one of those colorful little fabrics in the pocket. It's green. I try not to make assumptions about him for being rich; after all, I hope he's not going to judge me for being poor. He is incredibly handsome, it's just not a style I'm familiar with, given how I've lived my life.

He's so . . . polished. I've never felt polished. What if he expects a professionally buffed and styled and made-up wife? Could I learn to be that if we hit it off? It's something to think about.

I scroll down and see a tidy list of stats underneath his professional photo.

Age: 27

Height: 5'11"

Location: Wrightsville

Fixed Location: Yes

Match rate: 98%

Wants in a wife: A life partner who can appreciate the finer things and help build the family of our dreams together.

Ninety-eight percent? I'm floored. From what the class told us yesterday, anything above sixty-five or seventy percent is considered really solid. But ninety-eight? I didn't expect that. *Beckett.* I roll the name around in my mouth, testing it out.

Hmm. Well, hopefully he's nice in person, but at that high of a match rating, even if the differences in our financial status make me wary, I have to consider him.

Okay, next match—Fletcher. I scroll up again and tap his name in the notifications, and his detail page loads. *Holy cats, he is gorgeous.* The photo is casual, but he looks adventurous. He's leaning against a large tree, one arm bent behind and propping up his head against the bark, with a huge cliff drop off and a stunning mountain view behind him. But I can't focus on the epic scenery, because his eyes are so piercing, it feels like he's looking straight into my soul, right from the photo. I tear my gaze away from his eyes, and force myself to assess the rest of him frankly, like I did Beckett. He's got deep brown skin—more than a tan—and it's smooth and rippling with glorious muscles. I find myself with the ridiculous urge to run my fingertips over the strong shape of his bicep. *Slow down, killer. He's literally never met you before—paws off.*

I bite my lip as I take in Fletcher's shoulder length, curly brown hair. It's pulled back in the photo, but some curls are springing free and adding to his carefree look, his lips are curled up into a smile that looks like pure sin, and he's wearing a simple t-shirt and black hiking pants. If the speed of my pulse right now is any indication, he's a contender. But will we be as good of a match?

Quickly scrolling down, I read his stat list.

Age: 25

Height: 6'4"

Location: Montkota

Fixed Location: No

Match rate: 97%

Wants in a wife: A woman who's not afraid to laugh, and who loves adventure.

Ninety-seven percent! Relief washes over me. That's only one point lower, and still an amazing rating. And he seems more relaxed, like someone I might be able to get to know and be comfortable with. I mean, if we have to make a baby together, I don't want to be nervous around the guy. Though it's a lot to assume from a simple photo. I should keep moving, and check the last man's stats.

Scrolling back up, I pause a second longer than necessary on his photo, before quickly swiping past and tapping the last notification. Jax.

His page loads quickly, and I'm staring into stunning, deep blue eyes, and a cocky grin, the barest hint of straight white teeth shining through. He's wearing a black leather jacket, and some kind of black uniform underneath. It gives him a dark, edgy look that doesn't mesh with the fair hair and smirk. Strong brows and a straight nose give me the impression that he's forthright, if self-assured. He's posed in front of a building, all glinting glass windows, and some kind of sign on the door. Wait . . . is he a closer? That would explain the travel, but I wonder if it's a depressing job—boarding up whole towns when everyone leaves. I've been on the run for so long, though, that moving with him from city to city would feel like business as usual.

It seems wild to me that people put that much effort into preserving empty cities. The population's only recently stabilized, so it's not like there's going to be a huge wave of humans needing *more* space any time soon.

I scroll down, wishing there was a job description listed, but there's not.

Age: 23

Height: 6'2"

Location: Northwestern NAA

Fixed Location: No

Match rate: 95%

Wants in a wife: My other half.

My eyes stop dead on the high match rating. How is that *possible?* I'd thought after the first day of classes that the match percentage would be a dead giveaway of who I should pick, but they're only a few percentage points off from each other. Anything over eighty-five we were told had a high probability of producing children within the three-year time limit without being referred to reproductive assistance, or re-matched.

Based on what they'd told us *that* entailed, I'd love to avoid months of intensive monitoring, shots, scans, and doctor visits.

Wow. Three high matches, and—I scroll back up to take a second look at Jax's cocky grin, and short blonde hair—every single one of them drop-dead handsome. I bite my lip, more confused than ever. Today is the deadline to add additional matches, but do I need more than three men to juggle?

The wind chime alarm sounds suddenly from the tablet in my hands, and I startle so hard I fumble, and nearly drop the thing.

Training begins in five minutes.

Shoot. I got caught up in the Bachelor Book and missed breakfast. If I hurry, I can at least grab one of those pastries and a banana to eat in the class. Hopefully Susan won't mind; she seems laid-back enough. I jump to my feet, and scurry down the stairs and onto the twisty path, my mind spinning with images of three completely different, but incredibly gorgeous men, and try my best to ignore the fact that my stomach is a twisted knot of nerves.

This is getting more real by the minute, and my time of treating this like a vacation from being on the run is rapidly coming to a close.

I'm going to meet my husband in a few short days.

Maybe I don't need breakfast, after all.

The morning's classes pass in a blur, my mind too occupied to focus. When we break for lunch, the low rumble of my stomach protesting the skipped meal earlier is the only thing that pulls me into the present. Nell notices my distraction first, and bumps shoulders with me as soon as we sit down at our table in the dining room.

"What's on your mind, girlie?" Her blue eyes bore into me with the efficiency of an auger, and I quickly drop my eyes to my lap. That kind of *notice* makes me squirm and feels dangerous. Nell is older than us, street smart, *and* observant. It feels like she sees through me, and knows there's something different. At the same time, though, she's accepted me with open arms. Sometimes, it's off-putting, but I also really like her no-nonsense attitude.

Can I tell her how mixed-up and anxious I'm feeling? She's been in my shoes before, so maybe she'll have advice. Or she could tell me I'm overthinking it. I weigh the risks of showing some vulnerability against the possibility of her helping me somehow.

"I looked at my matches this morning. They're all handsome, and really high compatibility ratings. I just . . . I—I—" My mouth opens, and the words tumble out, almost before I realize what's happening, and I clench my jaw, unsure what I want to say.

Cammie leans forward, a wicked twinkle in her eyes. "Ooh, tell us, tell us! Are they handsome? Mine are. I added three extras too, just because, *phew*"—she fans her face—"they are *smoking* hot. I mean, give me an ice pack and a fainting couch, because I'm going to need it when they're all in the same room." She grins, last night's nerves seemingly forgotten.

"You are too much, Cammie. You can't *have* all of them—you know that, right? It's just going to be harder to pick with more guys," Leilani says over the rim of her water glass, pursing her lips.

"You're so pragmatic. This is all we get, you know? We get one shot—in most cases, no offense, Nell—"

"None taken," Nell says, waving her off, but I can see the shadow lingering in her eyes.

"Anyways," Cammie continues, "we don't get to date and flirt and get swept off our feet except here. This is all we get. Well, if this is it, I'm going to meet every guy I can, and I'm going to find the one that treats me how I want to be treated." She sets her jaw, the stubborn look defensive.

"There's nothing wrong with that at all. This is your life, and you get to choose. Do whatever feels right to you, but don't be afraid to release them back into the pool if they're jerks." Nell gives her a double thumbs up, and then turns back to me with her laser gaze. "It's also okay if you're not ready to jump into the deep end. You can take it slow. You can't tell everything from a photo and a list of genetic fertility ratings. Honestly, some of the girls got matched with some real stinkers in my last round of matches. Not all—my friend Sadie? She found the love of her life, and most of the girls have ended up happy in the last four years. Really. But you *can't* tell until you meet them. So, don't stress yet, okay?"

"But what if I don't like any of them?" Leilani says in a half-whisper, right as the wait staff drops heaping plates of food on the table in front of us. We wait a moment, thanking them as they walk away before continuing the conversation.

"Girl, if you don't like any, you can request three new matches. It's really going to be fine. Just let your beautiful personality shine through, and everything else will work itself out. You, though, Demy, what's going on with you?"

I swallow nervously and look down at my lap as I speak. "I hadn't looked, this whole time, because what if they all looked mean and we had low match rankings? But I had to look, so I could decide if I needed to add someone else." I swallowed. "They're all very handsome, and our match ratings are all over ninety percent, so, that's good—"

Cammie nearly choked on her fancy pressed sandwich. "I'm sorry, good? Nineties! I don't have a match above eighty percent, and all the rest are sixties and seventies!" She reached for a glass of strawberry soda and took a long sip. "Holy crap, girl, you must have super-genes. Who are your matches? We should all swap pictures."

"My matches are all in the fifties to seventies, too," Leilani added.

Nell held up a hand. "Hang on, hang on. Let's give this a beat. It's all new. I'm all for swapping notes, but after the guys arrive is the time. Trust me—we'll have plenty of time to dissect every little detail once they're here, and we're dating them all for weeks."

"Spoilsport," Cammie teased.

"Maybe so, but these two need a little more adjustment time before they flip into gossip mode." Nell gives me a reassuring shoulder squeeze, and some of the tension drains out of me. She's on my side. I take a deep breath through my nose before making eye contact with Nell, and then looking at Cammie and Leilani.

"I've never dated before, and I am worried it's going to be awkward. I don't want to hold back, because I know I need to put myself out there to get to know someone for real. But . . . do you think they'll care if I'm broke?" I ask, blurting out the crux of the issue.

Leilani purses her lips like she's thinking it over, but Nell's first to answer. "If they do, they're not the one," she says firmly.

"Okay . . ."

"I was poor, too, when my first husband and I met. He never cared; didn't even ask, actually. We did share our family backgrounds, which is when it eventually came up, but he didn't judge. He had plenty of money, and you get a paycheck for being in the New Lives Program. I'm pretty sure Sadie—ahh, the leadership—changed the rules last year so that you're paid weekly, and it starts immediately, not once you've gotten a confirmed pregnancy, like it used to." She jabs her fork into a piece of cantaloupe, and gestures with it as she continues, "So, you might have been broke before, but you've got your own money now."

I swallow the nibble of BLT in my mouth, processing that unexpected bit of news. "Okay, but, one of the men looks over-the-top wealthy. It's not a guarantee from a picture, of course, but . . . I suspect. Even if I've got some money now, it's not going to be in the same stratosphere as him."

Nell tilts her head to the side, giving me a kind look, but it's Cammie who speaks up, surprising me. "So freaking what? He's got money, you don't. You've got something he needs, that money *literally* can't buy. If he's as rich as you think, he'll understand that. Without us? No families, no heirs, nobody to pass all that money on to. But you're right; you can't hold yourself back and find the one. You've got to just make the leap. It's gonna be okay, even if you don't click with these three."

"Uhm, I hadn't thought of it that way."

"Well, you need to start. We're rarer than money. The program's mandatory for *every* woman, now. That's why all these men are bending over backwards to follow these program rules in the first place. No us? No babies." She twirls her fork dramatically in the air.

"Girl power!" Leilani says with a snort, then wrinkles up her nose. "It's not very flattering that all they care about is impregnating us, though. It's a cold way to start a relationship."

"They're not all bad, I promise," Nell says again. "A lot of the men really are family men, and this is the only way to go about it. My first husband was an amazing guy, and we were happy together, babies or no." She presses her lips into a thin line and pushes her food around on her plate with her fork.

"Do you miss him?" I ask.

Nell sighs. "I do. But I'm trying to put that aside for now. Focus on today." She gives me a smile, once again trying to reassure *me*, even though she's going through something really hard, too. *I can't imagine falling that hard for someone, and then being forced to split because you couldn't have kids.* A new worry settles into my stomach with all those anxious knots, and I push away my half-eaten BLT. For a place that looks like a slice of Eden, there seem to be pitfalls around every corner.

We walk back to class to Cammie's effervescent chatter about the various pros and cons of her *six* men, and I'm glad to have the distraction. I just have to get through a few more days of classes, and then I'll meet Jax, Beckett, and Fletcher. One way or another, I'll find out if they are who they seem to be in their photos.

Chapter Seven

GETTING READY

Demy

With my shoulders square and my chin up, I walk beside Nell, with Cammie and Leilani leading the way back from the final class. The midday sun is being swallowed by dark clouds overhead, threatening rain. The air has a bit more nip than before classes and feels heavy on my skin, despite the fact that we've only just had lunch.

The rest of training week has passed in a blur, but as the days have gone by, I've found myself growing in confidence. I know what's expected of me now in the program—I have six whole months, if I need them, to decide on these three guys or if I need new matches—and I've already gotten my first weekly pay deposit, just like Nell said. It's more money than I've ever gotten at one time from any of the crappy temp jobs I've taken in my life. It might not be a lot to a guy like Beckett, but it means the world to me to have some financial means.

Security. If I ever have to run again, I'll actually be able to afford a ticket to anywhere I want to go, even if this only lasts a few months.

Plus, I've started to form a plan for finding out who's chasing me, and why they killed my parents. This place has top notch security;

I won't be a pauper in this marriage. And Nell's constant rotation of textbooks has caught my interest, as well. I vow to myself to ask her about what she is studying, and how I can get into a study program, too. I need to finish my high school diploma so that whenever my time in the compulsory marriage program ends, I have options. This tiny reprieve has shown me that I need that. Security; options; a *future* where I'm not running. And if this program does what it is supposed to, I'll have a *child* to support. I can't do that on the run, with no education or life plan.

We walk into the dormitory and, all at once, our fertility meters vibrate and ring with alerts.

"Dresses delivered?" Leilani is the first to read aloud. "What dresses?"

"And where's room twelve?" Cammie mutters, tapping her fertility wristband with an annoyed frown as if it's going to answer her.

"Oh, you guys are going to like this part!" Nell says, excitement overflowing from her tone. "Upstairs, let's go!"

"What's going on?" I ask as Nell takes the stairs two at a time, and we trail up behind her.

"Tonight's the night we meet the guys—" She turns left at the top of the stairs, and darts down the hall. She stops outside one in the middle and pauses for effect while we all catch up to her. When we're all circled around, she pushes the door wide open with a flourish. "Which means, they've brought in racks and *racks* of gowns for us to choose from."

Cammie's squeal is so loud next to me, it nearly pierces my eardrum. "Good gracious, girl, chillax!" I call after her as she bolts into the room, the rest of us trailing behind more slowly.

Sure enough, Nell's right. This room is the same size as ours, but there's no bathroom, no furniture, and no closet. The whole thing is just lined and filled to the brim with clothing racks, fancy dresses spilling off of them like some sort of upscale boutique on crack. Each row has a name plaque hanging at the end. Cammie's already found her section, if the smalls oohs and intermittent squeals of delight are any indication.

My section is off to the right, so I slowly walk down the aisle, letting my fingertips run over the rainbow array of silken fabrics. The colors are lovely, and I force myself to stop, and push some of the hangers to the side so I can take a closer look at a deep purple gown. It's beautiful, covered in shiny pearl beads in a swirling floral pattern, a stark contrast to the deep cutouts on the sides, showing off more skin than I'd be comfortable with.

I continue down the aisle, stopping when a particular gown catches my eye. The closer I look, the more I begin to panic. These are all *huge* gowns, and flashy. Not one is simple, or looks like it would be easy to move in. The idea of being trapped in one of these while a room full of unknown men swirls around me feels like a death sentence. I start to breathe faster, panic clawing at my throat, the smells of the various gowns and sounds of the other girls chatting and comparing options pushes me under the swell of emotion.

I try, but it's like I can't draw in a full breath, like my lungs can't expand enough, and an ugly loop of images of me being caught in a lumbering ball gown, shoved against the wall by an angry-eyed man in a black cloak play on repeat in my head. My mouth tastes metallic, my ears are ringing, and, to my horror, tears are welling in my eyes as my face in the gown turns to my mother's, the life draining from her eyes as a cruel-eyed man looms—

I sink to the ground, finding a small gap between two racks, and wedge myself down into it, wrapping my arms around my knees, and dropping my forehead down on top. *Breathe, breathe, Demy.*

"Demelza!" The sharp hiss of my name combined with a hand shaking my forearm makes me snap my head up, terrified. Nell's crouched in front of me, worry etched into the lines of her beautiful face. "Hey, what's going on? Talk to me," she commands.

"I—" I try to answer her, I really do, but my throat feels like the sides are stuck closed, and the tears well over, spilling down my cheeks. I am such a mess, and now, she's going to know it. *Just another thing you've screwed up. Probably for the best. Everyone who gets close to you dies.*

"Demy! It's okay. Come on, on your feet. Let's go to your room and get some air." I must not move fast enough for her, because she wraps one hand around each wrist and pulls, yanking me up with a surprising amount of strength for how short she is.

"Everything okay?" Leilani calls from the other side of the room, and I see—almost through a long distance lens—her and Cammie with wide smiles, already holding up dress options and swishing the skirts around.

"We're fine, just need a break. You two have fun," Nell says and waves for them to carry on, still dragging me by the wrist with her other hand.

I follow, eyes unfocused as she drags me down the hall and to my room. She pushes the door open without asking for permission, and flicks on a few lights. She deposits me at the end of the bed. "Sit here, and don't move."

I obey the order without thought, sinking onto the too-comfortable mattress, and flinch at the sound of my balcony door sliding along its track. Fresh, cool, damp air washes over me with the scent of fresh rain, and I shudder as I suck in a lungful of it, and then another.

Nell crouches down in front of me, so I'm looking down at her. "How long have you had panic attacks, and are you on any medication for them?"

I try to focus, so I can answer her question. "For years, and no. No medication. I'll be fine," I say, but I sound wooden to my own ears, and distant. *That's not right. She's going to know that's not right.* A little voice whispers, but I can't focus on it.

"Okay, that's fine. I've got you. Would you feel better if you were to lie down? Take a shower? Stand by the balcony? What helps you?"

Help? I don't know—usually I just hide until the moment passes, and then go to bed as soon as humanly possible. I frown at her, not sure what to say. "Bed?"

"Great, lie down. On your side, if you want. The fetal position is actually a really restorative position."

None of that means anything to me, but she says it with confidence, and in a moment I'm lying on my side, hands wrapped around my knees, with Nell a foot away. She's mirroring my pose, her eyes holding mine steady. I breathe in and out through my nose, following her slow, deep pattern like it's a lifeline, and gradually my heart rate begins to slow. As I come back to myself, shame washes over me, hot and deep, like a burning beneath my skin. I close my eyes, and she clucks her tongue.

"No, Demy. Don't look embarrassed. Hey! Open your eyes again. Look at me."

I do, even though I don't want to.

"You have *nothing*, absolutely nothing, to be ashamed of. Do you hear me? We all have something, okay? Nobody's perfect, no matter how it seems."

"You have it all together, Nell. How can you say that?"

She laughs, the sound incongruous with my tumultuous emotions in the moment, but she throws her head back, lying flat beside me on the bed like a starfish for a few moments as laughter racks her body, before flipping back to her side, and propping her head on her elbow. Slowly, I realize that I can move again, too. I have no idea how much time has passed, though.

I fold my arm under my head, not having the energy yet to prop up like she has. Her smile is warm as she looks at me. "Demy, I absolutely promise you that I do not have it all together now, and never have before, either."

I shake my head lightly, not believing her, so she starts talking. The words are calm, quiet. Soothing, unlike Cammie's frenetic pace. I lie still and listen, glad to be out of my own head.

"You and I are more alike than you seem to think. I . . . didn't have a good life growing up. My mom died when I was young, and my dad was gone before that. I only remember little things about her. Our hair was the same color, but her eyes were green. When I was a little girl, I remember thinking she had somehow stolen beautiful emeralds and turned them into eyes. Weird, right? Anyways. I was raised by my aunt and uncle." She shifts a little, the light memories giving way to darkness shadowing her eyes, and I worry about what she's going to say next.

"My uncle drank. A lot. We never had any money, and what we did, he blew on alcohol. I was lucky to eat once, twice a day most of the time outside of school. School saved me, but I didn't have any friends there. My clothes never fit right, and even in a small, bass-ackwards school like mine, I didn't fit in."

I know that feeling. That's why I stopped going to school, once I was running; people started looking at me differently, and I didn't want to deal with the questions. I don't say any of that, though. I just lie quietly, letting her words soothe me.

"Between how I dressed, and looked, and my uncle's reputation around town—he owed almost everybody money—well, we weren't popular. I was alone a lot, and when I wasn't, I wanted to be. When he got too drunk, or the liquor money ran out, he'd get aggressive." She swallows hard, the words cutting off mid-stream as she closes her eyes.

I surprise myself by reaching out a hand, and resting it on her forearm. "I'm sorry he hurt you," I manage to say. My voice sounds hoarse, but even as bad at *people* as I am, I can see she needs to hear it.

Her eyes spring open, and she gives me a small smile. "Thanks. It was a long time ago, and my first husband . . . he took care of things back home for me." She clears her throat. "So, it's all in the past. Sometimes . . . sometimes the memories are still strong. But you know what?" She looks deadly serious, staring right into my eyes. "We're stronger. You and me? We're fighters. We're going to make the life we want; that we *deserve*. And you do deserve good things, Demy—I hope you know that. You don't have to tell me what happened until you're ready. I won't pry. But right now we have to get ready for the dinner tonight; there are no exceptions for the events, unfortunately. Can I help you get a dress, without you having to go back into the room? Avoid whatever triggered that attack?"

I swallow hard, unsure what to say. "The dresses are all so . . . big. Hard to move, hard to run. I need something simpler."

"Ahh, okay." She taps her fingers lightly on the duvet for a moment, before springing upright. "I'll be back in a few minutes. What's your favorite color? Wait, no. Don't answer that. With your complexion it's got to be red. Don't move!"

The door clicks softly shut behind her, and I roll to my back. It hits me that I've been curled up in bed with my shoes still on, so I toe them off, the twin thumps of them landing on the floor striking me as oddly funny.

I lie there only a few minutes before she quickly taps on the door and lets herself back in. "Okay, I've got the perfect dress. But we'll put that on later. Right now, do you think you're up to coming to the hair and makeup room? It's basically a whole salon in there, and Cammie has already styled Leilani within an inch of her life—we need to rescue her."

I snort, easily able to imagine a captive Leilani, hog-tied to the chair with hairdresser's capes, a gleeful Cammie behind her with a bottle of hairspray in each hand.

"Yeah, I'm feeling a lot better." I get up and follow her down the hall, but stop her with a hand on her arm before we go in. She turns to face me, hand on the doorknob. "Thank you, Nell. For everything."

"Don't mention it. We're in this together, okay? And listen," she pauses, gnawing her lip for a second. "Just . . . stay close tonight, okay? Don't go off with any of your guys alone—stay with the group, okay?"

"Uhm, okay," I agree, confused. She seems . . . worried. Though that could be post-panic-attack-anxiety talking. I always feel off-kilter for a while.

"Good. Now, let's get beautiful, so we can blow all their minds." Her worried expression is replaced with a wicked grin as I follow her into the mini salon, coughing on a cloud of hairspray.

"Cammie, I've got your next victim ready and waiting."

"Thank God," Leilani mutters, leaping from the chair. She's been curled, pinned, and sprayed to perfection, and heavy makeup applied to her features, exaggerating her high cheekbones, and straight nose. She looks like a movie star, and it's almost intimidating.

At any other time, I'd probably start worrying about being the least beautiful girl here, but before I can trundle down that dead-end road, Cammie steers me into her chair with hands on both shoulders and presses me into it.

"What color is your dress going to be?"

"Pure crimson," Nell answers for me from the chair next to mine, a mascara wand in hand as she does her own makeup.

"Ooh, yes! I love it. Knock their freakin' socks off from the get-go. I'm going with silver, and Leilani chose a stunning orange number. They'll be dazzled, I know it." She looks determined in the light-surrounded mirror in front of me, so I try to encourage her.

"They'll be smitten, I'm sure you're right."

She smiles and picks up a large round brush. "How do you feel about barrel curls?"

"Uh, what's a barrel curl?"

She rolls her eyes. "Never mind. Just don't move, and I'll make you fabulous."

"Deal." I close my eyes, the sensation of the brush running through my hair lulling me into contentment.

She pauses the brush, and then leans down to whisper in my ear, so the others can't hear, "We've got your back, girl. If you get overwhelmed, just find one of us. We're sisters now, and you're not doing this alone."

Tears prickle my eyes, and a lump rises in my throat at her kindness. There's no judgment, no teasing. Just love. This girl squad thing? It might be life changing.

CHAPTER EIGHT

THE MEETING

DEMY

Two hours later and only ten minutes late, the four of us glide-slash-stumble down the stairs, each wearing high heels and decked out head to toe in our chosen gowns. Our hair is perfect, our makeup looks like we're going to walk a red carpet, and Leilani even found a box of fertility meter bands in every color of the rainbow, so they at least don't clash with the overall effect. I wobble a little as my three-inch strappy heel lands on the parquet flooring of the ground level, but I catch myself on the banister. These are *definitely* not cloud flats.

You can't run in these shoes. The unease takes the form of an insidious whisper, and I swallow hard and glance to my left at Nell, looking radiant and bored in her blue gown, hair perfectly styled in short curls. She said to stick close to her, and after this afternoon I know she'll help me if I have another panic attack. No. I refuse to go down that path.

Jones is waiting for us, and his grin is wide as he takes the four of us in. "Ladies, you are absolutely stunning. These guys don't stand a chance. If there's not a proposal tonight, I'll be shocked."

He throws a hand over his heart, pretending to stagger backwards. "I mean it, if one of those lucky fools doesn't propose, I might," he jokes, and I can't help the eye roll at his cheesy offer. We look good, but I doubt anyone's going to hit one knee.

At least, I hope not.

Wiping that unlikely scenario out of my mind, I focus on the positive as we trail after Jones through the moonlight. The dress Nell found me is perfect, and I can move easily in the stretchy, clinging lace fabric. It does poof out at the bottom—covered in *feathers*, of all things—but it makes it easy to walk, and I have to admit the red looks good against my fair skin and dark hair.

Cammie did me up with a matching red lipstick, and "Hollywood curls," whatever that means. I look better than I've ever looked in my life, and I might even be a match for Beckett. Though I'm not *that* confident.

In fact, I'm nervous. I'm going to meet my future husband tonight. Spending six years chased by man after man in a creepy black robe has made me give pretty much all men a wide berth; I tried dating once, and a week later had to run again, so that put an end to that relationship. Trust is hard for me, and this is all going to move quickly.

The most important thing is that I stay sharp, and see who these men are as *people*. Cammie is obsessed with finding a hottie, but I want a man who's safe. Of course, that's hard to pin down. How do you even know? I haven't felt safe with a man since my father was killed. Frustration wells up inside me as we climb up the front stairs of the main building, the porch lights soft and lovely in the darkness, causing our dresses to shimmer as we ascend. Although, from what Nell told us, they'll be waiting inside.

I swallow hard, cursing my jumbled thoughts. This is the opposite of sharp, which is normal after one of my attacks. In through the nose, out through the mouth. I repeat the calming breaths as we swan down the familiar wood-paneled hallway to the dining room, noting the extra candles covering every surface even out here, and large, heavy-laden arrangements of fresh flowers perched on most surfaces. Their perfume hangs in the air, and it's like they've brought the outside gardens in for the occasion.

Jones stops in front of the large double doors to the dining room, and turns to us, his grin stretching so wide, it takes up his whole face.

"Are we ready, ladies? Tonight is the first night of the rest of your life."

Nell groans. "Jones, really? So cheesy. Just open the dang doors already."

He huffs. "Really, Nell, let me have a little fun with this. We only get to see their first impressions once. That's something," he grumbles, but pulls both doors wide, and steps inside with a pasted-on smile.

The lights are brighter, and we follow him into the familiar room single file. We loop around the tables to the front of the room and stop under the spotlights. Jones takes the mic and says . . . something. I weakly join in when everyone applauds, but my mind is spinning. A larger throng of men than I expected has gathered, waiting only a few feet away. That's not right. The *men* are larger than I expected, seeming to suck up all the oxygen in the room. I'm tempted to stare down at my feet—well, the feathered bell of my dress hem—but I force myself to look up, scan the crowd, and make eye contact with anyone who's looking back.

Then, I spot the first of my matches. Fletcher. He's standing off to the left side of the crowd, arms crossed over an impressively muscled chest, just like the photos. His curls have been tamed, gathered back in a bun at the nape of his neck, and I think I sense a hint of discomfort on his face, as if he's unused to wearing a fancy suit. Something about the way his jaw is clenched? I don't know him well enough to pinpoint it, but his expression shifts, and I realize I've been caught staring. His eyes meet mine, and heat sizzles between us, a tangible thing in the air.

Slowly, like honey spreading over a hot biscuit, his expression transforms into a grin, giving me a peek at straight white teeth hiding underneath his lips. I realize belatedly that I've been chewing my bottom lip. I let it go and feel my cheeks heat.

He's steady, though, and unbothered by my frank perusal. In fact, he lifts his right hand, and gives me a small, covert wave.

"Gentlemen, it's the moment you've been waiting for!" Jones's voice snaps me out of our bubble, and I realize that I have *absolutely no idea* what he's said since we walked in, or if he'd given instructions. *Crap, crap, crap!* I focus on Jones—though the heat in my chest is still acutely aware of Fletcher watching me—as he introduces Cammie first.

"Gentlemen, this is Cammie. It looks like there are several of you here for her! Will Maddox, Orlando, Alonso, Vince, Santi, and Fletcher step forward and greet this lovely lady?"

Confusion ripples through me. Is there more than one Fletcher? I whip my eyes back to where Fletcher was, only to find him on the move, and horror replaces confusion. Is he . . . is he *also* matched to Cammie? Is that even *possible*?

I watch, wooden, as a swarm of men descends upon Cammie, looking like a heartbreaker in her gorgeous, shining silver gown.

They vie to get to her first, most of them shaking her hand, others blatantly running their eyes over her, and the clinging silver gown. She's graceful, and brash—she's already laughing, head thrown back, at what one of them has whispered in her ear—and I know that I've got no chance of pulling a man's eye from her. Not that I'd want too—but I hadn't thought we'd be competing for the same guy, either.

How did that happen? Cammie and her barrage of suitors glide out of the way and towards a large, circular table with places already set, and Jones continues talking.

"Next up, we have Leilani. Isn't she striking, men? And I can attest from the past week of spending time with these girls, that Leilani is kind and sweet, everything you'd ever want in a life partner. Would Leilani's matches please step forward—Kellan, Campbell, and Esteban?" He waves a hand toward her, and I see a faint blush staining her tawny brown cheeks, offset perfectly by her tangerine gown. It's more flowing than mine, swishing hypnotically as she steps forward and greets her three men—only her highest genetic matches, no extras, like me.

Leilani is more reserved than Cammie, her hands knotted in front of her as she nods to each of her men in turn. One of them—a man with darker skin and handsome side-swept hair—offers her his elbow, and leads the smaller throng to another table, to begin their dinner.

I knew we weren't all sitting together—this is supposed to be our first *group date* after all—but it's only just now sinking in that I'm going to be alone at the table with three strangers for the rest of the night. My girl squad, while new, brought comfort. But I'm already back on my own, and it leaves a bitter taste on the back of my tongue. Nell steps forward next, positively beaming at Jones's side while he introduces her. I take in the remaining men—only four, and I easily pick out Beckett and Jax, both of them looking just like their photos. They each grin over at me, completely ignoring Nell's introduction, and I resist the urge to squirm in my fancy dress; the heat Fletcher brings out in me leaves with him as he walks away with Cammie.

I notice absently that Nell only has two matches; a mountain of a man, covered in tattoos and towering over her, his blond hair the only thing that looks *soft* about him. He sends a shiver of wariness through me, and I quickly glance at her second match, a black man who's only slightly shorter than the mountain he stands next to, head shaved, with a dark goatee that shows off the hard cut of his jaw. They're both handsome, and they've both only got eyes for Nell. She's got a grin bigger than I've ever seen as she goes right for Mr. Mountain, shocking me as she offers him a deep hug. She then turns and gives the second man the same, though they pull apart a fraction of a second quicker. Jones waves me closer, and I close the distance between us.

He gives me a warm smile, and then launches back into his announcer voice. "Gentlemen, I think you know by now that this is Demelza, your match. She is lovely, intelligent, and drop-dead gorgeous. You're very lucky to be in her consideration. Now, please step forward, Jax, Beckett, and ahh—there's Fletcher, back right on time." He gives me a brief pat on the shoulder, and then steps to the side, allowing the three men to surge forward. I have to fight not to step back as they surround me, the urge to run instinct by this point.

They're all smiling, though, and keeping their space—except Jax, who's the first to shove his hand out for me to shake.

"Demelza, hello! I'm Jax, and I'm so happy to meet you." I let my eyes roam up from his chest, past his square jaw, and into his eyes. They're intense, and dark. The sharpness I see there sends a small shiver down my spine as I offer him my hand in return. His grip is firm, but not bone-crushing.

"It's nice to meet you, too, Jax."

His calloused fingers slip from mine, and Beckett is right there, Mister Suave—and looking rankled to be second.

"Hello, Demelza. Can I be the first to say how utterly breathtaking you are this evening? Truly, you're a showstopper in that dress." He holds eye contact as he leans down over my hand, pressing warm lips to the tops of my knuckles. *Whoa.* When he straightens, a single strand of hair comes loose from his perfect style, and I step forward—our chests nearly touching—and tuck the wayward lock back into place.

"There you go. It's nice to meet you, too, Beckett. And you're too kind—I don't know what to say."

"You don't have to say a word." His voice is husky, and his eyes molten as I step away. I turn my focus to Fletcher, waiting patiently on my right side.

"Demelza, it's nice to meet you. I'm Fletcher, and I have to agree you look gorgeous this evening." His voice is deeper than the rest, and I can't help but notice the frisson of electricity it sends skittering down my arms. Goosebumps break out along my flesh, and I silently bless Nell for choosing a long-sleeved dress, so it isn't so obvious how physically attractive I find him.

"Fletcher, hi. I noticed . . . you're also matched to Cammie? I didn't know that was possible," I murmur, wanting to get it right out in the open. I didn't like it, had no desire to compete with one of the girls who was quickly becoming my friend, and the sooner we got it out in the open, the better.

"Yeah, uh, she chose me as one of her additional three. From what I understand, you and I are a higher match." He rubs his palms together and bobbles his head to either side as if he's unsure what to say. "I'm sure we'll make it work until one of you decides you're not interested." There's that grin again, but this time it doesn't hit me the same way.

"May I escort you to the table?" Beckett's there, arm extended, looking the picture of polish in his three-piece suit—a welcome distraction from my tangled thoughts over Fletcher and Cammie.

I slip my hand tentatively into the crook of his arm, the fabric silky over his firm bicep. Beckett leads all of us to a table towards the back of the dining room, a bit further away from the other three groups. Places have already been set with each of our names, and more fancy crystal than was laid out our first day here.

Beckett holds out my seat, and I sink carefully into it, tucking the large bottom of the dress under the table before he helps me slide in. Jax has claimed the seat on my right while he helped me, and Fletcher sits across from me, watching the interaction between Beckett and me with interest. Beckett settles to my left, and then the waiters descend with the first course, a warm lobster bisque, deep rusty orange with a juicy chunk of lobster resting on top of the broth.

"Well, this looks delicious," I say, pausing over the two spoons at the table. Why are there two? I sneak quick peeks around the table, and each of the men picks up the larger, outer spoon so I do the same.

"So, Demelza, please, we'd love to hear more about you," Jax says from my right. "Where are you from?"

I nearly choke on my bisque. Straight to the awkward questions, with all three of them here?

"Ahh, well. I've moved around a lot, actually. Most recently I was in Ionori for a job, but I'm from Wiscigan originally. What about you?" There, that didn't sound too bad, did it? Polished, even. *Don't get ahead of yourself, Demy.*

"I love it. A roamer spirit, like me." Jax grins, the devilish curve of his lips telling me a lot.

"Oh yeah? What do you do for a living?"

"I'm a closer," he says with pride.

"That makes sense, I saw a uniform in your photo, but I wasn't sure what it was for. That's a good job for someone who likes to stay on the move." I smile at him, and he beams back at me. "What about you, Beckett and Fletcher?" I turn towards them, trying to pull them into the conversation so it doesn't get too one-sided. But I also don't want to cut Jax off. This is hard already, and we were introduced less than ten minutes ago.

"What about us, what?" Beckett answers, one eyebrow raised. There's something . . . *off* about his tone, but I can't put my finger on it.

"Where are you from, and what do you do?" I repeat the question, trying to be polite. I flick my gaze to Fletcher, and see a quizzical expression on his face as he examines Beckett. So, *it's not just me. He's acting weird.*

"I'm from Wrightsville, and I manage my family's investment portfolio." He reaches up and smoothes his tie, though it already looks perfect to me. Nervous habit? "I presume you've heard of the Vaughn family?" There's that eyebrow, arching again as if I've failed a test I didn't realize I was taking.

Wrong answer or no, honesty is all I have. "Actually, no, I haven't. I'd love to hear everything about them, though."

"I haven't heard of them either. But I'm one step up from a wild man," Fletcher cuts in with a laugh, and I shoot him a grateful look. The waiters sweep our bisques away—mine barely touched, dang it—and replace them with a savory filled flaky pastry. I take a nibble, and find it filled with salty cheese and mushrooms. "Oh, wow," I say after I swallow the small bite.

"Good?" Fletcher asks, eyeing his own. "I don't usually eat fancy stuff like this, but it smells good."

"Very good, you should try it." I give him an encouraging smile, and he pops a hunk of pastry between his lips. I jerk my gaze away from the motion of his jaw as he chews, focusing back on Jax.

"So, what made you want to join the New Lives Program? I know it's optional for men."

Jax's eyes widen at the blunt question. "That's true, it is optional for men, but I've always wanted a family. My chances of having one any other way aren't so hot. Unless I want to chase an older woman."

"Oh, I hadn't thought of that. That was probably a dumb question." There is embarrassment burning in my cheeks, and I duck my head, shoving another bite of pastry into my mouth to stop the stupid questions flying out.

Beckett lays his fork down and shakes his head. "It's not a dumb question, actually. For me, it's more than just a wife and children. I want someone to build upon my family's legacy with, someone to carry on the name and tradition. This program vets us for genetic compatibility, yes, but it also ensures we're relationally compatible. If all that mattered was genetics, you'd be handed the top man, and that would be that."

"I agree there are other reasons for joining the program." Fletcher surprises me by agreeing with Beckett. "I'm hoping to find someone to adventure with. Someone who gets me. Of course, I want to have a wife and kids, but I don't want some ice princess who doesn't like me. That wouldn't work for the long run. I want a life partner." His eyes burn into mine with passion as he speaks, and once again I'm being swept away on the river Fletcher. He's a tangible *presence*, and it's a lot to take in.

A crumb of pastry sticks in my throat as I swallow, and I cough, my eyes watering as I try to dislodge the pesky particle. Jax reaches over and smacks me on the back—hard—while Beckett holds up a goblet of ice water. There's no alcohol provided in the program, so the wine glasses all hold soda or other non-alcoholic drinks.

I finally get it clear and suck in a full breath, gratefully accepting and sucking down the water Beckett offers. If I'd been a little embarrassed with my last question, my level of humiliation has now skyrocketed into the stratosphere.

I fight off a wheeze and take another sip of water. Condensation glides down the curve of the glass, melding under my finger, and I fixate on it instead of the three pairs of eyes I can feel boring into me.

And I'm going to be marrying one of them.

This is intense, but I'm saved from comment by Fletcher.

"Wow, Demelza, you really know how to command attention," he quips with a cheeky grin, and then the three of them start joking back and forth amongst themselves about who's got the best party trick, giving me a moment to compose myself.

My watering eyes wander away to the other tables, and all three of the other girls seem to be doing better than I am. Nell's chatting happily with her two men, and Cammie's got her entire table laughing. Leilani's harder to tell, but she's smiling at something one of her men is saying. I swallow hard and look away, noticing guards loitering at each exit to the room. Most of them are bored, shuffling feet and scanning the room idly, or talking to each other.

All except one. He's shaved bald, and from across the room all I can see is that his eyes are dark, reflecting his all-black uniform. The way he's watching me is unnerving, and a flutter of panic starts behind my ribcage. But then, his eyes skip away across the room, and I realize he's just doing his job. *Settle down, Demy. You're safe here.*

The water in the glass I'm still holding begins to ripple oddly, and I realize that my hand is shaking. I set it down a little too quickly, and some sloshes over the rim onto the linen tablecloth. Biting my lip, I take in another breath and look up, racking my brain for something to say that's neither awkward, panicked, nor stupid. All three men are watching me again, and I force a smile.

"Sorry," I say sheepishly. "That pastry is delicious, but—"

"It fought back!" Fletcher jokes. "No worries, Demelza. We get it. You were right, though, it's delicious." He raises another forkful in mock salute, before chomping it down happily.

"Indeed, the food here is exquisite," Beckett agrees.

"I'm not a fan of mushrooms, myself. But the soup was good," Jax chimes in. And just like that, the ice seems to have broken between us, and I can finally breathe a sigh of relief. Except . . . I throw a quick glance across the expansive dining room, and the bald guard is gone, someone else standing in his post.

Unease still lingers, rattling around uncomfortably underneath my ribs. I've been on the run so long, I'm seeing threats even here, inside the safest, most locked-down place I've ever been. It's utterly ridiculous, and I make a point to keep my thoughts on my matches, and *only* my matches, for the rest of the night. Paranoia isn't helping me focus on choosing the man I'm going to marry.

CHAPTER NINE

GROUP DATE

DEMY

I wake naturally the next morning for the first time since arriving at the New Life Center. There are no classes, so I don't actually have anywhere that I have to be until I get a date request, or request one myself. Not *happening*. *I'll let them drive things, until I get to know them better.* I lie on my side and check my tablet, finding a silent notification waiting.

When I tap it, it's a quiz about interests and dating preferences. *Interesting.* The app opens, and walks me through ten rounds of questions, finally ending with me selecting individual activities that I'm interested in. When the page of options loads, I'm floored. I've seen a gym, my dorm, and the main building where we eat, attend classes, and met the guys . . . but they've got more activities on here than I even recognize. Squirrel suit diving? Do I even want to know what that is? Ballroom dancing is going to be a no from me, as well as learning to play ice hockey—they must have an indoor rink.

I scroll past endless activities. Pampering. Dancing. Horseback riding. Crazy risk-taking adventures. When suddenly, something catches my eye. Self-defense classes!

I immediately click on the activity, and pore over the details. It can be a group date, or one-to-one plus an instructor, so I check that I'm interested in either option. They can also be booked as a recurring activity for me alone. Hmm, I'll definitely have to look into that. The gym is great, but self-defense training could be the difference between life and death if I ever get caught or am on the run again.

Next I pick the option to see more. A much shorter list loads, but I'm suddenly checking boxes left and right. Jiu Jitsu, archery, blade throwing, axe throwing, knife skills, basic survival, boxing . . . maybe this whole dating thing won't be so bad?

But the guys are all so intense. A group date where we're all learning how to fight or work with knives might end disastrously. I worry my bottom lip, thinking about it.

If they can't behave themselves, then I'm not going to choose them. Either way, I'll learn something about my matches. I decide to roll with it. This time is going to give me some safe breathing room *and* allow me to pick up new skills. Win-win.

I close the app, feeling good about my choices, and it hits me. There could be data on this very tablet which I could use to identify my parents' killers, and figure out why my family's been targeted. With shaking fingers, I flip through the different screens on the app. Most of it is directly tied to the program itself. There's a rules primer, scheduling app, the Bachelor Book, of course, and the messaging app my alerts come through that's linked to my fertility tracker. The only other thing on the screen is an e-learning app, so I click it.

It's a pretty basic app, all-white background with a series of icons representing the standard subjects. Dead end. I click it closed, letting out a sigh. Of course it wouldn't be *that* easy. But, that doesn't mean the data isn't here. Just that I don't have access to it.

Wait. Access. I jump off the bed, adrenaline surging as it hits me. *Someone here probably has a lot more access.* Who, though, and who could I convince to help me?

Still thinking, I wander into the bathroom and turn on the shower. I stare into the mirror as the water warms, drumming my fingers on the beautiful stone counter. The other girls have the same access as I do, so they're out. The director knows everything, but she's not going to share it. Same for Jones; he's friendly enough, but also aloof. I can't imagine him ponying up information I'm not meant to have. So who?

The mirror's beginning to steam when the vision of dark, serious eyes lingering on me in the dining room hits. *The guard.* The security team surely has information on threats, right? And if I could befriend one of them . . . maybe he'd tell me what I need to know? I'll start with him, the one who was watching me.

With that decided, I strip and reward myself with a luxurious shower. I shave, and wash my hair with all four products, taking the time for the deep condition to soak in. It's already been looking so much shinier with all the fancy products they provided, instead of the cheap stuff I used to scrounge from train station bathrooms. It's probably an hour later when I wander out, feeling like a steamed piece of broccoli wrapped in a towel, when I notice a notification dinging on the tablet again.

Date Request Received

My pulse picks up speed, and I suck in a deep breath. Already? I only just chose the options!

Tapping the icon, the message loads.

Your presence is requested in the indoor archery range at 10:30 for a group date.

Activity: Archery lesson followed by a picnic lunch

Attire: Athletic wear.

Length: Three hours.

Attendees: Beckett, Fletcher, and Jax

So, they're all in. This is happening, and it's happening right now. I check the time, and quickly hit accept before dropping the tablet to the bedside table. I've got to choose an outfit, then go get some breakfast, quick. Sending up a silent prayer to whoever's listening that the date goes well and my matches don't shoot each other, I dart for the closet, bee-lining for my favorite section full of buttery leggings and matching sports bras.

The forty-five minutes pass in a blur and before I know it, I've downed a banana and piece of toast, and am waiting on the covered porch for someone to take me to the gymnasium. I ran past Cammie and Nell on their way to dates, too, so it looks like we'll all have something to talk about tonight.

Nervous energy has me bouncing on the balls of my feet, and I'm really curious to see more of the grounds. This place is so freaking ritzy, I'm sure the range is going to be pristine and top-of-the-line. I don't want to get too used to this cushy life, because deep down I don't think it will last. Even if they can't breech the New Life

Center's security for the next few years, eventually I'll be back on my own.

But . . . not enjoying it now because it's going to go away again doesn't make any sense, either. I may as well enjoy whatever time I have, while I have it.

To my surprise, Beckett is the one who comes to meet me, and walk me to the range. He's dressed more casually than I've seen before, wearing a pair of navy joggers which hug his upper thighs, and a matching hoodie. He's got one hand slung into his pocket, and lifts the other in a brisk wave. His eyes, just like the first time we met, feel like they see straight through me.

I have to admit, he owns the more casual style, and he looks good. He stops at the bottom of the steps and gives me a warm smile. "So, you're an adventurous girl in more ways than one, I see. You picked all action dates." He lifts that eyebrow, and I can sense an unspoken question behind the words.

I shrug noncommittally. "It seemed like a good place to start."

"Fair enough. I'm looking forward to it—I've actually never practiced archery, so this will be a learning experience for me, too."

"Shame. I'm an old pro, and I'd hate to show you up on our first date," I say as I slowly take the steps down to where he's waiting.

"Seriously? Where did you learn?" He doesn't move, and I come to a stop right in front of his chest, having to look up a few inches to make eye contact.

I can't contain my wide grin at his shocked expression. "Nope, not serious in the least. I have never touched a bow before, and it seems like a fun activity."

He laughs, the sound deep and rich, causing warmth to spread through my chest. *I made him laugh; I didn't think I could do that.*

"You really had me going, you little liar." He wraps an arm around my shoulders and gives me a squeeze—it feels surprisingly natural, so I return the side hug. *Maybe I'm not completely terrible at this flirting thing, after all.* "You ready to go shoot some stuff?"

"Abso-freaking-lutely." I don't bother trying to hide my enthusiasm. For once in my life, instead of running, it feels like taking the first bit of my power back from the men hunting me. I'm taking charge. I'm in control. Maybe I'll be the one hunting *them* before long.

"—so, what do you think?"

Crap. Crap, crap, crap.

"Uhm, I'm sorry, I was distracted. What was the question?" I look up at him, guilt gnawing at my gut. What a bad date I am.

He rolls his eyes, and says, "I asked if you'll let me know when you're ready to move on to more . . . romantic dates. I don't want to push past where you're comfortable, but all this *sporting* isn't really my thing."

"Oh, yeah. Of course!" My eyes skitter over the sprawling lawn and islands of bursting plants, scrabbling for something better to say.

"So, what's got you so distracted over there?"

"Uhm," *the idea of sinking an arrow into one of the SOBs that killed my parents?* "Thinking about what you're thinking. How everyone's going to like archery. Not shooting myself in the foot with an arrow. You know, the usual stuff."

"Huh. Okay, then. I noticed you didn't pick anyone extra for yourself, like one of the other girls did. You not that excited about dating, or . . . ?" He trails off, and I can practically feel his eyes boring into my cheek.

"No, it's not that I'm not excited. I just . . . what's the point of picking other guys, when I haven't met you three yet? You're my best genetic matches. Picking anyone based solely off looks makes no sense to me, and it's not always easy to get a read off someone from a picture." I shrug. "It felt like muddying the waters."

"Makes sense. I can respect that; meet everyone before jumping in feet first." He gives me a smile, but it's overly polite, and it's clear I've somehow misstepped.

"What about you—am I your first match?"

"No, you're my second match."

"Oh, okay. That's cool. I guess it didn't work out with your first match?"

"No, we were compatible, actually. She was a lovely girl, really sweet. I was her one bonus pick, but in the end she went with her highest fertility match instead of me."

"Yeah, I can see that. I mean, no offense. It's just we've talked about it, and if you *can* avoid having to use reproductive assistance, it seems like an easier road."

"We?" he asks, looking off into the plush landscaping, instead of at me this time.

"Me and the other three girls; we're starting to become friends. It's nice to have someone else going through the same thing you are, even if we've all just met."

"I can imagine. It's a little different on our end, since all the men are in competition for the same woman. Well, not *all* of us." He sounds tense, but we come around the hedge right at that moment and I see the indoor archery range up ahead. The walls are floor-to-ceiling glass, much like the gym, and I can see both guys inside, along with an instructor choosing bows from the wall. In my excitement, I decide not to worry about Beckett and whatever

87

jealousy it seems like he's dealing with. I can't change that for him, so hopefully he and the guys will work it out amongst themselves.

"Come on, Beckett! Let's get in there before they get all the good bows!" I grab his arm, giving his bicep a little squeeze before jogging up the steps and up to the huge double doors. They're painted black—a surprising deviation from the grandiose and classic style of everything else here, and it feels modern and mysterious. Basically, I love everything about it, and I haven't stepped foot inside yet. Beckett catches up to me and pulls open the door, waving my hand away from the oversized handle.

"Demy, please. Let me take care of you." There's gentle chastisement in his tone, but something else, too. "You're a lady, and when you're on my arm, you'll be treated like one at all times."

"Thank you," I say, but my emotions are warring inside. I'm not some fancy lady, I'm just me. But does that mean I shouldn't accept his kindness? Should I argue that I'm *not worth it*? I shove it down and walk past him into the range.

It's everything I imagined, and more. The near wall is basically one big weapons rack, with bows of every shape, size, color, and type arrayed at eye level. Underneath are storage tubes bristling with hundreds of multi-colored arrows, and then racks of safety gear such as wrist and forearm protectors, gloves, and even a selection of quivers. I'm wide-eyed, staring longingly at all the impressive weaponry, when the other two guys approach.

"Hey, beautiful," Jax steps forward first, wrapping me in a hug. It takes me by surprise and I stiffen, but I manage to pat him on the shoulder like a normal human, instead of an unsocialized robot. He pulls back when Fletcher clears his throat but shoots him a sideways glance. Jax's hands linger on my shoulders a moment too long before he releases me, and I can greet Fletcher.

"Good morning, Demy, you look wonderful today. Are you enjoying the selection of fancy workout duds as much as I am?" Fletcher gives me a lazy grin but doesn't encroach on my personal space. His long, curling hair is pulled back into a bun today, and it gives him a totally different look. *Which I* dig.

"Yeah . . . the fancy gowns I could take or leave, but these workout pants feel like they're made of air. Or butter. I don't know—it sounds weird but they're the best thing I've ever worn. I might get married in them."

He throws his head back and laughs. "Well, now I've got to feel them. Can I?" His eyes are twinkling, and I feel myself nod, even though my brain has short-circuited at the warmth of his laugh. I pop my left leg up a little, and watch mesmerized as he reaches over and trails his fingertips over the pants, right above my knee. His touch is electric, and for a moment, I forget we're in a gym with three other men. I forget everything except the gentle, hypnotic touch. When he pulls his hand back a moment later, my eyes snap back up to his, the spell broken.

"You're right, those are amazing. If I were you, I'd never take them off either. But . . ." He pauses, then leans in close to whisper in my ear. "They don't make them in men's, so I guess I'll just have to snuggle up to you to get my fix."

My heart leaps into my throat at his simple, tantalizing words, and I find myself swallowing hard. My brain has gone on the fritz, and all I can process is the delicious heat of him *so close* to my ear, and the intoxicating smell of his shampoo—it's cedar and pine, and underneath is the masculine scent of *him*, and I'm in so much trouble.

"Hey, there—you must be Demelza, and Beckett?" For the second time in ten minutes, I'm snapped out of an inappropriate distraction. The instructor greets each of us with a friendly smile and a firm handshake, and I like him immediately. He's broad through the shoulders, which look well-defined under his tight, camo t-shirt, and his chestnut hair is thick and shining in the morning sunlight streaming through the windows. "I'm Peter, and I'm basically the weapons master around here, if this were a twelfth century fortress. If you're doing any sort of offensive or defensive training as part of your time, I'm the man you'll see. I checked your file, and it looks like somebody is really interested in self-defense." His gaze lands on me, and his eyes crinkle jovially at the corners when he smiles.

"Guilty as charged." I feel a blush rising to my cheeks. *It probably seems weird to them, doesn't it? Shoot.* I want to blend in, and not draw attention to my dangerous past . . . but also, I want to annihilate the next man in a robe who comes after me. I guess I'll be weird, then.

"Hey, don't look embarrassed. My baby sister is a real spitfire, and I think it's a good thing. This world needs strong women, and self-defense is a great confidence builder. So, follow your interests. Now, show of hands, since we're all here—Who's shot a bow before? Anyone?"

Jax raises his hand, but the rest of us all shake our heads.

"All right, noobs all around. Don't worry, we'll take it from the top, and we'll even give Jax a chance to show off some of his skills." He offers a fist, and Jax bumps it with his own, giving Peter a cocky grin and a nod.

"Nice. So, first thing's first, we need to choose the right bow for each of you, based on draw length and strength. Let's use the lady as a demonstration, then you fellas can test out what works for each of you. Demelza—"

"Peter, if you don't mind—call me Demy."

"Oh, sure thing. Demy, step right over here to this section, and we'll get you kitted out."

Twenty minutes later, we all have everything we need, and I am standing at the head of my firing lane, sleek black bow in my grip, listening to Peter's instructions from behind us and trying to mimic his exact stance when he gave the lesson.

Chin up, steady breath, don't let your elbow sag, touch the corner of my mouth, and . . . I release the string and watch as the arrow flies. It hits the ground with a clang, about three feet short of the target. A series of thuds follow, and I look down the row of targets to see everyone except Beckett has at least made contact with theirs.

Peter's arrow is sunk in a dead bullseye, and Jax's is embedded a little outside and to the left on his target.

Thirty minutes later, we're all starting to tire, but I *still* haven't hit the perfect bullseye. I'm willing to keep practicing—I didn't expect to master it in under an hour, of course—but everyone else has at least nicked that red target center. *Except me.* And that just won't do.

"Good work, everybody! Draw another, and when you're all ready I'll give the signal again," Peter calls, so I try again, aiming higher this time as I hold my stance. My breathing is steady and even, and I block out everything around me, except that target. The little holes in it from previous arrows are satisfying, but I only have eyes for the perfect, unblemished circle in the middle.

"On my mark, and . . . release!" Peter's crisp order has my fingers slipping free of the string, and I watch as the arrow flies down and down until . . . my arrow finds the bullseye with a satisfying *thwump*, embedding itself several inches into the target.

"Yes!" I let out a whoop of glee and throw both arms up in celebration.

"All right! Nice work, Demy!" Peter calls, and Jax whoops loudly from his lane at the end. Fletcher, however, bends forward and bolts towards me like an arrow himself.

I still have my arms up and am doing a victory dance when he reaches me. One second I'm bellowing like a Viking berserker on a distant shore, another my feet are off the ground, Fletcher's strong, warm hands encasing my ribcage as he hefts me up overhead. Suddenly he is the Viking, bellowing right along with me, and I can't stop a laugh from escaping as I look down at his face. He's the picture of exuberance; eyes bright and hair wild, escaped from its bun, with a wicked grin on his parted lips.

My breath catches in my throat as our eyes clash together, and heat blossoms where his hands gripped me. He is incredibly strong, but the touch is nonetheless light, just enough to keep me in the air as he slowly twirls us. When he finally begins to lower me, I slip down his broad chest, and the heat between us feels like enough to spark an explosion. We're staring into each other's eyes, and I don't immediately step back. He's sucked me in with his excitement, and I'm strangely breathless as the moment pulls taut like a bow string between us.

A throat clearing behind us snaps me out of it, though I can feel his magnetism trying to reel me right back in.

I spin on my heels to find an annoyed looking Jax and a softly smiling Beckett.

"Great work, Demy," Beckett says, holding up his fist for me to bump.

"Thank you! I had to work twice as hard to catch up with you guys. You were making me look bad," I tease, giving him a return grin.

"I don't think it's possible for you to look bad," Jax says, stepping between me and Beckett, and planting a sloppy kiss on my cheek. I tense as he lingers in my personal space, his whisper hot against my ear. "Especially not in those pants." When he pulls back, he makes a point of letting his gaze slide down my front, and unease ripples through me.

I don't have long to dwell on it though, because Peter joins our little circle and crushes me in a strong side hug. "That's what I'm talking about, Demy! You really pushed through today, and in time as you build up your shoulder strength, I think you could really be a great archer. You seem to have a knack for it, especially since this is your first lesson." He grins, the easy smile putting me back at ease. "So, am I going to see you again for some more lessons?"

"Absolutely!" I don't bother to hide my enthusiasm. I made real progress today, and for the first time in a long time, it feels like a little piece of control over my life is sliding back into my own hands in the shape of a black bow, and quiver of arrows. I'm not going to stay defenseless; and the next time one of the black-cloaked men finds me . . . he might find himself on the wrong side of my bow.

"Can I keep this?" I hold up the bow, and Peter quirks an eyebrow at the request.

"Well . . . technically I am supposed to keep all the weapons locked up. But . . . if you promise not to go out hunting for any of your suitors, I think we can make an exception." He winks, and Jax snorts obnoxiously at the idea of me hunting them.

"Promise."

"Well then you'd better grab a fresh set of arrows, too." He gestures to the wall of shiny, glorious archery accoutrements, and I practically skip over to choose some more arrows. I am trying to decide between the pink ones and some shiny silver ones with wicked metal fletching when Beckett's voice at my shoulder startles me.

"Demy?" When I jump, he holds up both hands in apology. "Whoa, there. Didn't mean to scare you. I just wanted to ask if you'd be open to having dinner with me one on one tonight? If you're too tired, dinner tomorrow would work, too." He smiles politely.

"Uhm, sure. Dinner tonight works."

"Excellent. I'll ask the chefs to whip up something special. You won't be disappointed." He nods, then turns to leave. "I'll see you tonight," he calls over his shoulder with a wave before leaving the archery range.

Peter has already begun taking down the tattered targets and tidying the room, which leaves me suddenly alone with Jax and Fletcher.

They both wait in silence, watching as I tuck the pink and silver arrows into my quiver. "So, um, this feels awkward," I admit, a fiery blush creeping up to paint my cheeks.

"Why? Because you just agreed to give him the first solo date in front of us?" Jax's tone is disgruntled, and it sets me on the defensive immediately.

"I'm sorry, I thought we were all adults who knew why we were here? Should I have taken him outside to answer his question, so I didn't hurt your delicate feelings?" I challenge, annoyed that he feels I'm playing favorites.

Jax shifts from his left foot to the right, anger tingeing his cheeks red. "Oh please, don't pretend I don't know why we're here. If he's your favorite, just come out and say so—at least then we'd know where we stand," he says.

"Hey, man, settle down." Fletcher's tone is calm with a hint of laughter. "If you wanted to be first, you should have asked first." He slugs him on the shoulder, and Jax turns his irritated gaze from me to Fletcher.

"Why don't you worry about your own game, huh?" he snaps, then turns and storms out of the range.

I stare after him in shock for a moment, unsure what to say to that outburst. "Was I in the wrong, there? I know I pushed him back pretty hard, but—"

"No. Absolutely not, don't even think that." Fletcher's tone is sharper than I expected, but when I look up, his eyes are kind. "Listen, that guy's a hothead. Plenty of men are, but he's young. He's got to learn to control that energy and put it somewhere positive. It's not on you to train him, or tiptoe around his feelings. Be you."

I bite my bottom lip and think over what he's said. Is that what I want to do? Tiptoe around someone for the next three plus years of my life?

"You're right," I agree, titling my chin higher. "If we're not compatible, we're not. And if he reacts like that over the first date, well . . . that may be that."

"That's what I'm talking about." Fletcher grins and offers me a fist to bump, so I do. "Can I walk you back to your room, or where are you headed next?"

"Uhm, well . . . I'd actually like to hit the gym next. But you're welcome to walk with me."

"Perfect. I've been meaning to check it out, so lead the way." His warm smile lights me up from the inside out, and I try my best not to think too hard about the fluttery feeling in my stomach Fletcher's giving me, when I've got a dinner date with another man in just a few hours.

I knew this would be complicated in theory, but the reality of this program just got confusing, fast.

CHAPTER TEN

MARRY THE COFFEE

DEMY

I spend an hour in the gym, working up a sweat on the rowing machine before hitting the showers back in my room at the dormitory. I'm standing in my closet in a towel, completely unsure what the heck to wear, when someone knocks at my door. Crossing the room with a sigh, I pull it open to find Nell waiting outside with a grin, and two cups of steaming coffee.

"Hey girl," she draws out the r, giving the word *girl* way too many syllables. "I heard through the lady-vine that you've got your first hot date tonight." She shimmies her shoulders ridiculously and offers me the coffee. "But, I thought you'd be dressed by now."

"I don't know what to wear, and thank you." I raise the cup appreciatively before taking a sip. It's coffee perfection, the rich, bitter flavor complemented by sugar and just enough cream. "I wish I could just marry the coffee. That would be easier."

Nell snorts, the sound indelicate and amused. "Don't we all, but you can't make a baby with a cup of caffeinated heaven. Now, you sit on the bed while I peruse the closet."

She shoos me with both hands, so I gratefully plunk myself down on the bed to enjoy the coffee boost while she does the brainwork of dressing me.

Her voice is muffled when it next comes from the closet. "So, you're spending the evening with Beckett. Is he your favorite? Or was he just the early bird?"

"Are you really comparing me to a worm right now?" I grouse, even though she's not wrong.

"That means yes. And, no—the date is the worm. You're a goddess in . . ." Her arm pops out of the closet, holding a slinky black dress. *Barely* a dress; it looks like it would be short on my five-foot-eight frame. "Black?"

"Too short," I call back, and the arm and dress disappear back inside.

"Longer, got it. Tell me about your dudes. How'd the group date go?" I hear the sounds of hangers scraping over the metal closet bar, and think about what to tell her.

"Well, the archery was great."

"Ooh, the guys were that bad, huh?" She pops out of the closet again, a frown on her face as she holds out a shimmery blue gown. This one is floor length and appears to have matching silk gloves over the hanger.

"Uhm, pass?"

"Fine. I wasn't even going to make you wear the gloves, sheesh. Though you would look like Beauty, ready to tame your own Beast." Nell waggles her eyebrows and disappears inside my closet again, so I take another sip of coffee and try to fight the image of each of my three matches in a cartoon beast mask. *Shudder.*

"The guys weren't that bad. During the activity they were great, and when I got my first bullseye—"

"I want to make an immature comment right now, and I think you should appreciate that I'm refraining," Nell says from inside the closet, tone tart.

"What are you, twelve? *Anyways*, they were all really excited and happy when I finally hit the bullseye. Fletcher was so excited he did this warrior chant thing and picked me up and spun me around."

Nell steps dramatically out of the closet, hand over heart, and pins me with an excited stare. "Like, picked you up overhead, picked you up, or more along the graceful clutching to his chest, as if you're his favorite teddy bear? Honey bear? Yeah, let's go with honey bear."

"Uhm, I don't know— it was higher than his chest. He was looking up at me and grinning, and his hair was all wild, and—"

"Ooh, please tell me he's the one you're going to dinner with tonight. He has *potential*."

"No, tonight is with Beckett."

"Oh." She deflates a little and leans against the door jamb. "Did he *also* pick you up and spin you around?"

"No, Nell. He's . . . not that type. He's serious. He wears a lot of suits—comfortably—and, I don't know. He's different. Mature, refined. That sort of guy. Okay, don't scrunch your nose at that. He *is* nice, in a different way."

"I guess so, if you like that sort of thing. In my opinion, go for a man with some nice muscles." She makes a cat clawing motion before reaching into the closet and pulling out a delicate yellow dress. "I should have led with this one. It's perfect, though now I'm not sure about wasting it on Beckett and his *maturity*. Though even he should like it; it's classy. What do you think?"

She holds the buttery dress aloft, and I'm instantly in love. It's simple silk, finely cut, and long enough that I won't be at risk of flashing Beckett anything inappropriate.

"I love it. I hadn't even seen that in there."

"Well then, come on—don't be shy, get in there and try it on." She passes me the hanger, and gestures me into the spacious closet.

I step inside the closet and hang up my towel on a hook inside the door and shimmy it over my head. Just like everything else in this closet the New Life Center provided, it fits me like a glove, and everything about it screams expensive. It's so soft, the fabric slips between my fingers without a whisper when I adjust one of the shoulder straps. One side is sleeveless, and the other has a big, bold ruffle which adds that extra *something*. It's perfect.

I step out, and Nell wolf whistles. "If that doesn't have him head over heels, well, send him home." She grins, and I know she's joking. That seems to be her coping mechanism for being here; everything's a joke, a bit over the top, and not taken too seriously.

The thought sobers me. This *is* serious. It's going to alter the rest of my life. It's bringing a baby—and a man—into my on-the-run lifestyle. I'm so tempted to open up to Nell, tell her about my life before coming to this place full of ease and luxury, but something makes me bite it back. It's too soon. And what if she resents me for putting her in danger? Because I have put her, and everyone else here, in danger. I didn't think of that before; I was only trying to find safety for myself. But now that I've met them all . . . I worry that me being here puts them in the line of fire, too. *Just another reason to figure out who's after me and how to stop it as soon as humanly possible.*

"Here, sit at the counter and I'll do your hair. I've been watching videos of these fancy waterfall updos, and I really want to try it but

100

my hair's too short." She practically skips into the bathroom and starts digging through the styling tools before I've agreed. Guilt gnaws at me as she fixes me with an enthusiastic grin, but I shove it down and smile back.

If I'm not ready to share my past, the least I can do is be there for her through the matching process like she has been for me, so I ask, "So, what about your guys? I saw you only have two. Is one of them still on the way?"

"Oh, no. This is a re-match, so I didn't have as many top matches." She starts doing something with a curling wand, waving off the question.

"Do you like either of them? Even if you don't have great genetic matches, you can still pull in up to three more guys, right?"

"Yep, that's a new rule that just went into place last year. It really has gotten better since last time. But I don't need more. One of my matches has a lot of promise."

"Which one? Atlas, or Easton?"

"Atlas," she smiles softly, and lays the perfect curl on my bare shoulder.

"He's the really tall one with the tattoos, right?"

"Mmhmm." She repeats the process with another section of my hair, working her way slowly around my head.

"I can see what you see in him, he is attractive, although . . . kind of intimidating."

"He's a teddy bear once you get to know him."

I chuckle. "And you've determined this in only a few days? What if it's an act?"

For a split second, her expression freezes before slipping back into her usual casual attitude. "Psh, when you know, you know. My gut is never wrong about who's safe and who's not."

We fall quiet for a while, as I process that. Is she right? Is my gut already telling me that one of my matches is *the one*?

I don't think so, though I know I feel *less* comfortable with Jax than with Beckett or Fletcher. His attitude today wasn't endearing, but this is a difficult situation. I'm not inclined to write him off over one incident unless it becomes a repeat occurrence.

But . . . him being so handsy so soon . . . it makes me shudder, and *not* in a good way. Not like when Fletcher was brushing his fingertips over my knee, or when I was standing chest-to-chest with Beckett.

"You getting cold? I can grab you a throw blanket out of your chest."

"No, I'm fine. My hair is looking amazing. I don't know how you do it." I lean forward slightly, inspecting her careful handiwork more closely. She's taken the curls and piled them up in a fluid cascade over my bare shoulder, and whatever product she applied has them gleaming like obsidian under the bathroom lights.

"Weren't you listening? Hair tutorial videos. Duh." She winks and drops the remaining handful of pins on the counter. "I think you're all set, but if you go do anything adventurous, you might lose some pins. Hopefully he doesn't mind a little windswept look."

"You're the best, Nell. Thank you." And then, I lean in and wrap her in a hug, surprising us both. She grips me fiercely in return before pulling back.

"Okay, okay. Let's get you out the door. You're already five min-utes late."

"Shoot!" I dart for the door, curls flying and giving me that *windswept look* earlier than anticipated. Nell tended to have that effect on people.

CHAPTER ELEVEN

FOIE GRAS AND FOOTWEAR

DEMY

W hen I arrive, Beckett's waiting on the front steps, looking impatient. Guilt swirls in my stomach for the second time in as many hours, and I practically jog up the steps.

"I'm so sorry! Nell stopped by to help with my hair, and time got away from us," the words come out in a breathless tumble, and as I stop at the top of the stairs, my chest is heaving.

His eyebrows shoot up, and his eyes roam down my appearance before stopping at my feet. My very inappropriately *bare* feet.

I ran out of my room without shoes. Embarrassment burns up my neck and into my cheeks with a healthy dose of self-loathing. The man is standing here in a very expensive suit, fiddling now with a watch that probably costs more money than I've ever made in the whole of my life, staring at my bare, grass-stained toes.

"You really were in a hurry," he finally says, his tone neutral.

"Yes, I really was," I murmur, unsure what to do now. "I'll go back for my shoes. Actually, you know what, we can reschedule. It's fine. I'm sorry again, I—"

I turn to flee as fast as I flew up the steps, panic dogging my heels and tightening my chest, but his gentle hand on my bare arm stops me mid-step.

"Hey, now. Canceling on me wouldn't help. This is no problem we can't fix. Come with me." I dare to look up at the command in his tone, and see an amused smile on his face, though there's still some tightness around his eyes. Because I wanted to leave, or because I'm an embarrassment?

I can't bring myself to ask. He strides confidently to the front double doors, pulling one open and flagging down one of the guards that always hovers in the hallways. It's him, the one who was watching me in the dining room the first night. I scan his chest and spot a name tag; *Lars*.

Lars scowls but steps forward, and I resist the urge to shrink back from his all-black uniform and unsmiling face. It's not a hooded cloak, but it's close enough to my pursuers to put me on edge.

"Yes? Is there a security problem?" He's no-nonsense with Beckett, but his hard eyes slide towards mine and soften slightly at the edges.

"No. Please radio in and tell the ladies' staff that my companion needs a pair of appropriate eveningwear shoes delivered, so that we can get back to our evening."

The guard narrows his eyes slightly—for a long moment, I think he's going to deny the request—until he suddenly reaches down. I instinctively flinch back, and he frowns at me now as he brings the comm device to his lips and passes along the message before stepping back, giving me a subtle nod. A moment later he's returned to statue mode against the gaudy wallpaper, leaving Beckett and me hovering in the enormous doorway.

"Let's wait on the veranda. I'm sure they'll be along shortly, and it's a nice enough evening for it." Beckett places one hand on the small of my back and holds the other out in the direction of the railing. I follow his lead, and we watch the sun sink below the distant hills for a few minutes, until a uniformed attendant appears with two pairs of heels in tow.

"Mr. Vaughn, I've selected two options from Ms. Carlisle's stylist closet. Would one of these be appropriate?" She looks to Beckett for approval, and my jaw nearly drops open at the audacity.

"Shouldn't you be asking *me* that? They're my shoes!" I take an angry step forward, but the woman doesn't budge. She waits patiently for *his* selection, and if looks could disintegrate a person, she'd be sawdust by now. She's wearing a badge, and I make a mental note to send some feedback about dear *Valerie* for the Bachelor Book people.

Beckett waves a dismissive hand. "Whichever pair she likes. Those both look fine."

Valerie finally turns to me, her mauve lipstick-covered lips pursed in irritation as she proffers the two shoes. Both heels are sky high, and I'm tempted to stay barefoot just to be stubborn. Grinding my back teeth together, I take the pair that's closest, so she'll leave, and lean against the railing to slip them onto my feet. Beckett fiddles with that watch again as he waits, and as soon as the second strap is buckled he clears his throat.

"Shall we? I've ordered a specific menu for us this evening, and it won't be nearly as good if it's cold or congealed."

I nod, the motion tight as the string on my bow, abandoned by the bathroom door. It's probably for the best, given how the night's gone.

This might be a fancied-up prison, but at least I'm not here for homicide. *Yet.*

The dinner with Beckett passes in a blur of one fancy dish after another, none of which I recognize. None have *congealed* as he so charmingly put it, but I pass on the foie gras and escargot regardless. It's not lost on him that I pass on some of his hand-selected dishes, but he doesn't comment out loud. His facial expression says plenty, and the feeling that I am an embarrassment only grows as the night goes on, and the Grand Canyon of food yawned wider between us. As soon as he drops me off at the dormitory steps, I shut myself inside and sink against the closed door.

Without thinking, I slide to the ground, and unstrap the torture implements Valerie thought were shoes, and fling them as hard as I can across the room. They smack the wall and bounce off with a deep, satisfying *thwack.*

"Whoa, Nellie. Everything okay over there?" The masculine voice shocks me into attention, and I look up with horror to see Fletcher wide-eyed and taking in the scene.

"Fletcher? What are you doing in the women's dorm?" I blurt, horrified to have made a fool out of myself in front of not one but *two* of my matches in the same day. And Jax is offended, because of the horrible first date. I'm zero for three today, and it's official—I suck at this dating thing. *And it's only day one, Demy. You're so screwed.*

"Cammie invited a few of us over for tea on her balcony. I'm not much of a tea drinker, so I was going to head out and grab a cheeseburger before I hit the sack early." He rubs one hand slowly over the back of his neck, and I have to work to keep my eyes on his face, and not the impressive display of bicep popping under his t-shirt sleeve. Nell's little cat-claw motion comes to mind, and suddenly I'm fighting off the urge to laugh like an utter loon.

"Sounds lovely. Don't let me keep you," I squeak out and shove myself to my feet so I'm not blocking the door.

"Hey, don't do that. Don't wrap your arms around yourself and shut me out. What's wrong? You look beautiful, but either that shoe personally wronged you, or you had a bad night. If it's the former, I've got a lighter back in my room, and we can deal with the shoe. If it's the latter, well . . . why don't you tell me about it?"

I look down at my crossed arms, debating. Is it bad form to tell one match about the debacle that was your date with another? He told me he was here to see Cammie, so I suppose he's not opposed to hearing about Beckett in theory.

"Come on, you can join me for a cheeseburger. They make 'em nice and greasy. It's sheer perfection in a paper wrap," he cajoles. I look up and see him grinning at me, hands in his front pockets as if this is no big deal. Relaxed.

I can't seem to find that kind of relaxation unless I've rowed myself into a lather, and here he is just walking around that way. I wish I could be more like that. Let go of some of the stress that's always dogged my heels. The anxiety that's plagued me since I watched my parents get murdered at thirteen. *Don't go down that road, Demy. Not tonight.*

"Are you sure? I don't want to mess up your plans, but . . . a cheeseburger does sound good. *Really* good." My stomach is half-empty, given the weirdness that was supposed to be dinner. I've only been here a little more than a week, and already I've gotten accustomed to regular, filling meals.

"It's not possible to mess up a cheeseburger, unless you put Swiss cheese on it. You don't like Swiss cheese, do you?"

"No. Cheddar is my favorite."

"I can work with that, but bleu cheese is better and I'm willing to prove it. You want to get some more comfortable shoes, or you wanna go like this? If you want I can go in and grab the burgers, and we can eat outside. I found a cool spot yesterday while I was exploring. I'm down for anything as long as—"

"As long as it's not Swiss. Got it." I wink at him. "I would like to change, if you're sure you don't mind? It should only be five minutes."

"Absolutely. I'll hang here until you're ready. I'm in no rush." The smile he gives me is heart-stopping, and I don't detect any traces of resentment in his eyes.

Turning, I jog up the stairs, holding the hem of the beautiful gown, and trying to tamp down the confusing tangle of emotions in my chest. Trying to juggle three men is confusing, and difficult; especially considering I've never truly dated even *one* guy before. I never thought it was wise to get close to anyone, since I never stayed in one place for long. I had a few crushes, sure. I also stole some kisses behind one restaurant or another on breaks. But that was all, and my inexperience feels like a flashing sign over my head: *Demelza is inept at relationships!*

I quickly shuck the masterpiece of a golden gown, feeling some regrets as I leave it abandoned in a crumpled heap on the bathroom floor. They abandon me in a heartbeat, though, when I slip into a comfortable green exercise set. The butter pants? I'm definitely getting married in them. Anyone who doesn't like it, doesn't have to come. I slip on my favorite tennis shoes, and jog back down the stairs only a few minutes later. Fletcher's right where I left him, except leaning against the door and grinning like the cat that stole the cream when he sees me.

"That's better. More comfortable now?" I bristle, wondering if it's a jab, but don't catch a trace of anything but genuine appreciation in his eyes. His stance hasn't changed, and there's no annoyed fidget about him, like Beckett's habit of playing with his watch.

"I am, thank you for waiting." I stop in front of him, and crane my head back to take in his smooth, russet skin and the plush line of his lips. He's handsome enough to be a statue, but he's so real, so warm. I want to trace the sharp cut of his jaw—a juxtaposition with everything that's so inviting about him—but manage to keep my hands to myself.

"Any time. You're worth waiting for." He trails a fingertip down my nose and taps the tip lightly. "Now, let's eat. I'm starved." Fletcher pulls open the door and holds it for me as I walk through, and we walk in companionable silence back towards the main hall. Halfway there, something strikes me.

"Why do you have a lighter in your room?"

"What?"

"You said we could take care of the shoes . . .?"

"Oh, that." He shakes his head slowly. "It was a gift from my dad. He smokes cigars, and thought it was a nice gift for my eighteenth birthday."

"Oh, okay. Kind of odd, but I guess it's nice that he wanted to share something with you."

"Yeah, I guess."

He sounds oddly defeated, and I want to ask if there's something more to it, but I don't want to push him if it's a sore subject. *I've messed up enough today not to pry into his relationship with his father.*

We arrive at the dining room late—it's after nine, and the place is a ghost town, with no one inside but the staff, and they're putting chairs up on tables and vacuuming underneath the tables. But Fletcher walks up to one of the servers with his usual confidence.

"Hey, Ricardo. Listen, Demy and I need cheeseburger therapy. Immediately. It's been a long day, and I can't let her go to bed hungry, you feel me? Can you hook us up? We'll take it to go so we don't mess the dining room back up, and I'll owe you a favor."

"Yeah man, give me fifteen. I'll have the kitchen bag them up for you."

Fletcher gives Ricardo a fist bump. "You're going to be my best man if I convince this girl to marry me."

Ricardo laughs and trots off to the kitchen shaking his head at Fletcher's antics. I can't deny that the idea of him *convincing me to marry him* sends shivers of anticipation sparking all over my skin. *Down, girl. It was a joke to get a cheeseburger.*

Ricardo is a man of his word, and in no time at all, he's back with a fancy kraft-paper box the size of a microwave. "I got them to throw in some extras, so you should be good to go. He and Fletcher exchange another fist bump and then we're on our way.

The cool night air kisses my skin as we exit the main hall, and I'm suddenly glad to be outside, the comforting scent of hot burgers and sweet jasmine an oddly perfect mix.

"You good with staying outside? I can take you to my spot."

"Lead the way," I say. He shifts the box of food so it's tucked under one arm, and grabs my hand with the other. We veer to the right, taking a narrower trail towards the back of the main hall. It twists and turns into a more traditional garden setting than most of the flat, manicured lawns that cover most of the sprawling, rolling grounds. We walk through the garden, passing several benches, and I'm starting to wonder where *exactly* he's taking me. Nell's warning to stay close the first day is pinging in my mind the further we get into the dark night, and away from the bright lights of the main areas, when I hear the gentle sound of burbling water.

A few more steps past a chest-height hedge laden with blossoms, and the soft glow of a mounted carriage light illuminates a curved wooden bench. It's nestled amongst the flowers as if they're a blanket wrapped around its shoulders in a warm hug, and it sits parallel to a small, clear creek running over smooth black stones. The sound is magical, and I let go of Fletcher's hand to step off the path, cross a swath of springy grass to the edge of the little creek, and suck in a lungful of the fresh, sweet air.

"Do you like it?" he asks, a tinge of hesitation in his tone.

"I love it. How did you find this place?" I turn back to face him with a grin.

"I didn't find it so much as got lost exploring yesterday, and followed the creek back until I found one of the paths." He sits down on the bench, plopping the box in the middle and gesturing for me to join him. I perch on the worn, wooden slats and gratefully accept the cheeseburger he passes me. It's got gooey cheddar cheese oozing out from under the bun, and I chomp into it gratefully, unable to stop the moan that slips out as the perfectly seasoned beef and cheddar combo hits my tongue.

Fletcher just stares, jaw flexing, as I make a scene over the cheeseburger. Embarrassment hits, and I duck my head—the delicious food suddenly feeling too large to swallow past the lump in my throat. I reach for a bottled lemonade, and gratefully suck down the cool, sweet-tart beverage.

He reaches over and lifts my chin with gentle fingertips, the touch whisper-soft, and runs his thumb over the corner of my mouth. "Don't be embarrassed about enjoying your food. I'm glad. I want you to enjoy all the good things in life—even if it's just a cheeseburger—and that's nothing to be ashamed of. Not ever."

Our eyes clash in a heated gaze, and the world around us narrows, condenses to him and me, and the shared breath between us. Without realizing it, we've both leaned forward—food forgotten—and we're hovering, frozen, inches apart. His eyes drop to my lips again, and his hand comes up to cup the side of my face. His hands are so big, his fingertips brush the nape of my neck, sliding into the cascade of curls Nell arranged earlier in the night.

He leans closer, and my eyes flutter closed in anticipation of his touch. But it doesn't come, and his hand on my neck stiffens.

"What the hell?"

My eyes snap open just as an alarm louder than a foghorn starts blaring, garish red flashing lights painting the side of Fletcher's face and turning his dark hair to a bloody aberration.

"Why would there be an alarm? Are we in trouble for staying out? Surely not, I mean they let us wander freely. What are we supposed to do?" My heart begins to race, visions of black-cloaked men descending on us en masse clicking rapid-fire behind my eyes like a kid's viewfinder toy changing images.

"Come on, let's head back to the dorms. Whatever this is, it's not good to be out in the open." His face is uncharacteristically grim, and he abandons the box of food in favor of gripping my hand tightly. We run down the quiet paths in silence, the red lights turning delicate flower petals into a washed-out blur of red as we pass them.

We're nearly back to the main hall when a hulking shadow leaps into our path, and I scream. Fletcher shoves me behind him, dropping my hand and throwing both fists up in a fighting stance.

The man takes a cautious step forward, and with the next flash of the lights, I recognize Nell's match—Atlas.

"You two, come with me! We need to get into the safe room immediately."

Fletcher lowers his fists and takes my hand again. I grip it harder than necessary, hoping it quells the shaking. Atlas starts jogging back towards the women's dorm rooms without waiting for us to answer, so we pick up the pace to keep up. My heart is pounding out of my chest, and the sick feeling in my stomach tells me this is my fault. The black-hooded men have found me, and even my last ditch effort of running away to an NLC isn't going to keep me safe.

CHAPTER TWELVE

SAFE (R∞M)

DEMY

Halfway to the women's dorm, Atlas veers sharply off the path, and runs toward an enormous hedge. When he reaches it, he turns sideways and shuffles through a small break I hadn't seen from a distance—barely large enough to admit his heavily-muscled frame.

I slip through without issue and find Atlas holding open the door to a run-down gardener's shed on the other side. Fletcher squeezes through behind me, and I hear a muffled *ow* as he takes a wayward twig to a pectoral muscle.

"Don't stop, we're not clear yet. Let's go, let's go!" He barks the orders, and I can't help but flinch back. Fletcher urges me forward with a protective hand on my shoulder, and ushers me through the door, keeping himself between me and Atlas, who opens a trap door revealing a four-foot-wide hole in the middle of the floor. A short ladder leads down to a circular silver platform eight feet below that's twice the size of the trap door. Lights dot the walls of the vertical tunnel, embedded every couple of feet in the smooth steel walls.

Fletcher doesn't hesitate, grabbing the top rung and swinging himself down into the hole, ignoring the ladder. He drops to the platform with a loud thump, and then holds up both arms.

"Demy, jump!"

Sucking in a deep breath, I plant my hands on the sides of the hole and lower myself straight down into Fletcher's waiting arms. He catches me with a small grunt, but he stays steady on his feet, clutching me against his chest with his arms around my waist. We pause there, breathing hard and gazing into each other's eyes for a heat-charged moment.

A scraping sound overhead draws our attention to the lid of the trap door, which is swinging closed—with Atlas still on the outside.

"Wait, stop! You need to get in, too!" I call up. If the men sent to get me kill Nell's favorite match . . . I couldn't live with that. Oh God, what if they kill one of the other girls? A sob catches in my throat, and I struggle to suck in a normal breath.

"I'll be fine. Press the button on the control panel as soon as this locks." He doesn't wait for my argument, and it dies on my lips as the trap door closes over us, sealing with a sucking sound that sends my panic ratcheting up another few notches. Fletcher lets me slide to my feet, releasing my waist once I'm steady so he can search for the button. We move around the platform in opposite directions, and I spot the big blue button after a moment.

"Got it," I call to Fletcher, and he steps to my side before I push it. When the button is pressed, it lights up, and the platform beneath us begins to lower.

"So, I knew the Cabal was a thing—we had to sign liability paperwork in our admittance applications, but I didn't realize they were this active. We've only been here a few days." He's got his arms crossed over his chest, watching as we slowly lower past more and more lights.

"Wait—the what? What do you think this is?"

"Well, I don't know for sure, but it's not like they would have gone to all this trouble for a tornado bunker. The Cabal's been known to use bombs in the past, so, this makes more sense. Bomb shelters are usually underground."

"Bombs? Cabal? What are you *talking* about?" Confusion wars with my usual panic; I've never considered there could be more than one reason for this alarm.

"You haven't heard of the Cabal? I'm pretty sure they put the notices in your welcome paperwork, too." He frowns. "They *should* have, at least. The Cabal is an extremist group who thinks humans should be allowed to die out, and let nature take back over as a way of resetting the balance of damage humans caused in the past. They actively attack NLCs and try to kidnap and kill the fertile women, so that the species continues to die out. It's real whack job stuff."

My jaw drops, and for a moment, I'm speechless. Have I leapt out of the frying pan and straight into an inferno?

"Yeah, crazy, I know. These loons even dress in a uniform. All black, and they wear these weird hood things? They're psychotic and aren't concerned about hurting innocent bystanders."

Wear all black. Cloaks. Psychotic killers. My brain freezes, and fixates on one thing.

"Do—do they shave their heads?" I hate the quavering in my voice, but I can't stop it any more than I can chisel a hole through the steel tube we're in with a toothpick.

"Uh, I can't say if they all do, but every picture I've seen in the headlines, they do usually have shaved heads, yeah. Why? You haven't seen one, have you?" His eyes sharpen, and he takes a step forward to grip my arms. The touch is gentle, grounding, and I lean forward so that my cheek rests against his chest.

"I don't know. Maybe?" The men who stabbed my parents fit that description to a T, and I've never seen one of them who didn't wear black, a hooded cloak, and have a shaved head. Am I being hunted by an organization? This Cabal?

"That's concerning. When this is over, we should talk to the security team," Fletcher says.

But if they attack NLCs, what the heck do they want with me?

The platform comes to a stop with a slight bounce, and I look up. There's a short hallway with an open door, leading into a much larger room. It's well lit, and appears to have furniture and a bank of monitors along one wall.

"Come on, let's get you sitting down. I don't like how pale you're looking."

I nod, words still eluding me for now. The realization that my parents might have been killed as part of some larger plot is hard to grasp after so many years of thinking they were only after my family for some reason. Unpaid debt; mafia connections; hit men; political espionage . . . My imagination has come up with plenty of wild reasons over the years. Never *that* wild, though.

We walk side by side into the safe room, and Fletcher closes the door to the metal tunnel behind us. There's no one else here, which immediately sets me to worrying. Even if this attack isn't because of me, I don't want any of my new friends to be hurt.

The room is bigger than it looked from the platform, and one entire wall is made up of screens showing various views of the campground. There's a red button embedded into a small gap in the screens, and Fletcher walks over and presses it, filing the room with voices.

"Channel two is secure. Repeat, channel two is secure."

"All four women are secure. The last one has just been registered inside of a shelter. Remaining matches are being airlifted out of the danger zone. Control room to Channel five, what's your status?"

Registered? What does that mean? I look around the room for any cameras, but I don't see anything obvious. Though, I'm sure they have some way to monitor us in here.

Atlas's voice answers, and my head snaps up. "Channel five still has bogeys. Going to assist. Easton, need you on my six."

"Copy, Cap. Headed to five for backup."

Easton. Why does that name ring a bell?

"Did you know Atlas was part of the security team here?" I ask Fletcher, whose eyes are riveted to one of the screens. It appears to be a live feed from a body cam, and whoever is wearing it is eating up the ground at a dead run.

"He's not, actually. He runs the top private security firm in the NAA and consults for the king and queen. We talked at a bachelor's mixer at lunch the day before we met all our matches."

"Oh. So, he's just helping because he's here? Then how does he know where all the safe rooms are?"

He shrugs. "It's his specialty, so he must not want to trust the security to someone else. I'm sure he asked to be keyed into the security himself since he knew there was a possible threat. Frankly, I'm glad he's here if you're in danger."

Don't ask, Demy.

Don't.

Ask.

"And Cammie, right?" *Stupid, stupid, stupid, stupid . . .*

He shoots a quick glance my way before continuing to watch the security footage. "Of course, I want all of you to stay safe." Absently, he reaches over and squeezes my shoulder.

Something about the answer causes me to deflate a little, though I can't put my finger on what. Turning away from the wall of monitors and trying my best to ignore the chatter over the various radios, I wander slowly around the room. There's a set of couches that seat eight, a stocked kitchenette, and a corner of the room dedicated to entertainment. It's got books, video game consoles, and even some light sporting equipment, like those sticky Velcro tennis balls.

How long do they expect us to be down here?

I wander past it to the only other door in here and find a sterile white locker room. One side has double lockers, the other sinks, and beyond that another door is open to bathroom and shower stalls. I idly check one of the lockers, and it swings open to reveal a soft black uniform hanging inside. There's a blank name tag patch on the front, and even a pair of boots sitting in the bottom of the locker. Next to them sits a slim silver device with a button on the side.

I pick it up and hit the button. Electricity sparks along a metal piece at the end, and I nearly drop it in surprise. *A taser might come in handy.* I stuff it into the thigh pocket of my pants and decide to add it to my newly minted weapons collection. A taser is way easier to keep on me than my bow, even if I do love it. The whole room shakes around me and I freeze, wondering what would cause that level of impact all the way down here.

"Demy? Where'd you go?" Fletcher calls from the other room.

"In here—we've got a locker room and bathrooms." I raise my voice so he can hear me over the rattling of the lockers.

He appears in the doorway, a grim look on his face.

"What is it? Did somebody get hurt?"

"No, they think everything is secure now. However, to be safe everyone's been instructed to hunker down for the night while they do a full sweep—Atlas's orders."

"Oh, okay. That's good, I guess. Did they confirm if it was actually the Cabal?"

"Nope, they haven't given us anything official. Only that everyone is unharmed, and the grounds are now believed to be secure."

"I see. Wait—there are no beds down here." I spin, looking for any other doors I might have missed that lead to sleeping quarters.

"They just told us that the couches pull out, and there are linens in one of these lockers."

I sigh; I can't help it. "I wish I'd actually gotten to eat that cheeseburger."

Fletcher snorts. "You and me both. Maybe we can scrounge up something in the kitchen, after we sort out beds?"

"Yep. Let's do it."

Half an hour later, we've found a set of king-sized linens, and realized that *one* couch pulls out. Making up the bed went quickly, and then we both opted for bowls of ice cream from the freezer. There is even a full selection of topping syrups, so I drowned my chocolate ice cream in caramel syrup. I guess they figured if you're ever stuck down here, things are bad enough to warrant a decent ice cream sundae. They were right.

But now, the ice cream's a melted puddle in the bottom of our bowls, the live feeds have one by one flickered out as the guards clear sections of the property, and Fletcher is walking toward the big red button which controls the audio feeds. He presses it, and the safe room falls into utter silence.

"Well, I'd like to grab a quick shower, and slip into one of their changes of clothes before we settle down for the night. Do you want to go first?"

"Oh, no. I'm okay. I showered right before I got dressed for my date, uh, with Beckett."

He gives me a crooked grin. "Okay, then. I'll be out in a few. And I'll take that couch, so you can have the bed." He nods and heads off for the showers before I can argue.

It's a king-sized bed, and he's way taller than me. If anyone's getting the bed, it's him. I wander over to the entertainment area and browse the books idly, eyes catching on one with a girl and a wolf on the front. I slip it from the shelf, and turn back to the remaining couches. One side is a chaise lounge, and I think with a pillow and throw, it'll be pretty comfy.

So, I steal one pillow from the bed, a few of the spare throw blankets from the lockers, and hunt around until I find the light control panel for this place. There's a night setting, and when I tap that option, the overhead lights gradually fade out, leaving only a thin strip of low lights around the floor. It's dim enough to sleep, but bright enough I can find the bathroom, so, perfect.

That done, I get cozy on the chaise lounge, click on the lamp, and start reading.

"Demy? Demelza!" The insistent tone wakes me, and I realize Fletcher's hand is on my arm. "Hey, sorry. You're so cold your teeth are chattering. I didn't want to wake you back up, but it's gotten really cold in here. Come get in the bed, and you'll warm up."

"What?" I mumble, still not fully processing. Though, after a moment, I realize he's right. My teeth are chattering, and his hand on my arm feels like a deliciously warm fire brand against my goosebump-covered skin. "Okay," I say, swinging my feet over onto the floor. It's so frigid, the cold cuts right through my thin athletic socks.

"Come on, right here." He holds up the heavy comforter, and I slide under. Warm bliss encapsulates me as soon as he drops the cover down and tucks it under my side, but I'm still shivering uncontrollably. He quickly moves around the other side of the bed and slides in, keeping a respectful distance on his side.

We're both silent for a moment, and now that I'm awake, the cold is miserable. My nose *hurts*.

"You'd warm up faster if we were to lie next to each other, but I didn't want to presume . . ." He trails off, and I can hear the uncertainty in his voice.

"Yes please. I'm so cold." I chatter the words out, and in the next instant, he's there, pressed to my side. His whole body is gloriously warm, and I curl on my side, pressing my nose against his chest to stop the bitter chill.

Fletcher chuckles and rests his chin on top of my head, before draping a heavy arm over the top of the covers, adding to my

122

cocoon. "I should have woken you up sooner, I'm sorry. It wasn't this cold when we first came down."

"It's okay. This is so much better, thank you. I love how warm you are." I freeze, the awkwardness of telling him I *love* something about him at this stage striking me a second too late to keep the words inside.

"You know, I've been complimented on a lot of things in my life, but that's the first time my temperature has made the cut."

I lightly smack his chest and roll my eyes at the teasing tone. "Well, clearly you've never been in this situation before, or you'd have heard it."

His voice drops lower. "No, I've definitely never been in this situation before. That's for sure."

Silence falls again, heavily this time.

"Do you regret joining the NLC program? I mean, putting yourself in danger to have a baby . . ." I ask, the words small in the large, open space.

"Nah. There's no point in regret. If I was going to regret anything, it would be that this is the world we live in—that we need all of this to have a family and that there are people out there who are willing to kill to stop us from having families. But, that wouldn't help anything, either."

"True, very true. I wish things could be simpler, sometimes."

He pulls his head back and looks down at my face, his features dim in the low light. "You don't seem very comfortable with all the extra luxuries around here. Is it very different from your life before?" There's no judgment in the question; just curiosity.

I take my time, thinking over what to tell him. "It *is* very different. I lived a good—average, but good—life as a kid. Then, my parents were killed in my teens, and after that I've been on my own. Times were lean. This place is . . . a lot. There's just so much excess everywhere."

His eyes widen at the news that I've been living on my own. "I'm so sorry about your parents—I can't imagine losing them at such a young age. I knew you were strong, but that's a whole other level."

I scrunch my eyes closed, unable to look at him when he's complimenting me for struggling through my trainwreck of a life.

"What is it? What did I say wrong?" His concerned tone cracks my self-pity, and I let out a shuddering breath.

"I don't know, Fletcher. I don't feel strong. I've never felt strong before. You don't know what it's like, being on the run. Always hunted. Nowhere to call home. A dropout, with no money, sleeping on bathroom floors—"

"Hey, hey. Please don't cry."

I hadn't realized I was, until he said that, and I dash away the traitorous tears leaking out of my eyes.

"You might not have *felt* strong, but you are. Stronger than me by a long shot."

Dubiously, I poke his enormous bicep where it cushions my head, and he snorts a laugh.

"Okay, so, you can't take me in an arm wrestling match. But, the fact that you made it on your own means you're a survivor, and you should be proud of that." He gives me a quick kiss on the top of my hair and scooches closer so that his chin rests on top of my head again.

The easy acceptance envelops me like a warm hug, and a little piece of something inside my chest clicks into place. He didn't shun me, or judge me, or freak out. He just rolled with it, and pulled me *closer*.

124

Somewhere, deep down, I had needed that even though I didn't realize it.

"I was worried you were going to think less of me. I don't even have a diploma."

"Do you want one? I can help you make that happen."

I'd considered enrolling in web-based school a few times over the years—those rare instances where I'd made it four, five, even six months in a single spot, with an okay-crappy job before I'd had to run again. But humiliation had always stopped me. Thinking about doing it now, though, feels . . . possible.

"I think I would." The words are barely a whisper, but I know he hears them because he squeezes me briefly in a hug, just that little bit closer to his tantalizingly warm chest.

"We'll make it happen, then. Hopefully things get a little easier from here on out, and you can focus on what you want," he murmurs.

Not while I'm being hunted by the Cabal, they won't. But I can't say that, so instead, I say, "I hope so, too."

CHAPTER THIRTEEN

THE AFTERMATH

DEMY

T he next morning, we're woken by the sound of the lift whirring to life, and within a few minutes, Jones and Director Churtle are standing in the entryway of the safe room, smiles pasted on as they take in our sleep-rumpled states.

"Good morning!" Jones's booming voice was not made for underground rooms, and bounces off the walls in an unpleasant clamor. It must bug him, too, because he lowers the volume slightly for the second go 'round. "We're just here to tell you that the threat has been eliminated, and you're free to resume your normal duties. Demelza, darling, it looks like you have a double date in an hour? You may want to get a move on." He gestures to the lift behind him, and shock floods my system.

"I'm sorry, what now? We just got *attacked* last night, spent the night in a freezing cold underground bunker, and you're just, what? Pretending it didn't happen? I want some answers! Who attacked this place? What are they after? Was anyone hurt? Are they going to come back?"

Director Churtle raises both hands, staying my rapid-fire questioning. "We understand your concerns, but at this time we don't have much information. No one was hurt, which is due to our excellent safety protocols. The intruders hadn't even made it past the gate line when the alarms started, and everyone made it either into one of our state-of-the-art safe bunkers, or an airlift off of the property before any danger could reach them. The guard staff has since cleared every inch of the property, and we're once again secure. These attacks are rare, but they do happen, unfortunately." She gives me a sharp nod, as if to say, "That's that."

"I'm glad no one was hurt, but don't you think this protocol should have been made known to us *before*—"

"Demelza," Jones's tone is placating, and it grates over my nerves like nails on a chalkboard.

"Demy. Call me Demy."

He clears his throat, and I catch the look of irritation before he quickly covers it. "Demy, I understand your questions. We will be putting together an information packet with our security team later this evening, and all of the women will be notified via your fertility trackers and in-room devices when that information Is available. In the meantime, however, there's nothing left to do but carry on with the program. Now, please, allow me to escort you back to your room so you can prepare for your morning activities."

He turns abruptly and walks back onto the platform without waiting for a response, Director Churtle hot on his heels.

"This is infuriating!" I spin towards Fletcher. "We were in real danger last night, and now we're supposed to pretend nothing happened, and go on with our regularly scheduled dates? I— Don't they care about us at all? Surely our safety is more important than getting us married off a week quicker. They can't breed us like cattle if we're *dead*, after all," I practically snarl at him.

The whole reason I came here was for safety, and after last night, that's beginning to feel like a hollow promise. Am I giving up my freedom, my body, and my future for *nothing*?

"I agree, but there's no point hanging out down here. Let's get up top, and see what we can find out from everyone else. I bet Atlas knows a lot more than these two are willing to tell us, and our date is a double with him and Nell."

I groan. "You're right. I should have thought of that. Come on." We gather up our few personal belongings and slip on our shoes, then head for the lift, where Jones and the director are waiting impatiently.

"I assume you two had a comfortable evening?" the director asks.

"It would have been a lot more comfortable had there been some heat," Fletcher says, cutting his eyes pointedly to the director's.

"Oh, dear, you two didn't find the control panel? What a shame." She shakes her head, feigning disappointment as the platform comes to a smooth stop. "Well, we'll make sure information on controlling the safe rooms is included in the informational packet this evening."

"Director, wait!" I demand, surprising myself. Usually I'd blanch back from an authority figure—I'm a runner, not a fighter, after all—but my anger is in control, and won't be denied.

She turns slowly on the heel of one black pump, her lips pursed in a sour expression when she looks back at me. "Yes?"

"I want a map. To *every* safe house. It's ridiculous that everyone has that information except the people they're supposed to protect."

She nods tightly. "Very well. We don't freely disseminate that, to reduce the stress it typically causes the girls to think of the attacks, which are fairly infrequent. And as you saw tonight, our security handled it swiftly and safely. However, if it will ease your mind, I will have that information sent along with the rest." Without another word, she climbs up the ladder, and out of the safe room, but I'll take my victories where I can get them. Jones is next, and by the time Fletcher and I are both at the top, she's nowhere in sight. Beckett, however, is waiting with a stack of to-go bowls in one hand, and silver spoons from the dining hall in the other.

"Beckett, what are you doing here?"

"Take a walk with me? I brought dessert." He holds the bowls aloft, before looking questioningly at Fletcher.

I turn to Fletcher, and he gives me a tight smile. "Y'all have fun." It stings a little that he just leaves, but I know that's stupid. I need to get to know all the guys; he's letting me do that, right?

So why does it feel like he's handing me off without a care? Why doesn't he fight a little harder when other guys are around?

"What have you got there?" I ask, crossing the few steps to Beckett, and letting him lead me down the path.

"Crème brûlée. It's my favorite dessert, and I wanted to share it with you last night, but things went sideways."

"What do you mean?" I hadn't enjoyed last night, but it seemed to go exactly how *he* wanted. After I was properly dressed, at least. We stop at a picnic blanket spread out on the lawn, with fancy tufted pillows for us to lean on, and a bottle of sparkling cider on ice.

"Demy . . . I know you hated our date, and it was completely my fault." He sets the bowls and spoons down on the blanket, and takes both of my hands in his.

"I—" I stop, not wanting to lie to him. I had hated the date, but it felt wrong to just say so.

"You can't even look at me right now. It's okay—I know it was all wrong. I was trying too hard to be someone I'm not. Not really."

I force myself to look up at his deep brown eyes, and see the honesty in them. So, I ask the only question I can think of.

"Who were you trying to be?"

"My dad. Or at least the version of me he thinks I should be. Always proper. Always looking the part of wealth and power, with a wife to match." He winces, and I look away again. "Here, let's sit. This conversation calls for sugar."

"O-kay," I agree warily, kneeling on the blanket and accepting the bowl and spoon he hands me. He's already taken the lid off, and the faint scent of burnt sugar hits my nose.

"I don't know how to woo a woman."

The frank statement takes me off guard. "Uhm . . . you're doing just fine today." I gesture at the beautiful setup with my spoon, giving him a questioning look.

"I know, I know. The kitchen staff helped me with this. But . . . Demy, I haven't dated anyone for ten years, outside of the brief weeks with my last match. When I was a teenager, all the girls I would have dated or flirted with were whisked off to this program, to find their genetic matches, and I was left behind to go to business school, intern at the family business, and then take over the investments. All my interactions with women cut off abruptly at age sixteen. Ever since, it's just been my dad, yammering in my ear about how women want to be *seen to*, and *taken care of* and what a responsibility it is to take on a wife in this day and age."

He puffs up his chest and adopts a stern facial expression as he says the last bit, and I bite back a chuckle at the impersonation of his father.

"I don't know how to just *be* with a woman anymore. Well, at all. Sixteen isn't quite a woman yet, and that's the last time I was around girls or women, outside my stepmother."

"I'm sorry, I can see how this would be hard for you, too. I've never actually thought about what it's like for the men who don't sign up in their teens or early twenties."

"I would have—I'm not some creepy older dude who's into younger women—but, I had to take my place at the family firm first. My dad was adamant that I needed something to offer a wife, so, here I am. Over ten years behind and utterly out of practice."

I reach over, resting my fingertips on top of his wrist. He stills, eyes laser-focused on the point of contact.

"I don't know what I'm doing either, Beckett. I've never dated outside this program, and last night it felt like I was screwing everything up, too. You're smart, wealthy, educated, and so . . . proper all the time. I don't have any of that, and I feel so out of place at your side."

He flips his wrist, capturing my fingers with his in one smooth move. The warm press of our palms together sends a tingle through my skin, and I tighten my fingers between his, holding onto him too.

"I don't want you to feel out of place. You're smart and beautiful, and I'm trying to take care of you, but I don't know what that looks like. The way my dad treats my stepmom . . ." He pulls a sour face. "That's out of the question."

"I don't know how to be taken care of, Beckett. I've been on my own for a long time, and I'm used to doing things myself. Maybe .

. . maybe we can meet in the middle." I give him a small smile, and he returns it.

"I'd like that, if you're willing to give me a second chance."

"Of course."

"Thank you, Demy. I'll do my best not to screw it up the second time around." He leans forward, enveloping me in a hug. He smells fresh and clean, like expensive cologne, where my nose rests against the soft skin of his throat, and I'm nearly overwhelmed by the ridiculous urge to kiss him there. He pulls back after a moment, though, saving me from the temptation.

"Now, you have got to try this crème brûlée. Have you ever had it before? It's my favorite dessert."

"No, I haven't. It smells a little burnt." I grimace down at my container, and he laughs.

"That's just the sugar topping. It's perfect with the sweet custard. Take your spoon like this, and just crack through it straight to the bottom."

He demonstrates, and then holds up his scoop and waits for me to get my own. I do, and the crunch is oddly satisfying. Our eyes lock as I slip the silky-smooth custard and crunchy sugar combo into my mouth, and he's right. It's pure bliss on a spoon.

Chapter Fourteen

BREAKING GRIPS

Atlas

I pace the gymnasium slowly, running through last night's attack as my eyes scan the perimeter through the floor-to-ceiling tempered glass walls. The floor is padded, muffling my bare footsteps.

Easton waits off to the side, arms crossed and face pensive as he watches me. He's my second in command, and he knows not to interrupt when I get like this. If not for him agreeing to come and be "matched" to Nell for additional security, I wouldn't have agreed to this mission, not even for Patrick and Sadie. Nell is priceless to me, and it goes against everything in my nature to put her in harm's way.

But the attack last night—it wasn't like the Cabal. I've studied reports of every single attack they've executed in the past twenty-four months prior to our arrival, and there is always a pattern.

Brute-force attack, maximum damage, with a few kidnappings sprinkled in—they took women, yes, but not as a primary objective. Last night the attackers swooped in with a delivery truck wired to explode. Of course, it failed the mandatory inspection at the gate, and triggered the alarm.

What they didn't expect us to catch was a secondary team of their people, breaching a side perimeter at the same time as their delivery truck distraction. Since all the women were safely underground, we allowed them to think they were undetected, tracked them on the surveillance system. Director Churtle put up a fight, but she isn't in charge—I am.

They went directly to the women's dormitory. They searched only the occupied rooms, before heading straight back toward the side of the compound they'd breached.

We stopped them, of course, but didn't manage to take anyone alive for questioning. As soon as my men fell in to scoop them up, they blew the delivery truck to divide our forces. It was a precise, calculated attack.

I stop pacing and turn to Easton.

"After this training session, I want you to get a cheek swab from one of the Cabal members who died by poison and contact Mav for delivery to Zanetti. We need their scientists on this. I want an antidote, so these lowlifes stop getting to take the easy way out. We need answers, and we can't get them from corpses."

"Do you think they'll be open to that? They haven't been . . . keen to work with outsiders."

"Tell them I'll consider it a personal favor, due upon request to the people of Zanetti. If that doesn't work, we'll throw in a personal request from Queen Sadie. Auntie can never turn her *protégé* down."

"Yes, sir. Consider it done."

Easton is a man of few words, like me. I appreciate that about him, in addition to his many talents in the field of security. "They have an inside man. It's the only way they could have known exactly which rooms the women were staying in, without searching them all. The question is, how did he make it past our screenings? We need to find out and catch him."

"That was my conclusion as well. Are you *sure* they couldn't have hacked into the surveillance system? That would have also given them the in."

I grind my back teeth together. "No. Nobody outside of Alaska Territories has Glitch's chops. He personally secured this location before our arrival, and he's monitoring the feeds twenty-four seven. The man is half caffeine at this point, but he's awake every time I call."

Easton snorts but doesn't comment. Glitch is a weird guy, but he's second to none at anything technology. After a long pause, he asks, "So you think our screening process is more fallible than his surveillance system?"

"People lie, Easton. It's fact. And if the Cabal has gotten organized enough to get a man through our checks, something has changed. And we need to get ahead of them, yesterday."

He nods, but I see Nell and her friend Demy heading this way, tailed a few steps behind by Demy's three matches. Nell insists that there's more to Demy that I'm not seeing, but her background check came back completely average. My wife has a sixth sense about these things, though, and I know not to write off her opinions. So, we're keeping a close eye on Demy, until we figure out what this is all about.

I keep the closest eye of all on Nell, of course, but she's my heart beating outside my chest. She's used to my hovering, though, four years into our marriage.

The group makes its way to the doors, and Nell's the one to open it. I narrow my eyes at the three men—one of them should have held the door—but they're too busy casting sideways looks at each other to notice me. Idiots.

"Welcome. Everyone kick off your shoes, and we'll get straight down to business." I clap loudly, and suddenly all eyes are on me as they hastily kick off their shoes and place them into the cubby next to the door. I watch them like hawks, looking for any signs that one of them might be the insider.

Beckett's well known and comes from money, but that doesn't rule him out. Corruption can be anywhere. Jax has been working as a closer, and they're almost as tightly vetted as the NLC guards—can't have the people sent to preserve cities looting, after all—but he has a reputation as a hot head, and he's been here less than a week. I'm going to keep an eye on him. And then there's Fletcher. His past is a bit more intriguing, but his file says he's been traveling the world and hiking for the last two years. It could be a son shirking his familial obligations, as it reads on paper . . . or it could be something else.

Once everyone's done, they form up on the mat in front of me. Nell's got her arm looped casually around Demy's shoulders, and I notice a drawn, worried look in the girl's eyes. It's almost as if she knows something, but I'll have to dig into that later. Nell likes her, and I hope there's nothing in her background that will break my wife's heart. When she gets attached, she's stubborn. There's no guarantee that the plant is a man, after all.

The men have arrayed themselves behind the two women, and Easton casually joins the group, after planting a chaste kiss on Nell's cheek. He positions himself behind her and to the side, so that he can see Nell, and the three other matches at all times.

"Show of hands—who's ever taken self-defense training before?" Nell, Easton, and Jax all raise their hands. "Okay, good. Fifty-fifty is a nice split. Now, the first thing we want to do is teach some defensive moves. You get grabbed; how do you get out of it? Someone *tries* to grab you, can you escape? That sort of thing is a great first step for beginners and has a lot of real-life applications. Learning how to hit is great, but for an inexperienced fighter, your best bet is almost always going to be to get free and run to safety. So, that said, let's see Jax and Demy, Easton and Nell, and Beckett and Fletcher. Don't worry, I'll rotate you three so you all get time with your lady."

The six of them partner up, and then we get down to business.

Demy

Atlas is a taskmaster. We've only been doing self-defense training for half an hour, and I'm completely winded. In between moves, he keeps making us go outside and run laps around the building. We're back in the gym now and Beckett is across from me, my hands are up, and I'm sluggishly bouncing from foot to foot, trying to catch him when he tries to sweep my legs out from under me. I'm supposed to avoid the sweep, but if I can't, he demonstrated a move to escape a ground attack that we're trying to replicate.

Nell's a freaking pro at this, and she's been hopping Easton's leg like it's a meaty jump rope. I want to be mad at her for making it look so easy, but I'm really proud. I want to get where she is. There's a loud smack and I glance to the side, to see that Fletcher and Jax are rolling around on the mat, aggressively fighting for the upper hand. My moment of distraction is the opening Beckett was waiting for, and between one blink and the next I'm flat on my back, staring up at the black-painted ceiling with the wind knocked out of me.

Beckett's solid presence appears on top of me, and it's only after he's pinned my wrists over my head that I remember I'm supposed to be bucking him off. *Dang it!* It's hard to process quickly when you can't suck in a breath. I finally get a fresh lungful of air, and try to snatch my wrists free of his iron grip, but it's fruitless. Beckett's suits might give him a polished look, but he is strong, and I'm no match for him. I attempt the bucking move Atlas showed us, but I'm not able to do more than rock the two of us on the floor. After a moment, I stop struggling, and just take a few breaths.

"You got distracted," he says.

"Oh, stop smirking at me. I'm not used to all the loud noises when somebody hits the mat." I stick out my tongue at him, and his grin just stretches wider.

"I'm not complaining. I don't mind a little one-on-one time with a beautiful woman. *My* beautiful woman." His eyes pointedly trace down from my eyes, past my lips, to the column of my throat.

I swallow hard, and suddenly my heart is racing for a different reason. He's right. We haven't been this close, and it's making my stomach flutter.

"Okay, break it up! Reset, and swap positions this time." Atlas barks out the order.

Beckett sighs, but pops back up to his feet with annoying ease, and extends a hand down to help me back to my feet. His palm is warm in mine, and he doesn't let me go when I stand. He squeezes lightly, and twines his fingers with mine.

"Can we have a water break, please?" Nell asks, wiping sweat off her forehead.

"Good idea—take five for a water break, but don't sit. There's a cooler by the bathroom." He points his thumb over his shoulder.

I head to the water cooler gratefully, pulling Beckett along with me. "Your man is relentless, Nell. Geez," I say as I catch up to her side.

She grins at me wickedly. "Yeah he is."

"I feel like you're being gross right now, and I'm choosing to ignore that because I'm worn out."

She snorts, and I even see a ghost of a smile on Easton's face on her other side. He's so quiet, it's like I know nothing about him, despite spending the past half hour in the same room together. Though, Atlas has only paired us with our own matches.

Jax beats us all to the water coolers—everything's a competition with him, it seems—and has a cup waiting for me when we round the corner where the cooler sits.

"Demy, for you." He passes it to me, and eyes mine and Beckett's intertwined fingers pointedly. Awkwardness washes over me. Do I pull away? Do I not, and stare him back down?

Surely they understand there will be some small touches with all three of them. I can't imagine choosing someone to marry whose hand I've never held, or shared a kiss with. It's not a battle I want to fight right now, so I free my fingers from Beckett's and reach for the cup with that hand.

"Thank you, Jax." I paste on a smile, but it feels forced. Jax is the only one who ever makes me feel *awkward*. Will we hit our stride and start to click, or should I just let him go, and focus on Beckett and Fletcher? *I'll ask Nell next time we get a few minutes alone.*

"You're welcome, Demy. I actually wanted to ask you if you'd consider a one-on-one date with me next? You've already spent time alone with Beckett during your date, *and* all night alone with Fletcher in your safe room." There's a bitter edge to his tone, and my feeling of discomfort grows. But, a one-on-one date is reasonable. I would be playing favorites if I said no.

Is he just a guy who needs to be the center of attention? He's proud of his accomplishments, but is there more to it? It's so hard to tell. Maybe a one-on-one will give me the answers I need.

"Of course, Jax. What would you like to do?"

His look is so triumphant, I expect him to start crowing. "Axe throwing. You and me. And we'll have them deliver dinner."

I so did not expect that, but it *does* sound fun. And at least he's honoring my choices for action-packed dates. Dinner with Beckett went so poorly—maybe this will be better.

Though Beckett's been completely chill today, and he's giving me warm vibes again. It's confusing enough I almost miss the days when I had *no* guys interested in me. But I can't wish myself back into being on the run.

"Sounds fun," I agree with a more genuine smile this time.

"Excellent." He takes a sip of his water and tosses the cup into the recycler. I scan the small group for Fletcher and realize that he and Atlas are still back in the practice area, heads craned together. They've got serious expressions on, and I bet Fletcher's trying to get more info on the attack last night.

"Well, I don't know about you guys, but I'm beat," Nell interjects. "All in favor of ending this little party?" She raises her hand, so Easton follows suit. Beckett's hand goes up, and a pang of disappointment hits me. This stuff really isn't *his* style. It's never been mine before—I never had the chance—but I'm really enjoying the physical challenges.

Plus, I learned three ways today to break free from an attacker, and that's knowledge I desperately needed, if my hunters—this Cabal—keep coming after me.

I reluctantly raise my hand, and so does Jax.

"All right! Shower time for me. I hate being sweaty, ugh, gross!" Nell practically skips back across the mats to tell Atlas that we're all leaving. He wraps her up in a hug, and then tosses her over his shoulder in a fireman's carry and carries her out of the gymnasium. She laughs the whole time and starts trying to tickle his sides as he hauls her off.

The sight brings a smile to my face, but deep down I wonder—will I ever be that comfortable with one of these men? How is she so easy with someone she's only just met?

They make it out onto the lawn before he retaliates and tickles the back of her thigh, and she starts hollering for Easton to rescue her. All three of my matches walk out with me a little slower, putting our shoes back on and chatting about the lesson. The walk back to the dorm is uneventful, and after three goodbyes I head inside to take my own shower.

I've got a lot of thinking to do.

Chapter Fifteen

Hunting for Answers

Demy

J ax sends me an invite for axe throwing, two days later in the afternoon. Unfortunately, I won't get an opportunity to talk to Nell about him, because after our self-defense class one of her matches whisked her away for a mini-getaway, and she's still not back yet. I didn't even know that was an option, but apparently it is if you ask and arrange it in advance.

The days are quiet, and it's a nice reprieve from the initial rush of dates. Sometimes I eat alone in my room, other times one or both of the other girls is free, and we eat together in the dining hall. I feel awkward around Cammie because she's also dating Fletcher. And liking him, from her talk at lunch at the beginning of the week. I'm trying not to focus on it, though it's hard not to think of him as mine after we spent a night cuddling together. Seeing him strolling across the lawn with her holding hands yesterday was a punch to the gut that I wasn't expecting.

Juvenile, probably, to avoid her because of my awkwardness. But, necessary. When the day finally comes around for my date with Jax, I'm restless. I already went to the gym, I'm tired of sitting in my room, but I don't really want to run into Cammie, until I can get my feelings under control. Finally, I decide to just get out of the dorm altogether and go for a walk. Or swing on the porch. *Something.*

I'm already dressed for my date in a black exercise set, and a new—but equally amazing—pair of sneakers that are also black, with hot pink streaks down the sides. I definitely look like I'm ready to smash some stuff with an axe. Without Nell to do my makeup and hair, I've kept it simple rather than pestering the other girls. Okay, yes, I'm being a chicken. They'd absolutely help me if I asked. But . . . I can't. So, a high pony and some lip gloss will have to do. I've got two hours left before he's coming to get me, and I'm going to wander over to the main hall to see if Lars is hanging around, and I can ask him about helping me find my parents' killer.

As I make my way down the stairs, I hear loud music coming from the kitchen. I'll have to walk right past it to get out the front door, but as I get closer, I can hear Leilani singing along loudly from inside. I poke my head in to wave, but find her and Cammie with spatulas, dancing back to back and gyrating to the song. Cammie opens her eyes before I can duck back out of the doorway, and squeals so loud she startles Leilani, and she stops singing mid-note.

"Demy! Get your tail in here, we are having a girls' date!" She does some exaggerated hip-swinging dance, and I shake my head furiously.

"No, I couldn't intrude on all this awesome. Plus, I have a date—"

Leilani turns around and waves her spatula at me accusingly. "You don't have a date for another *two hours*. Have you been avoiding us? You've been holed up in your room for two days, and we've barely seen you outside of meals. What's going on?"

Cammie holds her spatula up like a microphone again and parrots, "Yeah, what's going on?" Her smile is so wide, and they're having so much fun . . . and I feel like a total jerk for being jealous of Cammie dating Fletcher, too. Something must show through on my face, because Cammie's face falls.

"Are you really mad? Leilani thought so, but I didn't think . . . please tell us what's wrong. I don't want a rift in our girl squad." They both drop the spatulas, and now I can't walk away and not say something. But what do I say?

"It's nothing, really. I don't want to interrupt your fun, please. Please, just—go back to your singing." Leilani's got that look in her eye, and I know it's pointless. I'm committed. I suck in a deep breath, and just go for broke. "I've got feelings for Fletcher. I think . . . real feelings. And it's hard to hear you talking about dating him, too. You're allowed, of course. I don't want to stop you because you like him, too. It's just . . . hard. It sounds stupid admitting that out loud." I bite my lip to stop the word vomit that wants to keep pouring out.

Cammie fiddles with her long copper ponytail, and I wish the ground would open up and swallow me. *Yep, I am a jerk.*

"Okay, that's fine. You can have him." She flips her ponytail back over her shoulder and sashays back to the counter, like she didn't just floor me. She grabs her spatula, and another then another bright blue one which she waves at me. "Now, since I gave you Fletcher, you've got to come sing with us."

My mouth drops open. "You can't just . . . *what*? I thought you liked him?"

She rolls her eyes, and Leilani stands between us, her widened eyes going back and forth faster than a ping pong ball.

"I mean, yeah, I like him fine. He's hot as Hades's brother. But that's not the point. He's a low match score for me, and even if he wasn't—I don't like him enough that I'd avoid you over it. Simple. You like him more, he's yours. Now, take this spatula"—she presses it into my hand with determination—"and get your tush in here, and belt out this song with us."

"I don't know the words to the one you were singing," I admit sheepishly, still in shock over her decision to just *give* me Fletcher. What will he think about that? He might have liked her more, and then I'll be the jerk that kept him from someone he liked.

"That's no big deal, the sound system has everything. You just yell out any title and it'll play," Leilani says, brimming with excitement.

"You pick the next one," Cammie presses again.

"Oh. Okay then. Uhm." I think it over for a moment. "Oh! Play Single Ladies!" I throw my head back and yell towards the ceiling, and the bopping intro immediately starts.

Leilani groans at the ancient song, but Cammie laughs so hard, she doubles over. "This is perfect! Now sing it like you mean it!"

So, I fling my left hand in the air, and belt it for all I'm worth into my spatula.

An hour and a half later and with a much lighter heart, I leave the girls and jog over to the main hall. It's probably for the best that I got sidetracked; loitering for two straight hours would have caught someone's attention. I take the front steps two at a time, and have to stop to calm myself before I yank the door open. I'm pumped, but I need to scale it way back or someone's going to get suspicious. While it's not against the rules to talk to the guard staff, they make a point of not interacting with us ninety-nine percent of the time, and I doubt the director would look kindly on me asking for information I'm not supposed to have.

After I count to twenty to let my heartbeat slow, I pull the door open quietly, and step into the darker interior. It takes a moment for my eyes to adjust, and the pungent floral bouquet hanging heavy in the air takes a minute of adjustment, too. Once I can see clearly, I slowly scan the hall, noting the position of each of the guards.

No Lars, *dang it!* I stroll down the hallway to the dining room, and ask the maître d' for a glass of water. He bustles off to get it, and I scan the dining room slowly. There! All the way at the back corner, Lars stands with his back to the wall, eyes already pinned on me. But how to approach him?

I quickly look away, not wanting to draw the attention of the other two guards stationed inside the dining room. Slowly—painfully slowly—I walk towards the far wall, as if I'm engrossed in the very bland portraits of smiling families with small children and babies lining the wall. I force myself to stand in front of the first one for a count of ten, and then meander along the wall to the next, and then the next.

I pass the first guard with a polite head nod, and continue my way along the wall, passing some of the photographs more quickly, and lingering longer at others. From the corner of my eye I can see Lars watching my approach, but also scanning the room for non-existent threats.

"You're awfully interested in the alumni today." Lars's voice is sharp, but low, and when I look up, I see he's closed the distance, saving me two more boring portrait stops.

"Is that who these people are?"

He nods once, sharply. "Each one of them matched here over the years. Once you have your first child, you'll be expected to pose as well."

"Oh, I didn't know that," I say, casting around for a way to cut to what I want to ask him.

"What is really going on? You never pay any attention to these, and there's water in your dorms, and the gym where you spend all of your time."

A prickle of unease runs through me at his awareness of my habits. "How do you know that?" I stay facing the painting, but cut my eyes to clash with his.

He lifts one eyebrow lazily, as if it's a stupid question. "I'm on the security team. We're all debriefed on your tracking data at every shift change."

"Tracking data?"

He reaches out and taps one fingertip on my fertility tracker. "That's more than just a fancy piece of biotech. You think, with this place constantly under attack, we wouldn't have a way to know exactly where you are at all times?"

That was definitely not in the welcome packet.

"I . . . hadn't thought of that." The overwhelming feeling of naivete makes me blush and look away.

"You didn't answer my question," he says, and I can feel his eyes boring into the side of my face. Lars is *intense*.

"Uhm, well, I was hoping to talk to you, but it looks like you're working."

147

His eyebrows shoot up so far at that, his forehead crinkles when I sneak my next glance his way.

"Outside, five minutes. The eastside path, under the willow tree." His words are terse, and then he's gone, striding back to his post just as I hear the sound of a door swinging shut, and the maître d' hurries over with my water glass.

"Here you are, Ms. Carlisle. I hope you're finding the amenities to your liking? If there's ever anything you need, all you have to do is ask. We are here to serve."

The man's smile is genuine, but the little voice in my head argues that they're here to keep me happy enough that I don't complain I'm being forced to marry and have kids before I'm ready. I smile and thank him for the water, taking small sips as I cross the floor and out of the dining room. Once out front, I set the glass on the banister and bolt around the side of the building, eyes peeled for a willow tree. It's halfway behind the building, and there's not a soul in sight when I pull aside the trailing branches and duck under.

A small concrete bench waits nestled against the trunk, just big enough for two. I'm too nervous to sit, though, so I pace back and forth under the tree until the soft crunch of footsteps in thick grass makes me look up.

Lars steps between the branches silently, and crosses to the bench to sit down.

"I have ten minutes before I'm due back in the dining room, and your date starts in five. What's going on?"

"Uhm, well . . ." I swallow hard, and decide to just go for it. Worst case scenario, he tells someone and I get a slap on the wrist. Best case scenario, I find out who murdered my parents. "My parents were murdered, and I was hoping you could help me find out who did it."

"They were murdered recently? There's nothing about that in your file." He frowns and pulls a mini-tablet from his pocket, tapping in a password and immediately scrolling through something.

"No, not recently. It's been six years. I was barely thirteen when it happened, and I've been on the run ever since."

He freezes, and looks back up at me. "And why is none of this in your admittance questionnaire? It states that you're emancipated."

"Uhm, it's easier to get a job in the real world as an emancipated teen than make up lies about why I don't live with my dead parents. So, I filed the paperwork when I turned fifteen."

He groans. "And nobody else knows this?"

I shake my head.

"Tell me everything you remember about what happened, and I'll see what I can dig up. But, Demy, I should report this to the head of security *immediately*."

"Please don't!" I blurt the words, unsure why I feel so strongly that I don't want everyone to know, but I *don't*. Keeping my secret has kept me alive, and the idea of everyone around me knowing . . . doesn't sit well.

He narrows his eyes, and leans forward on his elbows. "You're asking me to keep a serious piece of information from my superiors. I could get fired, and this could create a gap in security."

"I don't want you to get fired, or for anyone to get hurt, I just . . . it can't hurt to look into it, and get some more information first, right? Then, if you have to report it, you'll actually know what happened."

He presses his lips into a firm line, and shakes his head a couple times. "I have a feeling I'm going to regret this, but okay. I'll do some digging first, and then we'll decide how to proceed. But this isn't *staying* out of your file. Are we clear?"

"Yes, thank you."

"You need to go. You're late."

"Shoot." I turn on my heel and jog towards the girls' dorm, where I'm supposed to meet Jax.

"I'll let you know when I have something." Lars's voice is low, but carries across the silent space just fine.

Chapter Sixteen

JAX WITH AN AXE

Demy

J ax picks me up a few minutes late, looking handsome in dark blue jeans and a button-up plaid shirt. It's a different look on him, but it suits him.

"Demy, you look divine, as usual." He smiles and peruses me from head to toe, his typical thorough inspection.

I sigh, deciding I'm done tiptoeing around him. Being blunt with Cammie worked out; maybe that's all I need to do with Jax, too. "Jax, why do you always do that?"

"Do what? Appreciate my beautiful match? You're too pretty not to appreciate, Demelza, surely you know that by now." He loops his arm around my waist, and half-pulls me down the steps with him.

"I get that you think it's a compliment—but it just feels like I'm a cow you're buying at an auction. That's not what this is."

He snorts. "It kind of is, though, I guess you'd be the buyer in this case, and I'm the grade-A cut of beef." He waggles his eyebrows jokingly, but I'm really not seeing the humor.

We take a turn down the path towards the archery range, and I debate whether to drop it, or push the issue.

"Jax, I'm serious. We're trying to find out if we're compatible to build a life together. It's about more than physical attraction."

"Relax, Demy. Geez." He lets go of my waist, his volume ratcheting up a few notches. "You think I don't know that? But we have to start somewhere, and where else do you start with a complete stranger? You're fine as hell. I'm sorry you don't think I'm funny, or as rich as the other two, but I *do* have some good things going for me, too, if you're not too blind to see it. This was supposed to be our night to get away from the two rich pricks, and show you what it could be like with somebody *fun*. Can we just drop the nit-picking, and try to have an enjoyable evening together at least once?"

I'm so flabbergasted by his tirade that I fall silent, trying to process what he's saying. He must take my silence as acquiescence, because he snakes his arm back around my waist, and pulls me back against his waist, just a little too hard. The weight of the taser in my thigh pocket gives me all sorts of naughty ideas, but I shove them aside and focus on what he just said.

Two rich pricks?

"What do you mean, the other two are rich? I know Beckett comes from a wealthy family, but Fletcher—"

He cuts me off with an annoyed grunt. "Really? You fell for the boy-next-door hiker routine? You really are blind. Fletcher's dad is the founder of the largest international biomedical company *in the world*. Fletcher is his only heir, which means he's richer than King Solomon. Or he will be, when his dad kicks it."

My mouth gapes open as we walk up the steps to the archery building. I did *not* expect that. While I suppose it might not be true—and I'm definitely going to ask Fletcher to confirm—that feels like a big secret to keep. He's so down to earth, and here he is secretly the sole heir to a massive fortune that probably comes with the same responsibilities that Beckett has.

Jax pulls the door open and holds it for me to walk in first, and Peter is once again waiting inside, the sunset behind him through the windows giving him an ethereal glow. "Demy! I knew you'd be back, but I missed you the last couple of days. Even if you don't have dates willing to come along for training, you're welcome to schedule time for yourself to sharpen your bow skills, or any other combat skills you'd like to hone."

"Thank you, Peter. I'll do that." It would be more productive than hitting the gym twice a day, at least.

"No problem, it's what I'm here for. Now, you two are all set up for some axe throwing this evening. It's a fun activity, but very dangerous. If you slip with your throw, you could injure yourself or bystanders. So, you'll be in individual cages for the activity, even though it's a date."

He points to the range, and sure enough, the ceiling has opened, and three heavy-gauge wire cages have been lowered all the way to the floor, and instead of the smaller arrow targets, heavy painted boards have been placed at the end of the throwing lanes.

Now, you'll stand to the side while I demonstrate the technique, and then you two can give it a whirl. He enters the first cage, drops the latch to close the gate, and then demonstrates in slow motion the proper form twice, before letting the axe fly. It embeds itself into the wood with an impressive thud, and several inches of blade have disappeared.

He does it twice more, and then it's our turn. We both enter and lock our cages, and I admire the selection of axes Peter's laid out for me with glee. They are wicked looking, and I can't imagine a member of the Cabal chasing me down if I had one of these strapped to my back, like some kind of Viking warrior of old. I pick up the first one, and take the throwing stance Peter showed us. It's heavier than it looks, and holding it cocked back over my shoulder puts strain on my triceps—I'm definitely spending too much time at the gym—and the throw is weak.

After that, I'm lost in the activity, and the fact that my date is a jerk who looks at me like a piece of meat fades to the back of my mind. It feels like only minutes later that Peter calls a halt, because our dinner has been delivered.

"And on that note, love birds, I'm going to let you have the place to yourselves. Do you need anything else before I go?" He shoots finger guns at us with a merry little wrist flick as he backs toward the door.

"This one's my favorite, can I keep it? Also, do you have back holsters for these?"

He laughs. "You're my favorite bachelorette, Demy—consider it yours. Don't skewer your date, and I'll see what I can do about a holster, too."

"Yes!" I pump my fist in the air, and he leaves us with a laugh. The dinner crew delivered not just food, but an intimate table for two with a full setup from the dining room, complete with linen tablecloth and napkins, fancy wine glasses, and full place settings. They've already plated the food under shiny silver domes, and as we trail over, they give us quick nods, and then leave, too.

I suddenly feel very, *very* alone with Jax. My palms feel sweaty, and it has nothing to do with the sparkly purple axe handle I'm gripping a little too tightly. He takes the seat on the far side of the table, leaving me the one closest to the door. I sink into it slowly and rest my axe against the table leg.

"So, what did you order us for dinner?" I ask, not lifting my dome yet.

"Something from my hometown. I hope you like pizza." He nods, and I pick the dome up from my plate. A fantastic smell hits me, of warm mozzarella and rich tomato sauce, and my mouth is watering. It's the polar opposite of the fancy nightmare meal I had with Beckett, and I actually love it.

"This is pizza? It has a top crust." I look up and see his grin. He likes sharing this with me. Maybe I've been overreacting, and he's been pushing so hard because he feels like he has to, since he's not wealthy. Something to think about.

"It's deep dish. Traditionally made in my home tri-state for centuries, and the best pizza on planet earth, bar none. Well, if they did it right. They tell me they have a chef from Wiscigan, but we'll have to taste it to see. Oh, here—let me cut it for you. The toppings are inside." He grabs a giant, plate-wide pizza cutter from a small side table they set up with two more domes on it.

It looks sharp, and I lean back slightly as he stands over the table to chop it down through my personal pizza.

"This is really cool, Jax. Thank you for sharing this with me." He cuts it into four tidy pieces—each oozing with cheese and showing peeks of pepperoni and sausage—and then repeats the process for his own pie.

"Absolutely. This is why I want a wife and a kid, you know? I want to share myself with them. Carry on my family traditions."

"That's lovely. And this . . ." I take the first bite, and close my eyes in bliss, chewing slowly to savor the intricate flavor. "This is heaven. Wow, you grew up eating this? Can you tell me about your family, and where you grew up?" I take another bite, and listen carefully as he launches into story after story about his family, the major city where he grew up, and the age-old debate about which pizza maker is the best. When we've eaten our fill of deep-dish pizza, he pulls off the other two domes, and a beautiful, perfectly square piece of tiramisu rests on each plate.

"You like coffee, so I thought this would be your favorite dessert. Though, cannoli goes well with pizza, too. We can try that next time, if you'd like."

"I've never had tiramisu, or cannoli. But I'm sure I'll love it. It's almost too pretty to eat."

"It's not nearly as pretty as you." This time, when he says it, his eyes don't stray from mine. The intensity is sending unexpected shivers through me, and I'm the first to duck my head and blush.

We finish our desserts while making small talk, and he walks me politely back to the women's dormitory. The night went shockingly well, and I feel like I finally saw the real Jax, underneath all the pushy bravado and hot-headedness. After he leaves, I shower and get in bed, and lie there even more confused about what to do. And I *really* need to talk to Nell, and the other girls.

CHAPTER SEVENTEEN

SECRETS REVEALED

DEMY

When my alarm goes off the next morning, I'm already awake and dressed. I head into the hallway and go next door to Nell's room. I knock, wait, and knock again, but there's still no answer. When is she coming back?

Determined to get a solid answer to that, I jog down the stairs, and straight to the main hall. I push through the double doors and start scanning for one of the ever-present attendants. A cluster of guards is debriefing in the corner, and Lars is there. He's leaning back against the wall, one booted foot propped against the gaudy, expensive wallpaper, and those dead eyes trained on me instead of on his fellow guards. I quickly look away, not wanting to draw attention to him again after he spoke to me in the dining room just yesterday. Especially not if he could get in trouble for protecting my secret.

I spot an attendant at the far end of the hall just outside the dining room, and I don't waste any time putting that distance between me and the security guard.

"Excuse me!" I flag down the blue-uniformed attendant, and he pastes on a proper smile.

"Yes, Miss Demelza, how can I help you?"

"I need to see Nell. Can you tell me—"

"Oh, of course. Miss Nell is right down the hall. Would you like me to take you to the executive suite?"

"Uh, yeah. Yes. That would be great. Lead the way, please." Executive suite? I know Atlas is an important private security firm owner, but what does that have to do with Nell disappearing for days and coming back to an executive suite instead of her room next to mine? Something's off.

The attendant is short, and as he walks ahead of me at a clipped pace, I can easily see the top of his head, and the perfectly circular bald spot on top of it. I nearly run into the back of him when he stops abruptly, and gestures to an ornately carved door that's several feet taller than I am.

"Here you are, Miss Demelza."

"Demy, please. And thank you . . . ?" I nod for him to give me his name.

"Stephens, miss. Leonidas Stephens."

"Thank you, Stephens. You've been very helpful."

"Certainly." He gives me a stiff little bow, and turns to walk crisply back the way we came, before disappearing into the main hallway.

I press my ear quietly to the door, and hear muffled voices on the other side of the thick oak. I'm pretty sure one of them belongs to Atlas—once someone yells at you and stuffs you in a safe room, you memorize their voice—there's a few I don't recognize, and then—Nell!

Without waiting, I knock on the door.

"Come in." Atlas's voice booms loud enough to be heard clearly through the three inch thick wood, no problem. It takes considerable muscle to wedge the heavy door open, but I slip inside, and am utterly confused by the scene in front of me.

Nell, Atlas, and Easton are seated at a massive conference table, with a holographic display in front of them depicting a man with glasses in front of a huge wall of blinking monitors, and in an apparently second location—is that the new king and queen of the NAA?

The man with the glasses is talking a mile a minute, unbothered by my barging into what appears to be a business meeting of some sort. "Atlas, your gut instinct was correct. I ran a full-scale evaluation of all prior Cabal attacks on New Life Centers, and this attack was unique. The flag in their database is still there, however, and it's becoming clearer and clearer that they are after a pin-point target this time, instead of their usual mayhem. What we don't know is what or who, and *why* they've changed their MO." He sucks in a breath, and he's about to launch into another round of discussions when the young Queen raises a hand to still him momentarily. "Nell, dear, you've got a visitor."

"You can set the breakfast down on the side table," Nell calls without looking over her shoulder. Atlas, however, turns around and frowns at me.

"What are you doing here, Demelza? You should *not* be in this room."

"Demy?" Nell spins in her seat at his use of my name. She shoots an apologetic glance at Atlas. "Well, I guess the cat's out of the bag. You should come sit down. We have some things to talk about."

"Nell, no. We cannot entrust the other women here with the details of this. It's a matter of national security."

She rolls her eyes, unfazed by the censure in the enormous man's tone. "Yeah, and it's also a matter of her *personal* security. This affects everyone here, and I'm not going to pretend it doesn't. Demy, come sit." She points to an open seat.

I walk on wooden legs, and sink into the rolling chair she pointed to. I'm facing the three of them on one side, and the three holographic people on the other. "Are you two . . . the king and queen of the NAA? Or . . ." I'm not sure, because they're both dressed very casually. They could be the same people, or perhaps their farmer cousins. On TV they're always decked out to the nines, and all glittery. I don't know what to do with the jeans, braid, and tank top version of a queen—though the longer I look at them, the more sure I am that she's the woman from the introductory video.

The man smiles, popping a dimple that would melt a thousand hearts. "Yes, I'm Patrick, and this is my beautiful bride Sadie."

Sadie rolls her eyes, but smiles at his sweet introduction. "It's nice to meet you, Demy. I'd love to hear about how you're finding the modifications we've made to the New Lives Program one day soon, but unfortunately we're in some hot water right now. Glitch was just explaining that the NLC where you're currently located seems to have been marked by the underground terrorist group, the Cabal. Their missions in the past have always been straightforward destruction, but this time . . . they're behaving differently. Does that about sum it up, Glitch?"

"Yep, you nailed it, Sadie. And I'm Glitch, by the way." The man pushes his glasses up his nose with one finger, and gives me a dorky wave. He's delightful.

"So, you three—" I turn to Nell and her two *matches*.

Atlas is the one who speaks up. "Nell and I are genetic matches. But we were matched in the same cohort as Sadie and Patrick, and we've been happily married ever since. Easton is my second-in-command at my security company and assigned personally to Nell while we're here undercover."

"Okay, listen, I see that look, and I get it. I hated lying to everyone, but we had to have a way to be here without raising suspicions, and still keep everyone safe. This made the most sense, and me being here gave Atlas cover to always be present. He's the one who's going to crack this, and take the Cabal out for good."

Sadie clears her throat and bobs her head to the side pointedly.

"With Glitch's super-brain, of course," Nell adds.

"I see. So, you're already married. Wow . . . I just . . . wow. Okay, so, why is the Cabal after this center? There are fifty or something, right—plus all the honeymoon destinations."

"Yes, which is what we're here to figure out."

"Okay. Is it safe for us to all stay here? Shouldn't they have moved us all as soon as they found about this 'mark?'"

Nell frowns. "That was my plan, but I got shot down. Glitch raised the good point that as long as we don't know why, we could just be moving whoever or whatever they're targeting with you all."

"That's correct," Atlas says. "We looked extensively at the situation, and decided it was best to lock down security here rather than try to move. It could be one of the matches, one of the girls, something in someone's possession, something in one of your *families'* possession—there are some very powerful men here, and

161

Cammie's mother is an important figure, as well. So, that's why any off-premises dates have been canceled for this match session, and the guard presence has been doubled at this location, heavily focusing on the border patrols. If you're inside the fence, we've made sure you're secure."

"Actually," Glitch interjects, "I've intercepted a new communication which I think rules out the possibility that it's a possession. They are after a person, but there's nothing identifying in the communication, not even the gender or age of the individual."

"Ahh." Panic starts to climb up my throat. I've been on the run for *six years* and suddenly this is all happening? What if it's me? They've never tried to blow me up, they've always tried to catch me. Is it possible this is a separate group, using the Cabal as cover? Or . . . is there something else going on? I wrestle with whether or not to tell them about my past, but hearing the listing of all the important people and families, it feels arrogant to think I could be the only target. Clearly Glitch and this team don't think so.

Thankfully, the conversation moves on while I'm still debating.

"I'm going to be digging into every individual on the premises anyways to ensure we don't have any moles, per Atlas's request, so I'll keep an eye out for anything that could flag a person as a likely target, such as—"

"Great work, Glitch. What's the word on the antidote?" Atlas stops another ramble before it can get fully rolling.

"Ahh, yes! Thank you for the reminder. The science team at—uh. Am I okay to discuss this in front of our new visitor? Auntie—"

"You're good, Glitch. Me and Demy are tight, and she won't let anything slip to the other girls, right, Demy?" She pins me with a winning smile, and guilt swamps me. She's letting me in in a big way, and I'm keeping something huge from her.

I have to tell her. Just . . . not with an audience. Nell, I can bare my ugly past to. But the King and Queen of the NAA? No. I'll tell her the very next time it's just the two of us, I promise myself. "Right. I can keep a secret." I smile at Glitch, and he continues as if the words had been building up behind his pause like a river freed from a dam.

"Zanetti is on it, and they've already identified the poison. There isn't a known antidote for the specific compound—chemically it's called hexathalogen, but the more common name is, ironically, maiden's blush. It's derived from a flowering plant, but what might give an unscrupulous deer a tummy ache in the wild has been concentrated so highly that it's lethal within ninety seconds of entering the mucosal lining. We were warned highly to avoid contact with any bodily fluids from an infected person going forward, because at this strength it's possible to have a secondary skin reaction to the substance. As far as the *antidote* is concerned, they are testing compounds known to relieve symptoms of another irritant plant in the genus Abrus. They'll get back to us every seventy-two hours until a resolution has been reached, or they determine one is not chemically feasible."

"That's rather chatty for Auntie, Glitch. I'm impressed." Atlas's droll tone has Glitch blushing to the roots of his dark, curly hair.

"I was assigned a liaison, actually. Her name's Lilah. She's a double-assigned citizen to both their technical communications division and their biological research team."

"Ooh, I think he's got a crush, Sadie! This Lilah sounds like the perfect match for *you*, Glitch. What does she look like? Have you run her genetic compatibility numbers with yours? I bet you have. Oh, you would make such smart babies! We need to hook you two up so you can raise the next generation of super-geniuses."

"Uhm, we haven't video-chatted yet, we've only messaged. She set us up a SCAD encrypted messaging app—" Glitch answers, wide-eyed at Nell's rapid-fire plans to marry him off to someone he's never met in person yet. *Par for the course, these days.*

I reach over and drop a hand on Nell's forearm. "Nell, Glitch seems a little overwhelmed. Maybe we could let him get to know her first? Also, who's aunt is this?"

"I can ask Mav about Lilah—she'll give me the scoop. *And* help me scheme. She's really come around to my team the last few years." Nell's grin is wicked, and Glitch pales at the expression of utter glee on her face. As an afterthought she adds, "Oh, and Auntie is actually Mav's aunt, but everyone calls her that. It's sort of like a title. She rules a secret, underground—"

"Okay, okay—I think that was the end of our itinerary for now," Patrick cuts in, and Glitch sinks back into his ergonomic chair gratefully. "I want you four to stay alert, stay careful—and do not take any unnecessary risks. Atlas, you're the man for this job. If I can do anything at all to make this mission more secure or successful, name it and it's yours. No exceptions." He levels Atlas with a questioning gaze.

"We have everything we need, Patrick, and more. We're going to bring this home for you, I have no doubt."

"Okay. We'll talk again if there are any updates from any team."

"Enjoy your dates!" Sadie says with a wave, and then their hologram blinks out of existence. Glitch gives another goofy wave, then he blinks out without another word.

The three of them all swivel towards me as if they're synchronized swimmers, and I stare back.

164

"This makes a lot more sense now. I know you're crazy brave, but cozying up to that guy in the first five minutes of meeting him did not make sense to me."

Nell chuckles, and reaches over to twine her fingers with Atlas's. "I know he's the size of a grizzly, but he's a teddy bear on the inside."

Atlas shakes his head lightly at the insinuation that he's a softie. "Only for you, Nell. Now, we've got to get back at it, or more people will be suspicious." He levels a pointed look on me.

"Sorry. I missed Nell, and I was getting worried."

"Told you we were besties," she trills, pushing back from her seat. "Now, where did those dadgum breakfast people get off to? I'm starved."

CHAPTER EIGHTEEN

STARGAZING

DEMY

The day flies by in a blur of activity. All of us girls are happy to have Nell back, so after our morning activities—I had my first solo bow practice, and it was epic—we cancel all plans with the guys and have a girls' movie night. Nell orders snacks that are definitely not standard hoity-toity NLC fare, but I have to say, the girl knows how to eat. We stuff ourselves to the gills on pigs in a blanket, bacon-wrapped dates, fluorescent cheese dip with nachos, skewers of all kinds, and an entire s'mores bar.

By ten p.m. we're all getting groggy, and part ways. So, it makes absolutely no sense that fifteen minutes after my shower, I'm still lying in bed, flat on my back, and staring at the ceiling as if it's got the secrets to all of life's problems.

Insomnia sucks.

With a sigh, I grab my tablet from my bedside, and unlock the screen. Then, an idea hits me. I can't fix much of my situation right now—the crazy people hunting me, for instance—but there is a question I never got an answer to. I tap out a quick message, and then lay the tablet down on my chest. I won't stare at it until he answers. I won't, I—the tablet dings.

I pick it up, and his response has me smiling and pulling on my favorite pair of flats, pajamas and all. Not five minutes later, Fletcher's waiting for me at the stairs, and pulls me to his chest for a big, warm bear hug.

"Missing me, huh? I was missing you, too. It was a jerk move for Jax to block your calendar for two whole days, but I don't want to talk about him right now." He chafes the backs of my arms lightly with his hands, giving me some of his warmth in the chilly night air. "What do you want to do?"

Hold the phone. Jax had intentionally kept me from the other guys the last couple days? Just when I think he's so sweet, I find out he was intentionally isolating me from the others. It makes me angry, but I don't want to think about Jax right now, either. I'm going to have to deal with him soon. The jealousy is too much.

"To be honest, I hadn't thought that far. I just had some things I wanted to talk to you about." I bite my lip as I look up at him.

"That sounds serious, so we need somewhere quiet." He thinks for a moment, then looks up at the sky. "Are you up for a micro-adventure?"

"Uh, yes?"

"Excellent. I know the perfect place, then. Come on." He wraps my hand in his, and we walk side by side down the path towards the main hall. But instead of stopping at the main hall, we go past it, and five minutes later we're standing in front of a near-identical dormitory.

"Is this where you're staying?"

"Yep. It's pretty nice inside, but not as frilly as the women's dorm."

That reminds me that he was in our dorm seeing Cammie, who's now let him go because of me. I mentally add it to the list of things to discuss tonight.

He leads me into the front door, holding his finger to his lips in the universal sign for quiet. We close the door carefully, and he leads me up the stairs. Everything inside is built identically, but decorated and furnished completely opposite. Our pale pink and baby portraits are a sharp contrast to their rich navy, and portraits of men in sharp suits, each with a woman on his arm, and a baby in her arms. My stomach clenches. The messaging is clear, just different. It's unsettling, and for the hundredth time I wonder what I've gotten myself into.

He leads me down the familiar-yet-different hall, and into a bedroom at the end. It's tidy, and the warm, masculine smell that is uniquely Fletcher envelops me when I step into his personal space. The bed is mussed, as if he was lying in it himself when I messaged.

"I didn't get you out of bed, did I?"

"Nah, I was just laying around, thinking. I'd much rather have company."

"Same. Do you want me to sit at the desk, or—"

He places a finger over my lips. "Does this seem adventurous to you? We're not done yet, come on." His grin is wicked, and it sends a delicious jolt of anticipation through me.

He leads me over to a large window, a massive sycamore right outside. "You ever climbed a tree before?" he asks over his shoulder.

"Uh, once or twice, but it's been a while."

"Good. It's just like riding a bike." With that, he climbs out the window, stepping onto a lower branch while holding onto one at about his chest height. Once he's moved further towards the trunk, he gestures for me to follow him.

"Uhm, Fletcher, we're on the second story." I lean out the window, and see the manicured lawn a full fifteen feet below.

"Uh-huh, not high enough to do serious damage. Now get out here, Miss Action-Adventure."

The challenge does it for me, and then I'm throwing my leg over the windowsill, and feeling for the limb with my toes. It gives slightly under my weight, and I have a fleeting moment of worry that it can't hold both me *and* Fletcher, and we're about to test his theory about no serious damage. The tree is strong, though, and the limb holds as I grasp the upper limb and shift the rest of my weight on it.

Fletcher gives a quiet whoop. "There she is. Come on, we're going up." He heads up the tree, not waiting around for me to follow.

I climb more cautiously but follow him up a few feet to another wide limb where he waits, straddling an adjacent limb with his back against the trunk. "You're a really good climber. Now we're just going to shimmy over to the roof."

"The roof?" I turn my back to the trunk, and sure enough, the limb he's sitting on extends only two feet from the roof, where it's been sawn off by the landscaping crew to protect the roof. "It looks like we'll have to jump."

"You will, but I'll go first. I promise to catch you. Do you trust me?"

"I'm up a tree with you in the middle of the night. I think that's your answer."

He pops easily to his feet, and in a few quick strides, he step-leaps over the small gap, and is standing on the angled roof

169

of the men's dorm. He holds up a hand for me, and I swallow hard. I'm not afraid of heights per se, but leaping across empty space to a *roof* is risky, that's all. I'm definitely not a chicken.

I step carefully over to his branch, and make my way more slowly to the end, holding a neighboring branch. But then I'm at the end, and I have to let go to make the jump.

"You've got this, Demy. I'll catch you."

Sucking in a deep breath, I jump. For a moment I'm flying, and then I crash-land into Fletcher's arms. He chuckles and tucks me tight against his chest. My heart is pounding so hard, I'm sure he can feel it where we're squished together.

"You're beautiful, Demy. Even more so under the moon, with the wind in your hair, and pink cheeks. Absolute perfection. I'm so tempted to kiss you." He brushes his thumb over my bottom lip, and the motion sends a zippy tingle along my nerves.

"Maybe you should give in to temptation." I try to keep the words light, teasing, but there's no hiding the heat building between us like a wildfire. One little spark, and we'll go up in flames.

"Maybe I will." He leans down and claims my mouth with his, soft and dominant all at once. His left hand sweeps up my back and into my loose hair, cradling the back of my head gently as he guides me into his kiss, his lips slanting against mine.

Fletcher's lips are smooth and firm, teasing mine in a way that I never want him to stop. After a few moments he pulls back, and I realize I've fisted my hands in the front of his shirt. I let it go, and rest my palms on his chest. Now his heart's thundering to keep pace with mine, too.

"Come here." He sits down, and then lays back on the roof, using his hands as a pillow behind his head. I carefully sit next to him, and use his bicep as my own pillow, crossing my hands over my stomach, instead.

For a few moments, we just lie there together, basking in the afterglow of that kiss and staring up at the stars. They're so bright up here, and feel closer, even though that's ridiculous. The sky stretches endlessly overhead like black silk, sprinkled with luminous diamonds. It's worth climbing a tree for.

"So, what did you want to talk about?" His voice is gravelly, muted in the cool night air. It runs over me like roughened velvet, and I resist the urge to shiver.

"Well, a few things."

He laughs. "Do I get to hear one of them?"

I jab him in the ribs with my elbow. "When I'm ready, Mr. Impatient."

"Okay, okay. No need to wound me," he teases.

That makes me smile. He's so laid back, and it is a sharp contrast to Jax's temper when the other guys are around. Which makes me think of him and Cammie, and the smile vanishes.

"So, I heard something, and I just wanted to find out if it's true."

"Okay . . . ?" He turns his head to the side, and I can feel his eyes boring into my cheek. How do I ask this without sounding like a gold digger? I don't care that he's rich, honestly. The steady job as a closer that Jax has feels rich to me, compared to living a half inch above the bottom of the barrel for the last six years.

"Well, you haven't shared what your job is. You talk about hiking, it was in your photos . . . but Jax mentioned that your dad owns some big biomedical company, and you're expected to take it over soon. It sounds an awful lot like Beckett's situation . . ." *There, that wasn't so bad, was it?*

171

He sighs, and the sound is so weary, I instantly regret the question. "Yeah, my dad founded Genexima Medical. It's big, and he expects me to take over. Well, he did. But I told him to stuff it and hit the trails. Does that change how you see me?"

"No, not really. I told you already that I'm broke. Did that change how you see me?"

"Of course not. You're a fighter, and that's admirable."

"Yeah, well, I'm a fighter with two whole NLC motherhood deposits and a ratty duffel bag to her name. If you can overlook that, I can overlook your impending wealth. Although, that's a big decision, turning him down. Do you not enjoy the field, or was it more than that?" I ask quietly. We're already into the conversation now, so I'm going to use this opportunity to understand him better.

"It's always more. I went along with the expected for so much of my life . . . the prep schools, the degree in biomedicine, the business internships along the way . . . I did it all. Until he asked for the one thing I couldn't do."

Dread fills me as his tone darkens. "What did he want?"

"He wanted me to marry his business partner and CFO's daughter, Flora. Even went so far as to run our genetic compatibility outside of the NLC's systems, to ensure we were capable of producing an heir." The words are bitter, and I hate that he's gone through this with his father.

"So, you two didn't get along well? You obviously weren't a love match, or else you wouldn't be here."

His sigh this time is sad. "Flora was an amazing woman, and we got along very well. We were childhood friends and attended the same prep school. But Flora was a lesbian. We weren't compatible, and a sham marriage would have made us both miserable. I knew it. Our fathers knew it. But it's still illegal for a woman to marry another woman, and they wanted to use me to cover it up, instead of using their *considerable* combined wealth to lobby for the laws to be changed. They have the technology that she could have stayed single, and used AI with a sperm donor to get pregnant on her own, no partner required. Knowing that, how could I marry her? Flora deserved better than a miserable, trapped life."

"I'm so sorry, Fletcher. That's awful for her, and for you. You *both* deserve better. So, you walked away, and your father didn't take it well."

"I told him no, he threw a tantrum, and then turned a company Christmas party into an unannounced *engagement* party. So, I walked out, and never went back. In his mind, I did the worst thing I could do—I didn't just break the rules; I made a fool out of him in the process."

"Well, if it helps, he deserved it. Trying to twist your arm into marrying someone is not okay." I turn on my side, placing a hand on his chest. "I'm proud of you for standing up to him. What about Flora? Did she get out, too?"

His face turns stony, and he's silent for so long, I think he's not going to answer. When he speaks, his voice is broken. "Flora's father got her a hand-picked match through the NLC, and less than two months later she was married off. She committed suicide sixty days after she married the man. She was already pregnant." A tear escapes the corner of his eye and slides down his cheek, and a sob breaks free from my chest.

I have no words. There are none that can handle the grief and horror that overwhelms me at what he just said. So, I do the next best thing; I throw my arms around him, pull him to a sitting position, and crush him to me in a hug. And I don't let go for a long, long time.

CHAPTER NINETEEN

ATTACK FROM WITHIN

DEMY

The next morning, it feels like I wake up five minutes after I closed my eyes. Fletcher and I stayed on the roof into the wee hours, and when I finally dragged myself across the grounds and back to bed, I tossed and turned for the rest of the night. Nightmares of poor Flora, and Fletcher's guilt-ridden face wrecked my dreams. That their own fathers could do that to them sickens me beyond belief.

I never did ask Fletcher his thoughts on splitting from Cammie, but after what he's shared, I've decided it's not important. He's a private man, and he has good reasons for keeping things close to the vest. Hopefully as we continue getting to know each other, he'll keep letting me in. He clearly needs time and space to open up more.

Deciding to skip the gym, I head downstairs to breakfast first thing. I'm too tired to row, and Peter won't care if I reschedule my bow practice for the afternoon. The other three girls are already there. Cammie's chattering away about her date with Vince—they're going to go ATVing—Leilani's nodding along enthusiastically, and Nell looks like she'd rather still be horizontal. *Same, girl; same.*

"Anyways, if today doesn't go well, I'm going to cut him loose. Four guys is plenty to manage. And honestly, Alonso's just got that *something* about him that I don't feel with Vince. Orlando doesn't give me the *same* fireworks, but he's so sweet. Vince doesn't seem to be trying as hard, which I take to mean he doesn't feel as strongly about me as he should if we're going to be a permanent match, you know?" Cammie looks around at the three of us, and I make a point to nod.

"We have to narrow it down at some point. It's okay if you're ready to start. You have the most matches, so it makes sense they wouldn't all hit it off with you," Leilani says.

"True. What do you guys think? Should I give it until the date to see, or should I just cut the cord now? It feels so cold, doing it via the app. I explained to Fletcher in person, before I released him from the app. It felt kinder, in a way."

"Go with your gut. If you think one more date will *really* make a difference, you can try. But if you don't think it will make a difference . . . prolonging something doesn't seem kinder, does it? Besides, that's precious date time you could be spending with one of your other four," I reason.

"That is *very* true. If I meet him at the date, and just explain that I don't think either one of us is feeling the vibes . . . Yep, I think that's what I'll do. You girls are the best." She gives Nell a quick hug, then high-fives me and Leilani across the table. "Okay, I've got to run. I want to get dressed for a breakup, and *also* see who is available this afternoon to console me. Toodles!" She gives us a flirty shoulder shimmy, then hurries towards the door.

"She is something else," Nell mumbles, taking a bite of breakfast sausage. "She's got good energy, though. What are you two doing?" she asks, waving the impaled sausage back and forth between Leilani and me.

"I actually have to run, too." Leilani blushes. "Kellan has a surprise date planned for me in half an hour. I thought we were going to go back to the art studio and work on our paintings, but he won't budge on a single hint." She sighs dreamily.

"That Kellan is a looker, and he's only got eyes for you, girl. I think he's got real keeper vibes." Nell wiggles her fingers like she's shooting magical energy at Leilani.

"I hope so. Wish me luck!"

"Good luck," Nell and I both chorus. And then it's just the two of us. She yawns widely and closes her eyes between bites of sausage. Now is not the time to bring up my crappy past. A server comes over and drops my usual breakfast eggs down in front of me, reminding me that there are more reasons—and ears—not to share in the middle of the dining room. *Later.* As he walks off, I see Lars in the closest guard position against the wall. He makes eye contact with me, and then jerks his head once, so quickly I almost think I imagined it, towards the far side of the building where we spoke under the willow tree.

Then, he speaks into his wrist comm, and takes the side exit out of the dining room.

I quickly polish off my plate with the half-asleep Nell. "Okay, girl, I'm heading to the archery range. See you later."

"See you later," she says with a yawn. A pang of guilt hits me at her trusting me while I'm keeping something so big from her, but as soon as I learn whatever Lars knows, I can share with her. And Atlas, who will *definitely* be angry. Large, muscled, intimidating, and furious. *Ugh.*

When I make it to the willow tree, Lars is already waiting with his arms crossed tightly over his chest.

"Did you find anything?"

"Yeah, I found something. Your parents were killed by the freaking Cabal, Demy! Do you realize what a big deal that is? The police investigation into their deaths didn't find physical evidence, but apparently a neighbor saw two black-cloaked men leaving the premises, and reported it to the cops. You were *also* marked dead, which is why you weren't put into the foster care system. It makes no sense, though, because you're here, and very alive."

"Someone marked me dead? But, how? I went on the run, but I didn't change my identity or anything. I mean, I filed the emancipation stuff and nobody said a word."

"I don't know, Demy. There's no information on it, but my best guess is that somebody tampered with your records to keep you from being found and put back into the system. Why, I don't know. This needs to get reported."

"Okay, yeah. I understand. Will you let me do it, though? I'll explain it to Atlas so you won't get into trouble." I swallow hard, pushing the fear aside. It's the right thing to do. I can't keep putting everyone else here in danger, especially if it was the Cabal who killed my parents. My throat tightens, and my pulse is going nuts. If I don't stop thinking about it, I'm going to spin out into another panic attack.

"Thank you, Lars. I really appreciate this." Tears sting my eyes, but I rub them away with the heel of my hand as I bolt from under the willow tree. The last thing I want is for the stoic guard to see me bawling like a baby.

I take a few minutes to clear my head, and then walk over to the archery range for a slightly belated archery practice with Peter.

We're working on my release form when his wrist comm starts alarming. He curses under his breath. "Demy, go right now—there's a panic room behind the water cooler. Reach behind the cooler, hit the blue button, and the wall will open. Once you're in, nobody can access it via the button. Go now, and take your bow!" As soon as I grab a handful of arrows, I bolt towards the water cooler, and he's out the door of the range.

I do as he says and find a blue button the size of my palm tucked behind the water cooler's stand. The wall hisses when it pops open, revealing a *much* smaller room than the one Fletcher and I spent the evening in. There's nothing inside but a love seat, a panel of wall monitors, and a bathroom. I watch sadly as the door seals shut behind me, locking me into the claustrophobic space.

The first thing I do is hit the big red button that controls the audio feeds. However, they're oddly quiet. There is the usual body cam footage of people running, but no sound. I press the button a couple more times, and the light switches on and off, but no audio comes pouring in no matter how many times I push it. With a sigh, I carefully deposit my bow and quiver of arrows onto the empty seat and settle onto the other cushion to wait out whatever the new threat is. I should be able to figure something out from the body cam footage, at least.

The thing is, though, that the running cam feeds keep cutting out. They all run down a dirt path, and then—boom, gone. There goes another one—I've now got five blank feeds. What is going on out there?

My chest feels like there are rubber bands squeezing it, and I jump to my feet. I can't just sit here and wonder, watching as one by one the feeds go dark. So, I pace. After about five laps, I shove the small couch in front of the monitors, to give myself a little more open space.

When pacing gets old—have I been in here five minutes, or fifty?—I do wall sits. Then high knees. Then—a chime fills the previously silent room, and I freeze, panic rushing back up. Spinning to face the wall of monitors, I see Beckett's face.

"Demy? I'm coming in. The threat's been cleared, okay?" Almost every other video feed has gone dark, so I have no choice but to trust him.

The door hisses, and slides open, revealing Beckett on the other side. His face is grim.

"Beckett, hey!" We meet in the middle, and squeeze each other in a relieved hug for several heartbeats. It starts to sink in, though, that he feels tense. So, I pull back. "What's going on? Is everyone okay? What was that attack? The audio didn't work in this safe room, and the feeds kept cutting out—"

"The audio was turned off, due to the nature of the attack."

The air whooshes out of my lungs in a single gust. "So, it was another attack? How did they clear things so fast, though? Last time it took all night—"

"Demy, I have some bad news. They wanted a friendly face, so each of the girls has one of their matches—"

"Oh, no. No, no. Beckett, don't do that. Just spit it out. Who got hurt?" He doesn't answer immediately. Instead, he takes both of my hands in his.

"Demy, it's going to be okay, and she is going to be okay. All right? They told me to start with that—she is going to be fine in a few weeks—"

"Beckett! I can't breathe here, just spit it out!"

"It's Cammie, Demelza. She went out with Vincenzo, and he didn't take the news well that he was being released. He's never gotten a match before, and when she told him, he—well, she's got some injuries. Nothing irreparable, thank God. The fight was loud enough it spooked some of the horses, so one of the stable hands came running, thinking it was a wild animal, and, well—"

"Where is she? Where is Cammie right now?"

"Demy, they aren't going to let any of you see her. They think it will just make everything worse, for her and for you. She's in pretty bad shape. One of her eyes is swollen shut, she's got cracked ribs, and—"

I snatch my hands out of his, and look him dead in the eye. "Beckett, so help me if you don't figure out a way to get me to Cammie's bedside in the next hour, you'll be going home right behind Vince. This is not a joke, and it is not a game. Take me to her, now!"

He takes a step back, and an angry look crosses his face briefly, but he shuts it down. "I'll see what I can do." He turns and strides out of the room stiffly, and doesn't wait for me to catch up to him.

I grab my bow and jog after him. He's got a slim black cell phone pressed to his ear, and he's speaking so quietly I can't make out what he's saying, or who he's talking to. He presses a button and slides the phone into the inside pocket of his suit jacket.

"My chopper will be here in half an hour."

"Your chopper? Where did they take her?"

"The closest trauma medical center is at the other end of the tri-state. They had the center's chopper here within minutes, and she was already in the air. They've landed and triaged her, and know enough of her injuries to know she's going to be okay. Unfortunately, though, even with the chopper, we still won't make it across the tri-state in under an hour from now. So if you'd like to go alone—"

"Beckett, I'm sorry. I don't want to go alone, and I'd appreciate your company, if you're still willing to give it. I shouldn't have—" Tears well up, blurring my vision, and the back of my throat burns. Beckett has been nothing but kind, and here we are in a crisis and I'm treating him terribly. "I'm so sorry."

"Shh, now. It's going to be okay. Cammie is in rough shape, but she will recover physically in a few short weeks. They've got a plastic surgeon flying in from York tonight to handle a few stitches, and truly she's getting the best possible care given the situation."

"I can't believe one of her matches *attacked* her." I pull back enough to see his face, peering down at me. "It's so awful, Beckett. Aren't the men vetted before they let them into this program?"

"They are, but unfortunately with enough influence and greasing the right palms, almost anything can be swept under the rug. I would bet that with some pointed digging, we'll find a few skeletons in Vincenzo's past." He cups the back of my head and pulls me back against his chest. We stay like that for a while, until the sound of chopper blades grabs our attention. It's not in sight yet, but it has to be close.

"Are you angry with me?" I ask Beckett, not daring to look at him.

He chuckles. "I was annoyed at first, but no. While I'd rather you didn't use that command on me, personally, it will serve you well in your role as my wife." He turns away from the sound of the chopper, and looks into my eyes, so I reluctantly mirror his position. "There are expectations, Demy. When you're in the public eye like I am, people will expect you to dress and behave in certain ways, and to always keep your composure. You have to decide if you're ready for a life like that. I can offer you a lot—the whole world, if you want it—but it doesn't come freely."

The helicopter clears the tree line, and the sound of the blades and the air pushing us back quickly becomes too much for us to talk over.

As we board the sleek black-and-gold chopper, the words hang on me, dragging me down. *Am I ready for that kind of life?*

In just under an hour we're walking into the sliding doors of the trauma center. The harsh lighting stings my eyes after the dimmer helicopter interior, but I ignore the unpleasantness and arrow straight towards the information center.

"We're here to see Cammie Tinsley. Can you tell us where to find her?"

"Are you family?"

"Well, no. We're friends. Good friends."

"I'm sorry, miss, but we can't let anyone back who isn't family. No visitor list has been established, and—"

"Please, we've gone to a lot of trouble, and I know she'd want to see me. Can you ask?"

She looks down her glasses at me, and at Beckett looming quietly over my shoulder. "One moment." She walks to the back wall, faces away from us, and speaks quietly into a wall mounted comm device. She walks back over to us. "First and last name, please."

"Demelza Carlisle and Beckett Vaughn."

She nods, and walks back to the comm. It feels like forever before she has an answer, but when she comes back, she directs us up the elevator into the trauma ward, and then how to page to be let in. We do, and we're paged back immediately. Two more hallways, and we're standing outside Cammie's door.

"Do you mind waiting here?" I ask Beckett over my shoulder.

"Of course, take all the time you need. I have some calls to make, anyways." He gives me a tight smile, but leans against the window, and pulls out his phone again.

"Thank you, Beckett, really. This means a lot to me."

"You're welcome. Now, get in there. We only have an hour before we have to head back to the NLC."

I don't waste any more time after that. A quick knock, and I peek inside. Cammie raises one hand weakly to wave me in, and I have to bite back a sob. Her face is black and purple, her lip is split, and one eye is swollen shut. She's got bandages and machines everywhere, IVs, and I can't see any spot I can hug her without hurting her. To see the bright, beautiful woman from this morning only a few hours later, looking like this . . . I want to murder the S-O-B who did this to her. But right now, I have to focus on her—not on that douchebag.

"Hi, Cammie. I'm so sorry, girl. I can't believe this has happened to you. And it's all my fault. I told you to go meet him." I choke back a sniffle. "I really don't know what to say. Sorry feels like not nearly enough."

"I'm so glad you're here." The words are raspy, not at all her usual high and laughing voice. She lifts her left hand—miraculously un-bruised, poked, or monitored—a few inches off the bed, and I take the invitation to grip it tightly. "I didn't think they'd let anyone leave the facility with all of the—attacks." Her words are slow and slightly slurred, and I assume one of the many IV bags is a painkiller making her drowsy.

"I didn't ask for permission, but I did give Beckett an ultimatum. I feel slightly guilty about that, but not guilty that it got me here. God, I wish I could rewind the clock. What happened? They didn't tell us a whole lot, only that Vince . . ."

She nods, the movement jerky. "I met him at the stables, which is where you pick up ATVs. It's close to the trails. I started to tell him—that it wasn't working out." She clears her throat, and points to a small cup of water on a nearby table, so I grab it for her and bend the straw so it meets her lips.

She takes a sip, and tries to smile but winces as it pulls her lip. "Thanks. Geez, I'm a mess, sorry."

"Hush, this is not your fault. Don't you dare apologize. This was *him*, and you did nothing wrong. We've all got your back."

Tears gather at the corner of her undamaged eye, and her lower lip trembles.

"I'm sorry. I'm terrible. I should have sent Leilani, she's so sooth-ing—"

Cammie squeezes my fingers so tightly, it feels like my bones are gonna crack. "You're doing just fine. Anyway, I told him I didn't think we were a good fit, and he grabbed me. Tried to kiss me anyways, so I kneed him in the balls." She coughs, and her right hand flies to her ribs. "That set him off. He started swinging. I tried to run and screamed my head off, but he caught me by the ponytail, and then . . ." A tear trickles down her cheek. "Thank God for the stable hand. He came with a shotgun. When Vince saw it, he jumped onto one of the ATVs and took off."

"They caught him. Atlas had him locked up before we left—he doesn't mess around. Beckett says Vince is going to get serious time for this, Cammie. He won't be able to hurt you—or anyone else—ever again."

"Good, because if he ever tried I'd shoot the POS myself."

"You can borrow my bow."

She chuckles, and then winces. "Don't make me laugh. Laughing hurts."

"Sorry, sorry."

She waves away the apology. "So, Beckett, huh?"

"Yeah, Beckett. He's waiting outside the room."

She nods. "Good. He seems nice. Helicopter Ken doll," she murmurs, eyes drifting closed.

"You rest. I can stay for an hour, and if you need anything at all, I'm your girl."

"Okay." The quiet murmur is the last sound besides her soft, even breathing and the steady chirps and beeps from the monitors. The hour passes too quickly, and it's with regret that I tuck her pale hand under her blankets to leave.

"Love you, Cammie," I whisper before I slip out the door.

CHAPTER TWENTY

SPARKLING

DEMY

The next day dawns with all the grace of a sledgehammer. My head is pounding, and I'm not in any mood to see people or talk to people. Leaving Cammie alone in that hospital was one of the worst things I've ever had to do, and I argued with Beckett half the flight home that we should get regular visits with her. So when my tablet starts trilling excitedly on my night stand, I'm more than tempted to throw it against the wall, or smash it with my sparkly purple axe.

Instead, I pick it up to ignore whatever the alarm is—events can kiss my butt, today—but sit bolt upright when I see the screen.

I'm out of bed and down the hall in sixty seconds flat, pounding on Leilani's door. Nell appears a moment later, and after we both start pounding, Leilani reluctantly opens the door.

"Why in the blue blazes did we just get a *wedding* notification?" Nell shouts, at the same time I screech, "You're getting *married*?!"

"I know it's a lot, and you guys don't have to come. I'm upset for Cammie too, I just . . . I can't do this any more. We're getting attacked, stuffed in safe rooms. Cammie got *beaten*—" Her voice

186

breaks off in a pitiful sob, and she buries her face in her hands. Nell wraps her up in a hug, even though she barely comes to Leilani's chin.

"It's gonna be okay, sugar." Nell shushes her.

"This is the only way out, and I'm done. I'm sorry. I hate to leave you two here, with the weight of all this . . . I just can't—"

"Don't apologize, Leilani. If you have a match you're comfortable with . . . it's okay to go." *At least one of us should be safe.*

"Thank you. Really, thank you. They told me that it's tradition to have a spa day to prep for the wedding, and, since it's the same day, I'll have to make all the choices while we're there. But if you two don't want to come, I understand. Given the circumstances." She looks down at her feet, the fluffy green slippers matching the pink ones they left in my closet.

The last thing on the planet I want to do is go sit through a spa day, especially now. But Leilani is clearly miserable, and despite raising holy hell last night outside the director's office, they won't let me—any of us—see Cammie again until she's cleared for travel back here. They are at least sending her matches to her, and they confirmed that her parents have already arrived, so she's not alone.

There's nothing more I can do for Cammie right now, and miserable and alone isn't how I want Leilani to spend her wedding day, even if it's going to suck for us all to act happy today.

"Of course we're coming," I insist, and her eyes lift. Her smile is watery, but it's better than her staring at the floor. She moves from Nell's arms to mine, and we hug it out.

"We have half an hour before the first appointment," Nell says. "We'd better all get dressed to get this wedding show on the road."

"So, where are you and Kellan going on the honeymoon?" Nell asks from her pedicure tub.

"Uh, well, we haven't actually decided. We were looking at British Washegon, or maybe Costa-Ma."

I can't help a small chuckle at that. "Those couldn't be further apart, unless you headed to Nunavland, and it's literally solid ice. Who wants which destination?"

"Well, there's a lot of cultural significance to Washegon. And I've heard the coast is lovely, even though it's cold. Sweater weather is appealing. But Kellan really wants to lay on the beach in bathing suits."

Nell snorts.

"What?"

"Nothing, nothing. Zero percent surprised by that split. Here's what you do: propose that you start with your place now, while the weather's warm. And then when it cools off too much, you escape down to Costa-Ma. Perfect plan. And you'll have more time to get comfortable around each other *before* you whip out bikinis."

Leilani's cheeks turn pink with her insinuation, and she ducks her head. The pink-uniformed women doing our pedicures are all older, with silver-threaded hair. Margie's my attendant for our spa day, and she looks up at that advice. "You should listen to your friend, sweetie. You have a couple years of honeymooning ahead—the weather will be much nicer up north now than if you wait. "

"I hadn't thought about the weather. I'm sure Kellan won't mind as long as we have a plan to see both places." Leilani smiles warmly at Margie.

She nods happily and goes back to beautifying a part of me that's never been beautified before. I'm sure my feet will look great when she's done, but nobody told me that pedicures *tickle*. I've been making an absolute fool out of myself giggling the entire time. I'm pretty sure Margie's making it tickle extra for kicks, at this point.

There's a knock at the door, and we all six look over.

"Are we expecting anyone else? After this we're moving to hair and makeup, and the wedding starts in two hours." Nell cocks an eyebrow suspiciously at the door.

"Who is it?" Margie calls.

"Delivery for one of the ladies," a masculine voice calls back.

"Bring it in, please," she instructs. He walks in holding a medium-sized box, tied with an oversized crimson ribbon.

"Miss . . . Carlisle?" He looks up, and I lift a hand timidly. Who's sending me presents?

He places the box in my hands and skedaddles, clearly not interested in hanging around and having his toenails painted. I resist the urge to beg him to take me with him—barely.

"Are you going to open that, or let us all die of suspense?" Nell's tone is equal parts excitement and exasperation.

"Sorry, sorry." I grab the end of a ribbon, and tug. It slips apart easily, dissolving into a pool of silky smoothness in my lap. I waste no time before lifting the lid, and find a square card with a hand-written note nestled on top of the tissue paper inside.

Dear Demelza,

This life comes with expectations, but there are also benefits to enjoy along the way.

189

Yours,

B.V.

"So, who's it from?" Leilani practically squeals with excitement as I set the card aside.

"Beckett."

"Okay, so it's going to be amazing. That man has excellent taste!" She claps excitedly.

"Or he hires people with taste," Nell points out as I lift the tissue paper.

"A distinction with no real difference, Nell," Leilani shushes her.

Oh. *Oh.*

Nestled on a pale cushion are a pair of bright red heels, completely covered in sparkling stones, but . . . are those actual gems? Rubies, based on the color.

I lift one of the thin, elegant heels in my hands, admiring the sweeping curve of the sole, and the delicate gem-crusted straps that are long enough they'll crisscross over and around my foot and ankle, and then continue all the way up my calf.

"Holy crap on a cracker, he gave you diamond-studded shoes." Nell starts laughing, but it cuts off with a grunt. *Thank you, Leilani.* I'm too shocked to say anything, because I'm pretty sure this pair of shoes costs more than any house I've ever slept in. That alone is mind-boggling, and on closer inspection, she's right—there is a delicate arc of diamonds matching the flare of the sole.

"Demy, look down." Leilani's voice is practically delirious with excitement, so I do. When I picked up the left shoe, a small velvet box slid into the depression it left behind.

"I think he got you jewelry, too!" She squeals, and I start to feel faint. I pass the sparkly shoe in my hands to Leilani, and reach down for the palm-sized box.

I almost don't want to open it, but based on the five pairs of eagle eyes I can feel on the box right now, I know that would cause a mutiny. So, I crack open the lid. Nestled on black velvet is a pair of pear-shaped ruby earrings, dangling from a delicate white-gold thread. There's also a white-gold ring, mounted with another pear-shaped ruby the size of the knuckle on my thumb.

Holy mother of rubies. I feel light-headed.

"This is too much—I can't accept something this expensive from him. This . . . this is too much even if I was sure I was going to pick him. If I wear these, he's going to expect—"

"He better not expect a dadgum thing except a sincere thank you." Nell cuts me off, leveling me with a pointed stare. "This is a government-run program with strict rules, Demy. The choice is *yours*, and—gift or no gift—you don't have to choose him. If it makes you that uncomfortable, though, you can refuse it. We can get another deliveryman to take it right back to him with an apology, if that's what you want."

"She can't send it back! That would be incredibly rude. You don't refuse gifts, Nell."

"She's worried about his expectations, and she has a right to be!"

My panic at this overwhelming display of wealth is thrumming in my ears, the crushing weight of Beckett's expectations beginning to drown out their argument. He wants more than a wife; he wants a prize to be shown off, to glitter and sparkle like these rubies to prove his success in the eyes of all his business acquaintances.

The room narrows, darkness gathers, and a tunnel-like feeling comes over me . . . until a gentle touch on my shin pulls me back from the edge of the chasm. I look down, and Margie's expression is grave.

"I understand where you're coming from, Demy, but a gift like that . . . he can afford to give it. Don't make a rash decision that you may later regret."

She's right, I need to think this through objectively. A gift like this could buy me a lot of security in the future, if I ever have to run again. How different would my life have been so far if I'd had a nest egg the size that these could buy, to make sure I was always a step ahead of my pursuers? The words hold more weight than Maggie knows, and I decide to keep the gift, no matter how uncomfortable it makes me.

Whatever happens here, I'm never going to be so poor that I can't buy a train ticket out of danger again.

"Thank you, Margie. I think you're right." My words sound distant and my breaths are coming short, but there's resolve underneath my panic now.

Nell and Leilani are still arguing, so I raise my voice to be heard. "Guys! Stop! I'm going to keep them. Nell's right; it doesn't mean I have to choose him. But I do need to send a thank you note. Can you help me write something?"

Two hours later, the sun is setting, and Nell and I are standing in custom-fitted gowns to the right of an outdoor altar, the heady scents of flowers perfuming the air. A flautist is playing a chipper tune as Leilani walks down the aisle, and Kellan's grinning ear to ear as he watches her approach.

As sweet as the moment is, it takes everything in me to keep my eyes from wandering back to the second row of seats, where my three matches sit shoulder-to-shoulder. Jax looks bored on one side, while Beckett and Fletcher studiously watch the proceedings—though Fletcher's gaze has flickered to my bouquet more than once, and the massive ruby resting on the ring finger of my right hand.

I can feel the questions in his gaze, and I don't have any good answers. Unsurprisingly, the bridesmaid gowns Nell and I were given are both crimson red, and have hi-lo hems, so our shoes are visible. The perfect display for the stunning—surprisingly comfortable—strappy heels twining from my feet up to my calves. *No coincidence there.* It no longer shocks me that Beckett would arrange something like this. It's like he's staking a claim, but also proving a point. He can provide a lifestyle the others can't, if I'm willing to step into the role he wants.

The three of them are somehow all completely different, and I'm torn on how to proceed. Nell is already secretly married, Leilani sliced through her options in a matter of weeks, and is saying her vows right in front of me. Cammie . . . well, she's got a long road ahead of her. My heart aches thinking about her, bruised and broken in that hospital bed, all her light and effervescent personality smothered under the weight of a man's unchecked rage.

And here I am, stuck. Right where I started, and no closer to a decision. I need to make at least *one* decision. I let my gaze stray back to the three men; so different, and yet each calling to a different piece of me.

But which piece is the right piece?

The small crowd stands and cheers, and I realize I've zoned out through the entire wedding ceremony. Leilani and Kellan share a tender kiss, the sweet, hopeful moment bringing the first genuine smile I've had since Cammie's attack. I raise my bouquet of roses and cheer along with everyone else as they walk down the aisle, hand in hand, with stars in their eyes.

I say a silent prayer to anyone who's listening that their story ends with the same joy it's starting with. My beautiful, peaceful friend deserves that, and more.

CHAPTER TWENTY-ONE

POWER OUTAGE

DEMY

To no one's surprise, the reception is held in the dining hall. The staff has pulled out huge swags of greenery, and sprays of beautiful flowers adorn every surface like frosting on a cake. The cake itself at three tiers in height is significantly larger than our small party requires, but hopefully the staff will get to enjoy some, too. They work hard. I make a mental note to invite them all to my wedding when it's my turn.

Turning to my left, I see Leilani and Kellan at the head of the table, heads ducked together, and a pale blush on Leilani's olive complexion. She's a beautiful bride, the gown a shade of cream silk, with a skirt that moves around her like ocean waves.

I should be happier, but I can't seem to force a jovial spirit. After the fifth course of rich, fancy food, Kellan stands from the table, a grin consuming his features. He taps his champagne flute lightly with a spoon, and everyone at the table quiets. Jax is on my right side, and gives my knee a squeeze under the table. When I look over at him, he rolls his eyes, then scooches his hand a little further up my thigh.

Stiffening, I reach down and grab his wandering fingers, and capture them in mine. He scowls but stops prodding me.

"—just wanted to say thank you all for your support and encouragement through this process. You ladies have become true friends to Leilani in such a short time, and the men here have all formed a brotherhood of sorts." He clears his throat and looks down at Leilani. She nods, encouraging him, and he continues, "We are heading up to Washegon for our honeymoon tonight, and we'd be overjoyed to have any of you couples join us, when it's your time. We've meshed so well through this experience, it would be great to extend that support to the next phase, where we focus on growing our families."

There's a smattering of applause, but instead of sitting, he pulls a smiling Leilani gently to her feet. "And on that note . . . it's time to get out of here!"

The men explode in cheers, and I shrink back into my seat from the sudden noise, my heart thundering and chest tightening in an instant. Reaching down into the seam-pocket of my dress, I finger the slim taser tucked there. It soothes me a little, and I take a few deliberate breaths in and out through my nose as I try to calm the tide of panic before it grows into something unmanageable.

Fletcher leans over, and whispers in my ear, "Can we go somewhere quieter and talk?"

His warm breath against my neck sends a shiver through me, and I nod my agreement. As soon as Leilani and Kellan are out the door, he rises and buttons his dinner jacket, taking my hand and pulling me after him.

Before we make it two steps from the table, though, Jax calls out, "Where are you two going?"

"We'll be back in a few," Fletcher says without breaking stride.

We exit through a side door, into a small garden surrounded by a stone wall. Ivy crawls over almost every inch, but peeks of the smooth gray stones show through here and there.

The space feels blissfully calm and soothing after the raucous noise inside, and the moonless night sky makes it feel like we're cocooned away, only the two of us in the whole world. "I didn't know this was here," I murmur, not wanting to break the spell of this tiny garden.

Fletcher leads me to the lone bench—it's made of poured concrete and just big enough for two—and sits down on it. I make to sit on the side next to him, but he intercepts me halfway, and redirects me to sit sideways across his lap, hugging me close to his chest.

"I'm sorry about Cammie, Demy. It's absolutely awful what happened to her, and I wanted to check and see how you were doing. I've been aching to hold you ever since they told us, but Beckett was closer. And today they had you women locked up all day, preparing for the wedding."

I sink into his warmth, soaking in the warm, cedar-and-man smell that is so uniquely Fletcher, and take my time responding. The tightness in my chest loosens as I slip my arms around his neck, and that's a miracle in itself—let alone my emotional reaction to being this close to him. I'm content and warm sitting sideways on his lap, but my stomach's doing strange flips at the nearness. He's warm and solid and everything I never knew I needed, rolled up into one man. Surely this feeling has to mean something.

"Thank you, Fletcher. It was awful, and I hated leaving her in the hospital. Beckett broke a few rules but managed to get me in to see her, at least. She just looked so . . . small. And fragile. She was covered in bruises and wires. Even her face—" I'm unable to continue, swallowing hard past the lump that's lodged itself like a tumbleweed of twisted emotions.

"I can't even imagine, Demy. That never should have happened. They've already shipped Vince off to the federal prison to await trial. He's going before the high justice, and the king himself has already committed to personally attend the trial. He is going to pay for what he's done to her."

"Good!" The word comes out savage as I pour all of my rage into it. He chuckles, and rubs my back lightly with his hand before settling it onto my hip, where I can feel the warmth through my red satin gown.

"So, those are some lovely new accessories you've got there. Is that an engagement ring?"

"What? No!" I turn and face him, confusion warring over my face. "Do you think I'd be out here sitting with you"—*on you*, I add silently—"if I was engaged to Beckett?"

"I did kind of steal you away. You might have felt the need to let me down easy. I'd understand if you picked him."

My head feels like it's spinning, and the moment of blissful ease I'd felt when he'd first settled me down in his lap vanishes into nothing. He'd understand if I picked Beckett? What does that mean? We never talked about Cammie letting him go; what if he doesn't *want* me to pick him? Dread and confusion dance a sick tango in my stomach, and I push myself to my feet.

"I need some space," I croak out, and turn for the door.

"Demy, wait—what's wrong? What did I say?"

"Not now, Fletcher. Just— I'm going back in." I yank on the door handle, but the door won't budge. Twisting the handle has no effect, and Fletcher is already looming over my shoulder. "The door is stuck. Can you open it?" I hate the way my voice is shaking, and I clench my jaw to stop myself from saying anything else I'll regret later. Anything like, *You're supposed to hold me like that forever, not be happy to hand me off to another man.*

Fletcher applies his considerable muscle to the door, but it won't budge, either. I stare down at my feet in misery and realize that the little strip of light underneath the door is gone. "Are the lights off inside?"

"What?"

I point down at our feet, and he swears. "Something's wrong. This door shouldn't be able to lock with someone out here."

Panic flares, and I grip my taser tightly in my pocket. Think, Demy. How can we get out of here? The sound of running out front hits us, and that confirms my fears. Here we are, sitting ducks and there's another attack happening.

"I'm going to try to find something to break the knob off with, but if that doesn't work we're going to go over the wall. We're not exactly exposed here, but if they've been watching and know we're out here, this wall won't stop them. There's a safe room close to here, and we should be able to get to it."

"Even if we get to it, how will we get in if there's no power?"

"Each room has its own power redundancy. They'll function unless the individual room has been destroyed, which would be next to impossible."

Don't fixate on the next to, just don't do it, Demy. He begins searching the ground, and I split off in the other direction. The tiny garden is annoyingly well-manicured, though, and the only thing of any substance in the entire area is the lone concrete bench.

Fletcher crosses to it and attempts to lift it, but it's been anchored into the ground.

"Come on, we're going to have to go over," he whispers. "As soon as you're on the other side, run straight for the exercise gym. The others are probably heading for the same one, since it's closest. There's a safe room inside. The blue button is behind the last treadmill by the mirrors. Don't wait for me, I'll catch up to you. Are we clear?"

I nod, too deep in the grips of panic for any more words.

He crosses to the wall and holds up his hands for me to step into. I do, the strappy, sparkly heel looking ridiculous for this use, and lift my hands up to rest lightly on the wall, ready to grab the top and pull myself over.

"On the count of three. One, two, and up!" He presses me up so quickly, I almost miss the top of the wall and go tumbling over headfirst. I manage to grab the top of the wall and steady myself at the last minute, and hear a shout.

"There she is!" I whip my head around, and see Jax, Nell, and Atlas running straight towards me. I nearly sob with release as I swing my legs over and drop to my knees with a painful thud on the other side. Nell practically tackles me in a hug, but it only lasts a moment.

"Move, move, move!" Atlas's booming voice dominates the chaotic night, and then Nell and I are running towards the gym, Atlas and Jax on either side. I'm so focused on not breaking my ankle trying to run in my heels that I startle when Fletcher appears on Jax's other side and mis-step, knocking into Nell. She grabs my arm and hangs onto me as she keeps running, steadying me.

It seems like we're going to make it unscathed, until I hear the sickening staccato pattern of gunfire off to the right. Both mine and Nell's steps falter and stop, as we look to the side and see a cadre of black-clad men closing on us. I feel a scream rising in my throat, but Easton darts to the side, returning fire and causing the men to stop their advance and duck for cover.

"Keep moving!" Atlas booms at us, and we bolt for the gym again, not stopping until we make it to the front steps of the gym and fling the doors open.

Sickness churns in my gut at the idea of Easton facing down those gunmen alone, and I peer out into the night behind us to see if I can spot him, but everything is pitch black, and I can't see far into the darkness outside.

It's the only time I've ever seen the gym without the usual cheerful overhead lighting. We all fumble a bit as we head into the foyer; the nicely spaced rows of equipment that are easy to navigate with full lighting becoming treacherous in the dark. The windows make me feel exposed, and I hurry along behind Atlas and Nell towards the far back corner of the gym.

"Incoming! We need to hurry!" Jax shouts from the back, and Atlas spins, shoving Nell and me to the front to keep going. I risk a look to the right and see a line of black-clad men in hoods crossing the lawn, though it's hard to tell how many without any lights on the grounds.

Nell lunges forward, swinging on the frame of a treadmill to smack the big, blue button that opens the safe room while Atlas barks orders to the guys. Easton arrived at some point during our run, and he's standing right behind me, facing out with his gun drawn and pointed towards the floor. Gratefulness that he's alive swamps me, and I fling an arm around his shoulders and squeeze. He gives me a short smile, but peels my arm off of him.

"I have to stay free to move. You're okay, though. We've got you, and the glass is bullet-proof," Easton says.

The familiar whoosh of the wall moving aside and opening the safe room hits me a second before a blinding illumination from inside the wall. This one looks like a more traditional elevator, except the small, square room has a lone button on the wall, to take you down. Easton ushers us inside, when Jax starts shouting.

"You are out of your mind if you think we're sending her down there alone! Fletcher might be a pushover, but you can't keep me from her! Get out of my way or I'll move you myself!"

I whip around to see what's going on, only to be blocked by the enormous sight of Atlas's back, unmoving between the safe room doors and my two matches.

"You can try, pup, but I'd hate to break your arms when we need them to deal with the Cabal. You have two options; you fight with me and deal with those guys, or you run for the helipad. Going down with my wife and your temper is *not* an option. Easton, push the button!" The final bark sends Easton into motion, and he slaps the button without hesitation.

The door quickly slides shut, the last thing I hear before we're sealed inside is Fletcher's calm voice cutting underneath Jax's protests, "Where's the gun cache?"

This safe room is about the size of the first one, and clearly meant to hold either more people, or at least hold you for a longer time. Nell and I both move slowly getting inside, while Easton arrows to the control wall, turning on the audio feeds and immediately scanning each of the monitors in detail. With no lights anywhere outside, most of what we see is dark. That is, until, my eyes lock onto one with an ongoing fight. It must be Atlas's from right above us, because I see Jax take a swing at him, his own lip already busted and bloody.

Easton raises his wrist comm and says, "Atlas, time to cut your feed."

He appears to dodge the punch, and a second later that monitor goes completely black, leaving us in the dark.

"I can't believe Jax is picking a fight right now with the Cabal ten feet away!" I spin towards Nell, gripping the skirt of my dress like it's going to hold me together. She puts her hands on my shoulders, and guides me towards the couches.

It's bad enough being locked underground when unknown security guards clear out a threat. It's about a hundred times worse when three people you know are straight above you, directly in the line of fire and outnumbered. A thought hits me, and I spin back to where Easton is stationed in front of the monitors, hands clasped behind his back. "Fletcher said something about a gun cache—are they going to be able to arm themselves before the Cabal get to them?"

He turns and nods, his demeanor as calm as if he's out for a Sunday stroll. "Every building inside the perimeter has a weapons cache in addition to a safe room. They'll be fine. The glass up there is bullet-proof hurricane glass, And Atlas has a direct line to the full security team for back up. They'll hunker down and won't end up with a scratch. Well . . . any inflicted by the Cabal," he corrects himself, and the memory of Jax's bloodied lip swims back into my vision sickeningly.

"I know it's hard but try not to worry about them. They *will* be okay, I promise. Atlas will get Jax cooled down—one way or another—and the Cabal will be dealt with. Right now, we need to get you sitting down, and take care of your legs."

I frown at her. "What?" When I look down, I'm shocked to see blood coating the fronts of both shins in rivulets all the way down to my feet.

"You didn't feel that? Your adrenaline must be going a mile a minute. I'm afraid you're going to feel it when I clean them, unfortunately. Easton, can you grab the first aid kit, bandages, whatever pain med options are back there, and a couple of towels from the locker room? One warm, one dry. Thanks." She rattles off the list methodically, inspecting my legs more closely now that I've sat down.

"Ugh, these shoes did a number on you. Those rubies tore your skin to shreds. It looks like the straps twisted and dug in while we were running." She sighs softly, then begins untying the first one, and I wince as the jewel-encrusted straps are lifted from my tender flesh. "I'll take it easy as I can, but I'm afraid this is going to hurt until the pain medication kicks in."

"It's fine, I can handle it," I grit out between clenched teeth, and dig my fingernails into the backs of my crossed arms to distract myself from what she's doing.

Time all but ceases to exist while Nell works on my damaged skin, and by the time she's done, I'm wrung out. So many highs and lows in one day, to end the way it did . . . I'm spent. But I can't let myself sleep, not yet.

I suck in a deep breath, bracing myself for her reaction. "There's something I need to tell you, Nell . . ."

Chapter Twenty-Two

ALL CLEAR

Demy

"Why does that phrase never mean something good?" She ties off the bandage wrap with an efficient knot, tucking it under at the top of my calf. "Why can't it be, 'I need to tell you something . . . I've cured world hunger. Or, ooh! I figured out how to make childbirth completely painless! That would be one most of us could appreciate at some point.'"

I stay quiet, and stare at her drowsily until she finishes the small tirade.

"Sorry, sorry. I'm not serious, it's a coping mechanism. What do you need to tell me?" She packs the roll of bandage away into the first aid kit and looks up at me. She's serious, now that her hands are still and in her lap.

"I think the Cabal is after me. I don't know why, I don't know for sure, but—" Easton spins on his heel, suddenly much more interested in our conversation than whatever's on the screen, and his laser-focus causes my words to grind to a halt.

Nell notices the direction of my gaze and makes a shooing gesture towards him. "Back as you were, Captain Nosey-Pants. This talk doesn't concern you yet, but you and Atlas are welcome to overanalyze it like teenage girls with their first crush *after* she gets the story out."

He rolls his eyes, but doesn't take offense, and turns to face back towards the monitor bank. I know he's still listening, but it helps that he's not staring anymore.

"Thanks. This is difficult to talk about." I clear my throat, and weariness hits me like a wave. I've been keeping it all in for so long, hiding who I really am and what I've been through. Can I pour it all out now? Do I have a choice if I want the madness to stop?

"Take your time, Demy. We're not going anywhere fast."

That makes me snort. "True. Okay, so, it started when I was thirteen. I was walking back home from school one afternoon when I heard a scream. It was my mom—I just knew, in my gut. So I started running, but the screams stopped. I—I walked up to the back door, and something made me pause. I didn't charge in, even though I wanted to see what was wrong. When I looked through the window, I saw . . ." I pause, sucking in air through my nose. I've actually never said this out loud before, and I don't know if I can.

Nell wraps her fingers around mine, and that small touch gives me the push to keep going.

"My dad, he was on the kitchen floor. There was a puddle of blood spreading on the tile, and I couldn't see my mom anywhere. But then I heard a crash. I was so scared I froze, and my mom ran into the living room. She was looking back, over her shoulder, and it slowed her down. She was trying to head out the front door when he caught her." I swallow hard, blinking back tears as I stare down at our joined hands. For some reason the smell of the day comes back to me, like it was yesterday. Azalea bushes blooming, and the metallic tang of gunfire. It makes me queasy.

"Take your time, Demy, this is an awful memory. But I'm here for you."

"Thanks. It's just hard to—yeah. It was a man wearing all black. He had a shaved head, and the coldest eyes you've ever seen—I couldn't see what color, but his eyebrows were so pale they were almost white. He had been chasing her, so his hood was back, and when he stabbed her, his face was just . . . blank. No care, no worry as he took my mother from me. I didn't stop to see what happened next. I unfroze and ran back the way I came. Then I realized they might know where I went to school, so I turned off and ran into the woods, and didn't stop until I couldn't breathe anymore. I hid behind a fallen log, and waited until the sirens came."

"So, they killed your parents in front of you, but we don't know why. That is truly awful, but is there a reason you think you're after *you*, specifically? Maybe they were after your parents, and left you alive because you weren't involved."

"I wanted to know more, so I spoke to one of the security guards about it, and he says that the police reports confirmed that it was the Cabal who killed my parents. But . . . they've been hunting *me* ever since." Nell sucks in a breath, and my words falter. I can't stop now, though. She has to know all of it.

"I've spent the last six years running, and anytime I stay in one place too long, one of them shows up. So, I run again. They were getting close again, which is why I joined the New Lives Program. I don't care about getting married yet, but I needed somewhere with better security, somewhere I could rest for a little while." Those last words are barely a whisper, so heavy is my shame. I've put everyone in danger, and then I made it worse by keeping my secret after I found out who Nell and Atlas were. She's going to hate me, they're going to kick me out, and then I'll be right back on the streets, and—

She leans forward and crushes me in a hug. And then the tears flow, like a long-repressed waterfall. My shoulder is damp, and I realize she's crying, too. After a few moments of sobbing, she pulls back, wiping her eyes. "We're going to figure it out, okay, Demy? This is not your fault, and Atlas is going to find out why. We knew—well, we suspected—based on some stuff Glitch found, that they were chasing something on the move. We just didn't know what, or why. It looks like you fell right into our laps, though."

"Lucky me," I tease.

"It's all a puzzle, but Glitch and Atlas love puzzles. You're not alone anymore, Demy, and we're going to put a stop to this. You're not running anymore. Right, Easton?"

"Right," he answers, still pretending to watch the monitors, instead of listening to our every word. "And it needs to be said, there's no guarantee this is because of you, even if it seems likely. The Cabal has always targeted NLCs, because that's where the fertile women are. Let's all try not to jump to conclusions."

I nod sleepily, the adrenaline crash and the late hour dragging my eyelids down low, now that I've spilled my guts. I feel lighter, at least. I'm not keeping secrets anymore.

"You should rest," Nell says, soothing a cool hand over my forehead. "Atlas will be down to update us as soon as everything's clear."

"Okay," I murmur, eyes already sinking closed. It's been a long day.

Chapter Twenty-Three

GRAZE WOUNDS

Demy

I'm awoken sometime later by the sound of the safe room lift. Nell is already on her feet, hair mussed from sleep, and rubbing her eyes, but darting into Atlas's arms as soon as the lift comes to a stop. He staggers back a step with the force of her flying against his chest, and my own heart squeezes in response. *I want that.* My eyes immediately shift to the men waiting behind him, and the two of them couldn't be more different if they tried.

Fletcher is calm, patiently leaned against the wall with his arms crossed over his chest. He's relaxed, even after what must have been a long, unpleasant night. When we make eye contact, a lazy smile crosses his face, and he pushes off the wall to come and greet me.

Jax, on the other hand, is *pissed off*. Tension and anger radiate off him so thickly, I can practically see it hanging in the air like a toxic cloud. He's the first to jump out of the elevator, shooting Fletcher a pointed look as he cuts in front of him. To my dismay, Fletcher pauses and holds both hands up, letting Jax go first. *Why does he always do that?* It's another tiny thing that undermines my security about his feelings. Is he all in? Is he hoping I'll pick someone else?

I don't know where I stand with him, and it bothers me. Jax is charging me like a bull, though, and it's going to have to wait.

I push off the blanket Nell tucked me under and stand, feeling a little wobbly on my feet. Jax doesn't stop or give me a moment to steady myself, though; he thunders into my personal space and crushes me to his chest. The feeling reminds me of how my panic attacks start; with a tightness in my chest that won't let in enough air, no matter how hard I try to push past it.

"Jax," I wheeze, pulling at his shoulder. He doesn't budge, keeping me pressed too hard to his chest, so I try again. "Jax, please, I can't breathe!"

He huffs, and loosens his arms a fraction, allowing me to get a lungful of air, at least.

"I was worried sick. I can't believe that controlling bastard *separated* us. Are you okay? I know no one got down here, but you must have been freaking out."

He leans back to take in my drowsy face and frowns. "Or not."

"I was worried, but Nell and Easton assured me you were surrounded by bullet-proof glass and sitting on a literal armory. By the time Nell finished cleaning up the wounds on my legs—"

"True, we had protection. I guess I'm glad you got some sleep." He charges ahead as if he didn't hear me, and I start to get angry. It starts out as a slow thing, building and building like a campfire with too much fuel.

The way he doesn't respect my personal space. How he only cares about himself. His endless jealousy. The angry way he just shoved past Fletcher, as if he has more *right* to me for some reason. He's still talking, and the well-fed fire turns into an inferno.

"We have a one-on-one this afternoon, so at least you'll be rested for it. Can't have you getting bags under your eyes." He snorts. But then, his hands wander dangerously low on my back, as if he's trying to feel me up *right in front of everyone*, and that does me in.

"Enough, Jax. Enough. Let me go." I shove his shoulder harder, and his pissed-off expression returns.

"What the hell, Demy? Don't you want to see me after I just *risked my life for you?*"

"Of course I did! But this is too much! You're pushy, and arrogant, and self-centered! I've had enough."

"What are you saying?" He growls the words, and I grab his hands from off my backside, forcibly shoving them away so I can take a step back. His eyes are as cold as a glacier, and every bit as sharp.

"I'm saying we're not a good fit. I'm releasing you back into the program."

"You've got to be joking!" He's yelling, now, and I can't help but flinch involuntarily. "Gotta land yourself a pretty little rich boy, huh? Well, good luck with that. Neither one of these hypocrites is as real as you and me. We had something, and I guess you're stupid enough to throw that away!"

Easton appears over his shoulder, but as soon as he lays a hand on him to get his attention, Jax snaps.

"Don't friggin' touch me!" He whirls on Easton and throws a punch. Easton dodges, and Fletcher appears at my side like a genie.

"Come with me," he urges, hand gentle on my arm.

"There's nowhere to go, Fletcher."

"You can't just drag me away from her! I want to have a conversation about this like adults! She's making a mistake, and I should get to prove that to her!" Jax shouts at Atlas and Easton, both slowly closing in on him from both sides. Realizing he's trapped down here with the two of them, he spins wildly, his eyes landing on mine. "Demy! Demelza! Tell them you were wrong. Tell them you're not sending me home, that you were just emotional. Tell them!"

I shake my head. "I'm sorry, Jax, but it's not going to work between us. It's time to go home."

"You stuck-up little bi—" He lunges in my direction, but Atlas shoots an arm out and clotheslines him across the throat, cutting off his words in a strangled garble. His back hits the floor with an echoing thud, and I wince back.

Fletcher steps in front of me, blocking my sight with his broad shoulders as Atlas and Easton deal with Jax. There are scuffling sounds, and the sound of rubber soles being dragged across the polished floors, and then I hear the lift ticking upward.

"Hey, it's going to be okay. Please don't cry," Fletcher murmurs, reaching up to swipe away a tear I hadn't realized was rolling down my cheek. I'm so tired of the ugliness. I've been running from it for years, and it follows me everywhere like a stalker. If it's not the Cabal, it's something else. Someone else.

"Sorry," I murmur, reaching up to wipe away another escapee.

"Don't apologize, Demy. It's been a long day. Did I hear you say you had an injury on your legs? What happened—was it from climbing the wall?"

Of course. Of course he would be the one to fixate on that, and ask how I was. Why did it always seem so hot and cold with him? He made me think he cared when it was just us, but then . . . I realized belatedly that he was still waiting on an answer.

"I'm fine. Nell patched me up. It wasn't the wall, it was from the shoes. Those diamonds and rubies on the straps cut in while we ran. They're probably ruined, too."

"Shh, it's okay. The shoes aren't important. You're okay, we're all okay, and that's all that matters. Shoes can be replaced; you can't."

I look down, taking in the blood- and grass-stained front of his once-pristine white dress shirt. His suit jacket is long gone, and I frown.

"Nell said you three would be safe inside the gym. What happened? Is this your blood?"

"We went out to fight when our backup arrived so we could surround them. A little of it's mine—don't make that face, it's just a scratch from a dagger—but most of it's not my blood. Unfortunately we still didn't catch any of them alive." He grimaces, as I find the slit in his shirt, where he's got a gash on his side.

"This needs to be taken care of. Can I bandage it for you? We've got all the stuff down here."

"If you want to. If not, I'm sure the medical facility will get me sorted out after they take care of the more serious injuries."

My blood runs cold at the mention of serious injuries. "No, come on. There's no telling how long that could take, and I can take care of it now." I nod towards the bathroom, and grab his hand, pulling him towards it.

He follows easily, twining his fingers with mine. Nell's already curled back up on the couch, cuddled under her own blanket. She winks at me as we walk past, and then makes a point of closing her eyes and folding her hands over her stomach in the perfect mimicry of sleep. *Crazy woman.*

The first aid kit is still sitting out on the bathroom counter when we walk in, so I cross to it and flip it open, inspecting our options.

213

"What about Beckett?" I ask idly, as I flip through the supplies. It's still fully stocked, less a bit of bandage from the roll Nell used on me earlier.

"He grabbed a helicopter out. He's fine, and he'll be back in the morning."

"Good, I'm glad." Am I? Glad he's safe, of course. But, he left. I was in danger, and he didn't look for me, he just . . . left. Unease stirs in my stomach, and I mentally shake myself. *Stay on the task at hand, and the man right in front of you, Demy.*

Fletcher waits patiently while I pull out the supplies I need to bandage him up, and when I turn to face him, he's leaning against the counter, closer than I realized.

I clear my throat, suddenly *very* aware of how alone we are, and thoughts of Beckett flying out of my head. Nell is in the other room, but that wink told me she's playing dead for the duration of our time down here.

Don't focus on hormones right now. He's hurt; be professional.

"Can you lift your shirt for me, so I can clean the wound?"

He shrugs out of the suit jacket wordlessly, but I can't miss the flinch when he tries to pull it over his right shoulder.

"Here, let me help." I walk around behind him, taking over and carefully pulling the sleeve off of his arm, so he can hold still and not stretch the wound further.

"Thank you," he murmurs, holding himself stiffly as I lay the jacket across the toilet lid.

"Of course. I don't want to make it worse. We're trying to fix things here, not break them." I give him a playful wink, and he grins back.

"Much appreciated. Do you want me to hold this up, or take it off?" He gestures to the stained button up shirt, and I bite my lip in indecision.

"Which would be more comfortable for you while I work?" I finally ask.

"I don't mind taking it off. The scrape stretches pretty far around the back." He begins unbuttoning the shirt with slow, practiced movements. I've always thought that Beckett was the one who looked at home in a suit and wore it with ease. But something about the confident way Fletcher flicks each button open while never breaking eye contact tells me it's something he's done many times.

The air grows heated between us, and I look down, rearranging the supplies in the first aid kit—anything to stop watching him strip off his shirt, and thinking very *unprofessional* thoughts—until he clears his throat.

"Can you help me with this shoulder again? If you don't mind."

I glance back up, and see an apologetic look on his face as I hurry around to help him get the clinging fabric off. "You don't have to look like that, Fletcher. I don't mind helping." I ease the shirt down and lay it next to the jacket, and when I turn back around I finally get a look at the entire wound. It stretches from the front of his ribs, all the way around and stops barely an inch from his spine. His thick, beautiful muscles have been bisected by an angry, weeping gash.

"Oh, Fletcher, that might need stitches. You might end up in the medical center after all."

"Well, just do what you can for now, and then at least I won't be bleeding everywhere in the meantime."

"Okay. We should clean it first. Do you want to lean against the sink? It's probably going to sting."

"No sugarcoating it, then, huh?" He leans gingerly against the sink, and the smirk on his face doesn't fool me a bit that he's really hurting.

"No, but you don't seem like you need me to kiss your boo-boos all better," I retort, trying to keep it light. When I look back up with the antiseptic in my hand, though, the smirk has been erased by smoldering heat.

"I wouldn't turn down a kiss, whatever the reason you wanted to give it."

"Well, in that case, if you're a very good boy while I clean you up, maybe I'll give you one."

He snorts. "Yes ma'am."

After that he falls silent, gritting his teeth through me swiping an antiseptic-soaked cotton pad over his gash, and getting debris out of it. Most of it is thankfully shallow, but there is one deeper spot towards his back that definitely needs stitches. Next up is the antibiotic ointment, and a thick layer of gauze before finishing it up with a stretchy bandage. I carefully rub the bandage on his opposite side so it will seal to itself, and then straighten to admire my work. It's clean, covered, and I managed to rein in any inappropriate thoughts while I was at it. I'm calling it a win-win.

Setting the bandage back down in the kit, I turn back to him. "Okay, do you want me to grab you a shirt out of the locker room? It's pretty chilly, and we might be down here a while yet. Nell and I didn't bother to pull out the beds, but—"

He reaches forward, hooking one of his hands behind my waist and pulling me forward a step. We're so close, I can feel the warmth radiating off his bare chest.

"I need something else, first."

"What is it? Oh! Pain medicine. Yes, let me get you a couple tablets—" I try to pull away, but he's got me anchored tightly against his body, and my heart pounds like a rabbit caught in a snare. A very, very attractive snare.

"Excuse me, nurse, I was an excellent patient, and I was promised a reward for good behavior."

I freeze, half-turned away from him, and a furious blush crawls up my neck. "Uhm . . . were you serious about that?"

"Deadly. I never joke about something as important as a kiss from my girl."

"Your girl?" I half-whisper, afraid to breathe wrong and have him change his mind, or pull away again.

He leans forward, a promising gleam in his eyes, and when he stops an inch from my mouth, I can feel his words on my lips, like a sultry promise of what's to come. "My girl." When he closes the gap between us, it's like being subsumed by an inferno. He's everywhere, consuming me, all at once. One hand twines into my sleep-mussed hair, the carefully placed pins long gone, his other skims along the back of my triceps, sending a delicate shiver through me. And his lips . . . they're all-consuming. I'm so lost in him, I stumble forward a step when he eventually pulls back, immediately missing the velvet softness of his skin under my fingertips.

"Someone's coming down." He gives the back of my arm a gentle squeeze before he releases me, and steps around the frame of the bathroom door to see who our visitor is. I brush my fingertips lightly over my lips as I follow him, the warm tingle left behind the only evidence of his earth-shattering kiss.

It's only Atlas this time, and he looks world-weary, but deter-mined. He crosses the room to where Nell's sleeping—for real now, with her jaw slack and soft snores rolling out on every breath. He lays a hand on her forehead softly, before looking up at the two of us. I try not to look *too* suspicious, and give away the fact that we'd just been kissing in the bathroom, while Fletcher's still shirtless from his bandaging.

"You two can head on up to your rooms and get some rest. We'll give Glitch a few days to run with this, and then we'll meet back in the conference room to discuss the new information you shared with Nell this evening."

My mouth goes dry at his words, and Fletcher shifts to stare at me; his gaze feels like a spotlight, highlighting all the things I *haven't* shared with him—or Beckett, for that matter—yet. I swal-low hard, nodding at the order.

"Go get some rest, both of you," he says again, and my feet start moving of their own accord, even though I can *feel* the question Fletcher's not asking.

It's a heaviness hanging between Fletcher and me as we walk toward the lift, and I find myself feeling unexpectedly sad. The kiss and his sweet words had felt like a huge step forward, and now, suddenly, things unsaid are pushing us back to square one.

And it's all my fault.

Chapter Twenty-Four

MODIFIED

Demy

Another week passes in a tense haze of rotating dates and meals that taste like sawdust as I wait anxiously for news. Despite my constant exhaustion, I barely sleep each night after climbing into bed. The sun is already rising on the tenth day before my eyes began to close, and when I get an alert at eleven a.m. to get ready for a noon meeting with Atlas, I feel like warmed-over roadkill. Tired, puffy, and in desperate need of some cleanup.

My legs are wooden as I make my way through the main hall and down the side corridor lined with the conference rooms. The night in the safe room, and Fletcher's face when we parted ways at my dorms are playing on repeat in my mental theater.

He looked deflated, and every time we've seen each other since, he's been aloof. I know it's because I am keeping something from him. But dang it, I haven't even had time to process it all, myself, and him pulling away without giving me the chance to explain hurts. He just said I was his girl, and now he's pulled away like those words meant nothing.

How am I supposed to tell him that I've been on the run from my parents' killers for six years, and that I'm the reason the Cabal is attacking over and over again? I freeze mid-step, and stagger to the side to lean against the fancy brocade wallpaper, crushing the heels of my hands against my eyes to stop the tears that suddenly want to fall.

I came here for a fresh start, and all I've done is drag my problems onto everyone else's heads. Maybe I should go. I could run. I've got some cash now, enough to give me a good head start on the Cabal. And if I could time it with one of my dates off campus—or even better, secure one of those getaways like Nell took with Atlas—I could be so far away, it would take them months to find me again. Then everyone here would be safe, at least.

Of course . . . I have no idea what would happen to me if I went MIA from the mandatory government marriage program, but I can't imagine it would be anything *good*. So, I'd have to hide really well. Stay off the grid, find a tiny, one-stoplight town that was on the verge of being closed. I've heard rumors that there are a ton of those up north, and I could actually make it that far with my deposit money. And I could sell the ring and shoes somewhere along the way.

I lower my hands, letting the possibility sink into me. I don't *want* to run again. But if they keep attacking—at least I'll have a plan. It will be better for everyone, if I'm gone. I straighten from my position leaning on the wall, and nearly scream when I look up. Lars is standing barely two feet away—and I didn't see or hear him approach.

"Hey, whoa, there! You okay? I was just coming down to check on you." He holds up both hands and gives me a smile, but it doesn't reach his eyes. They're colder than well water in the dead of winter, and I feel the itch to run, and run now.

"I'm fine, thanks. I won't bother you any more, I don't want to get you in trouble." I say as I spin on my heel. His arm snakes out and grabs my wrist before I can take a second step away, and my heart starts hammering in double time. Slowly, I turn back to face him, and pointedly look down at my arm, where he's gripping me a little *too* tightly.

"Listen, I really didn't mean to spook you. It seems like you're having a rough day, and I wanted you to know that I'm here for you. If you ever need anything else—even if it's just an escape—I'm your man. We can be friends."

"An escape?" *Is he seriously offering to get me out of here? Wouldn't he lose his job?*

He laughs. "Nothing too crazy, just a little down time. I know all the good hidey-holes around here." His winks and lets go of my wrist. "You've had a rough go of it, Demy. It's understandable that you'd need some time to yourself. I hope you're not thinking of *actually* running, right? You need to tell me if you are. There are bad men out there, and this is the safest place you can be."

"No, of course not." I scan the front of his uniform to avoid his penetrating gaze. I can't let on that that's *exactly* what I was thinking.

"Okay, then. The offer stands if ever you need to take me up on it."

"I'm fine, Lars. But thanks." I force a smile with my answer, then turn on my heel and half-jog down the hallway. I nearly pass the conference room in my eagerness to get away from him.

The sound of Nell's ebullient laughter reaches me in time to stop, though, and I pull the heavy door open without knocking or waiting. One last glance over my shoulder as I step inside shows Lars, still watching me from the exact spot I left him, and a shudder rolls through me as I step through the door. It feels like he's onto me, but I don't know how.

Nell's practically beaming at me. "There she is! You're just in the nick of time. I think Glitch is going to *explode* if he has to wait thirty more seconds to tell us what he's dug up."

"Don't pick at him, Nell," Atlas chides.

"I'm not picking at anyone, just observing."

"In your capacity as *medical officer*?" Easton says with a laugh. I can see Queen Sadie grinning from her holographic position beside a stoic King Patrick.

"Hey, you know I'm right. If we were ever to have a space exploration party, I'd be the medical officer, *clearly*, since I have four years of training under my belt. You two would be security officer and arms master, Patrick would be the Captain, and Glitch—"

"Would very much like to get this started. Please," he interjects, shifting forward in his seat, and pushing his glasses up his nose in the holograph.

"Fine," Nell grumbles, and crosses her arms over her chest.

I sink silently into the chair next to her, and Glitch doesn't wait another second. "Okay, so, here's the dealio. The second-round of background checks on every person inside the perimeter came back completely clear. Everything I've found points to the fact that Nell's suspicions are correct. I light-fingered a bit of Demy's payment tracking data, and it aligns nicely with several of the Cabal-related incidents we were unable to make heads or tails of earlier in the year. In fact, there was only *one* incident that didn't match her tracking data or a direct assault on an NLC." He sucks

222

in a lungful of air, and then taps something we can't see, causing the conference table in front of us to flare to life.

A blue outline map of the North American Alliance appears dead center, with the rest of the world map rolled out to either side. Little red dots march across the screen slowly, like oversized ants. Except these flash in and out of existence as a scroll bar runs along the side of the table.

"Okay, so, these are the typical Cabal attack locations from before, then this is the last six months, when the activity picked up. Interestingly enough, these picked up the same month as your eighteenth birthday, correct, Demy?" He pauses the motion and looks at me.

"Uhm, yes," I agree, seeing the date-time stamp at the top right of the table. That was the month I turned eighteen.

"Okay, so, starting at this date, I'm going to add a green line showing Demy's movements, and run you through the entire nine months day by day, starting . . . now."

He sits back, and we all watch in silence as a little yellow squiggle appears over New Texas, back and forth for a few beats until there's a cluster of red-ant-dots representing the Cabal, and my yellow line shoots east, towards Missiana. The squiggling back and forth resumes over the little town where I'd holed up in Missiana for a few beats, and then there's another cluster of the Cabal attacks. Over and over, we watch my ping-pong-like flight across the middle of the NAA, and the Cabal hot on my heels.

It makes me feel tired just watching it. Thankfully, after the third time the angry red dots almost catch me, Atlas puts a stop to it.

"We get it, Glitch. We don't need to watch the full replay. Do you have any insights as to *why*?"

"I have a hunch, but I'd like a little more information from Demy first, if that's okay?"

Atlas nods, and Glitch turns to me. "This all started with your parents' deaths when you were thirteen, right?"

"Right."

"Okay. If my theory is correct, that doesn't make sense. What I want to know is if anything changed right before that. Did you guys move? Did you get a new neighbor who seemed weird? Did either of your parents quit or change jobs?"

"No? Not that I remember. We moved every few years, but that was for my mom's job. She was on some committee? We were always put up in a company house."

"Hmm." He purses his lips, and fidgets with something off-screen, causing his arm to jingle nervously. "We're still missing something. Did you have any illnesses? Strange medical concerns, swap schools, get a new best friend . . . *anything* that stands out in the few weeks before their death?"

"Well . . . actually, that does ring a bell. I got the flu really badly a couple weeks before. I had a fever that wouldn't quit, and they ended up having to call out a doctor in the middle of the night. He gave me a shot, and I got better the next day. But . . . what does that have to do with anything? People get sick all the time." *Not me, granted, but other people.*

"He gave you a shot? Where did he give you the shot?" Glitch leans forward excitedly, and his glasses slip down his nose again.

"That's kind of weird, actually. It was the back of my neck. Something about getting the medication into my bloodstream quicker?"

"Nell, can you look and see if she has a scar on the back of her neck?"

224

"Sure." Nell pops out of her chair like she's spring loaded, and a moment later she's pulling my hair off to one side. "Yep, she has a tiny scar, well healed and directly over her spinal cord." Nell gently runs her fingertips over my neck, feeling it out. "The scar is about . . . three fingers down from the base of her skull. Hidden in the hairline, and hard to spot if you aren't looking for it."

"And you've never had surgery there that you're aware of, right, Demy?"

"No? I was a really healthy kid. I only got sick a few times in my entire life."

"I knew it!"

Glitch pumps his fist in victory, and Patrick's tone is wry when he asks, "Care to share with the class why this is significant, Glitch?"

"Sorry, sorry. I think you had a tracking device, and it was removed. Whether or not your parents knew, I can't say—only that the scar supports this theory. It's possible your body rejected it, or it was infected somehow and the doctor found it. However it happened, it would explain why they've been hunting you ever since. Whoever put you up for adoption lost their tracker, and they want you back."

"No, that doesn't explain anything. Why would they be tracking me in the first place? Who embeds a tracking device in a kid?" My voice is shrill, and my pulse is pounding angrily in my temples. What is this craziness? Why would I have had a *tracking device* removed? And my parents, in on it? No way. No *frigging* way.

"Sorry, I did skip over that part, didn't I? You've been genetically modified. I'm not sure how yet, given that any sort of modification of the human genome is *highly* illegal and has been since months after the discovery of the Sterilization Vector. I was able to trace all the way back to your parents' adoption paperwork, and it looks like your adoption was through a normal, reputable agency at the time, and—"

"Wait . . . I'm sorry, *what*? What did you just say?" I interrupt his endless, meaningless words as I fixate on one that leaps out at me. Adoption.

"Uhh, reputable adoption agency?" he stammers, looking confused.

"I'm not adopted. What are you saying?"

"Oh, dear." Glitch's eyes widen, and Nell wraps her fingers around mine. "I'm afraid . . . perhaps because your parents were killed while you were still so young, it never came up, but . . . you were, in fact, adopted. As an infant, only a few days old. Your mother was completely sterile according to her medical records, so it wasn't possible for you to be their biological child."

"I— I—"

"It's going to be okay, Demy," Nell soothes, and I grip her fingers tighter in mine.

I'm adopted, and I'm some kind of genetically modified freak? *Illegal* freak?

"No, Demy, you're not a freak at all. Please don't take it to mean that!" Glitch sounds horrified, and I realize I inadvertently blurted the words aloud. "The changes we've uncovered so far were quite minor, and if it weren't for this strangeness with the Cabal, you likely would have never known, aside from your above-average fertility. The standard DNA matching process at the NLC didn't even catch the changes. It wasn't until I ran your DNA results against historical data that I found a hit. We're still digging into exactly what alterations were made—and, hopefully, identifying those differences will lead us to discover how you even came to be, since everything on record shows that all illegally modified embryos were destroyed throughout history as they were discovered."

Illegal. Adopted. Cabal. Destroyed. I lurch out of the chair and stagger to the nearest wastebasket in the corner of the room and heave my guts up.

"I think we need to give her some time." Sadie's words come from a distance, and they sound tinny in between bouts of heaving. A moment later, Nell's at my side, her cool hand pressing softly to the back of my neck in stark juxtaposition to the orders she's now barking out to the two giant men in the room.

I hear the conference room door close, and after a few moments my stomach settles, the heaves finally stopping. Panic is still clawing at my now-raw throat, but one horrifying thought has risen to the surface.

"It was my fault, wasn't it?"

"What?" Nell asks, confused.

"My fault that they died," I whisper, barely able to choke the poisoned words out. "I got sick. I reacted to the stupid tracker, so they called the doctor and, and—"

"Hey, now. It was *not* your fault. You were an innocent kid who didn't ask for *any* of this. Do you hear me? Kids aren't responsible for the messed-up choices made by the adults around them. Not one bit."

Tears cloud my vision, and I sink down onto the plush carpet, letting my back hit the wall next to the trash can with a rough thud. The pain helps. It makes me feel anchored, at least, as everything I know about my life crashes down around me.

Nell drops to the ground next to me, wrapping me up in a bear hug, and I return the embrace woodenly. Eventually Atlas and Easton come back, both of them carrying the supplies Nell asked for. She straightens up to snatch the wet rag from Atlas's hands, deftly folds it into thirds and lays it on the back of my neck.

I stiffen at the cold, but the shock brings some clarity, too.

"We should probably get off the floor."

The men lay the other supplies on the seat of a nearby chair where she can reach them if needed, then they walk to the other end of the room and start talking quietly to give us a little space.

"Whenever you're ready. There's no rush. This has been . . . a lot. And it's not uncommon for severe anxiety spikes to lead to nausea, or even vomiting. So, we can take it slow."

"I didn't know that. I usually just feel like I can't breathe, or my chest gets tight."

"You haven't been in medical school for four years." She boops me on the nose sarcastically, and a small smile pulls at my lips. She's irrepressible, and I envy that. "You ready to try standing up? I think you'll feel better when you're off the floor."

"Yeah, let's." She scoops me up by the forearms rather easily for her small size, and in a moment I'm wobbling on my feet.

"How's that?"

"Fine . . . good. I'm good, just want to sit on a regular chair."

"Perfect. I also got you some of this lemon fizzy soda . . . sounds weird, but it's delightful for nausea. Sadie swears by the stuff every time she gets knocked up."

I look up in surprise at the casual way she's referring to the queen, and she laughs.

"Me and Sadie go way back. She's a wonder of fertility, much like you. She's already on her second kid, with number three on the way."

"You mean her genes were . . ." I trail off, sipping the soda she hands me. It is sweet and tangy and bubbly all at once, and I'm immediately addicted.

"No, not that we know of, anyways. Although now that you mentioned it, we can ask Glitch to check for similarities. I'm sure with that big ol' brain of his, he's already checked."

"Oh, okay." I'm strangely crestfallen. It's bad enough to be a genetic weirdo, but to be the *only weirdo on the planet* feels just a bit worse than that. "So, what now?"

"Ah. That's a question for the rest of the team. You okay to keep talking?"

"I'm as ready as I'll ever be." I force a smile I don't feel, and she levels a knowing look on me.

"Listen, I know this is a lot. But you're not alone, okay? We're in this together, and we're going to make sure you stay safe. Right, Atlas?" She calls over her shoulder without turning.

"Right, Nell."

She grins wickedly. "Do you even know what I just said?"

"No, but I assume it was soothing in some way." He saunters over and snakes his giant arm around her waist possessively, and I'm hit with another pang of jealousy. They really are perfect together, despite what an odd picture they make.

"I just told her that she and I were going to run away to the Polynesian Islands for a round of expensive spa treatments in paradise while you hunt down all the bad guys for us."

He arches an eyebrow and looks down at her, as if he's trying to decide if she's serious or not. "You know I'll never say no to you being out of danger, if that's what you'd like."

She rolls her eyes, and smacks him lightly on the chest. "And leave my cuddle mountain? I don't think so."

His longsuffering sigh at the ridiculous nickname makes me laugh, and Nell's wicked grin makes me laugh even harder.

While we're joking around, Easton has already gotten the holographs up and running again, so we all settle back into our original seats. Glitch is slumped slightly in his chair and Sadie's cheeks are pink, as if they'd been having a sidebar while Nell sorted me out.

"So, where were we?" Patrick starts off, rubbing Sadie's shoulders while he talks.

"Action plan. What's next?" Nell surprises me by going straight to the bottom line.

"I think it's time we move Demy to a safe house inside our network. There are too many variables here, and too much outside of our control. A smaller, more remote location would be better for her safety while we sort out how to get the Cabal permanently taken care of." Easton chimes in next, surprising me. He's usually so quiet, it's unlike him to speak out of turn.

"Agreed," Atlas says.

"Well, hold on, though. She's in the middle of the New Lives Program. She's involved here. You can't just snatch her away from the men she's building a connection with," Sadie chimes in.

Oh, God. I haven't even thought of what I'm going to say to Beckett and Fletcher. I have to tell them, now that we know for sure it's me the Cabal's after. What if they're angry? What if they want to leave? They have that option, and I wouldn't blame them. But starting this whole mess over from scratch? Tears prickle the backs of my eyes, and I close them to prevent any from escaping. I am not about to sit here and cry like a baby in front of all these important people. Absolutely not.

"She doesn't have to be snatched; it can be up to her how to proceed. If she wants, they can both come. Or just one, if she's ready to decide. But as we all know from personal experience, the honeymoon centers aren't set up for the level of defensibility we'd need if they keep coming after her at this pace. Although I don't think both of your matches would agree to lockdown, I'm willing to try if that's what you want, Demy." Atlas shifts his shrewd gaze to me instead of the holograms, and I want to shrink into the seat and disappear.

Who doesn't he think would agree to come with me? And only *one*? Beckett is from an important family, and he's left a time or two during the attacks rather than stick around. But Fletcher is so hard to read. Just when I think we're getting closer, there's a wall between us again. It's unnerving that Atlas feels like he has a better grip on which of my matches is more committed to me than I do.

"How long do I have to decide?" I ask, worrying the soda can tab between my thumb and ducking his calculating looks.

"We can give you a day or two, but not much more. The attacks are growing in intensity, and they aren't going to stop until you're gone from here." The blunt words hurt, and my mind flips back to my idle planning in the hallways. Wouldn't everyone be better off if I just disappeared?

"Will I be going there alone?" The question is quieter than I intended, but my chest is tightening again, and I'm lucky to get the words out at all.

"Of course not!" Nell butts in. "There's no way I'm leaving you alone until this is completely resolved, and I know everyone else feels the same. Right, guys?"

"Right," Atlas and Easton agree one after the other.

"So it's settled. No going off alone. We're in this together for the long haul, you got it, lady?"

Relief floods me, and the tears I was so determined not to let loose escape me anyways.

"Aww, don't cry. It's going to be okay." She hugs me fiercely, scrubbing up and down on my back as she talks.

"It would be better, though, if you were prepared to choose one match. The smaller our footprint is, the less likely we are to be discovered before we can get this sorted out. Are you close to a decision?" Atlas is all business, and completely unfazed by my tears.

Am I close to a decision? Morbid amusement bubbles up my throat. *Not in the slightest.*

"I'll decide by tomorrow night."

CHAPTER TWENTY-FIVE
GETTING SERIOUS
DEMY

That night, I can't bring myself to schedule a date. My brain is too clouded, too confused to know what questions to ask the guys, what to *decide*, and what to base the decision on. So, I don't. I push it all off for one last day and invite Nell to have a movie night in the living room downstairs. She accepts, and cancels her evening plans with her guys on the spot. We gather after dinner. I haul blankets and pillows from our beds and she raids the pantry for a junk food smorgasbord, as is her specialty. For a girl studying medicine, she doesn't care much about nutrition, and I kind of love her for it.

I'm rearranging the couches so the biggest one faces the TV head on, when the front door clicks open. *Great. One of the guys clearly didn't get the message.* Abandoning the couch mission, I stomp towards the foyer, already scolding whoever it is as I round the doorway.

"Listen, I know we had plans tonight, but, Nell and I just need a little girl time, and we will be back together *tomorrow*, so if you don't mind—"

"Geez, I'm gone for over a week, and this is the welcome I get?" Cammie's cheerful sarcasm hits me like a lightning bolt, and I freeze, as if my ears are tricking me. But it's her, her bruises are yellowish-green and mottled, but she's grinning, and holding her arms out wide for a hug. I'm across the floor in three seconds flat, wrapping her in a hug.

"Nell! Get your butt in here, Cammie's back!"

"Okay, killer, my ribs still hurt and my ears don't need to start ringing again."

"Sorry!" I immediately release her, and straighten guiltily as Nell bounds out of the kitchen and starts a chain reaction of weird handshake moves with Cammie.

"I missed you, too," Cammie says with a grin that encompasses us both.

"So, how are you feeling? You scared the crap out of us," Nell says.

"I'm . . . here. I'm still sore, and the cracked ribs are going to take a while to heal up." She lets one of her hands flutter over the sore area before pointedly dropping it back to her side.

"Right, but getting attacked is as much *mental* as it is physical. How are you doing with the matches you have left?"

"I still have them all. I asked them to let me get back here before we resumed our matching activities. I didn't really want all those drool-worthy dudes hanging out over my hospital bed while I was looking like dog doo."

I snort at that description. "I don't think they would have cared how you looked, Cam. And if they did? Ditch 'em. Hopefully they were all supportive?"

"They were all *pissed*. And at least two flew out to give reports to the justice about his sketchy behavior, to help with his legal charges. Anyways. I really don't want to talk about it. I just want to be here with my girls."

She wraps one arm around both of our necks and squeezes us to her for a long moment. When she pulls back, the usual naughty glimmer is back in her eyes.

"Did anything interesting happen while I was gone? Tell me that all the hotties are still here, and then give me a play-by-play. I don't want to miss *anything*." She waggles her eyebrows saucily. "Wait, where's Leilani, anyway? Off on a date?"

"Well, actually . . . Leilani is already gone on her honeymoon," I answer.

Her jaw drops, and for the first time in our short acquaintance, Cammie is completely speechless.

"That little *tramp*! She got married without me?" She props both fists on her hips. "Which honeymoon resort did they get off to? I'm going to pick this week, and go give her a piece of my mind. We had a pact! Ooh, wait. She didn't marry that Campbell guy, did she? I do *not* want to honeymoon with him. I want to lay on a beach in a skimpy bikini with eye candy, and that guy is *not* it. Ya feel me?"

"You're a psycho. No worries—she picked Kellan. Now, save any more questions for after movie night, capiche? I've got to go grab the salt round." Nell points two fingers back and forth between her eyes and Cammie's a few times before skating back to the kitchen to gather another batch of snacks.

"The salt round?" Cammie questions as she trails me back into the living room.

"She's got some weird theory about how as the night progresses you have to change flavors? So far we've got sweet, sour, and she's working on salty. She was muttering about creamy, but I don't know how she expects us to eat more than this." I point to the overburdened coffee table, and Cammie grins.

"God, I've missed you guys. Even if Leilani is dead to me now." She grabs a package of sour gummies, and rips it open with a savage expression.

"Oh, give her a break." I go back to moving the couch. "You getting attacked freaked her out. She didn't want to stay here without *you*."

"Aww. Okay, that kind of makes sense. I guess she's actually a goddess." She pops three gummies into her mouth and puckers her mouth as she drops onto the couch mid-move.

"Do you mind?"

"Nope, not at all."

I sigh, but don't make her get up as I shove it the last foot into place. Either she's a featherweight, or my excessive gym time has really paid off. Maybe both.

Nell bustles in, arms full of chip bags, a bowl full of some kind of conglomeration of snacks coated in what looks like peanut butter with sprinkles, and a fistful of spoons. "Okay, salty is here and creamy has been staged in the fridge. It's time to roll the movie."

"What are we watching, anyways?" I ask, settling on one end of the couch and grabbing a package of tiny, multi-colored candies. They're all oddly shaped, but I'm pretty sure all the colors are the same flavor: sugar.

"It's a classic that perfectly suits our current situation: How to Lose a Guy in Ten Days."

I nearly suck a candy up my nose. "I'm sorry, what?"

"You've never seen it? This is going to be even better than I planned! You'll laugh, you'll cry, you'll want to steal a canary di-amond necklace and put an ugly sweater on a dog." She laughs darkly and hits a button on her fertility tracker, and the opening credits start. "Now everybody be quiet. This is a classic for a reason."

When the movie ends, the three of us are floating on a cloud of feelings and junk food. We've all spread out on the couch, legs entangled and blankets half-pooled on the floor. The credits roll, and I stare at the ceiling.

"Guys, I need some advice."

"Don't eat all the marshmallows next time if you don't want to be elbowed in the ribs," Nell snarks, and I huff out a laugh.

"I'm *serious*, real advice. About who to pick," I say, the last part barely a whisper.

"Ooh, I love it!" Cammie springs upright like a rabbit on speed and starts braiding her hair back from her face. "Let's do it. Lay it out for us, and we'll help you. Are you ready to choose?"

I make brief eye contact with Nell, and tell her the only part that matters. "I'm going to decide tomorrow. But . . . I just have such conflicting feelings. I know it's time, but . . . they're completely different."

"Don't focus on the decision. Just walk us through the conflicts. No pressure." Nell's still reclining on the other arm of the couch, but her gaze is intent.

"Yeah, you can't decide until you untangle it all. Consider us your personal detanglers." Tying off her braid, she shifts so she's facing me square on, and nods for me to start talking.

"Well . . . They're both really nice. They're both handsome, and they've been perfect gentlemen, unlike Jax." I shudder at the reminder of his toxic behavior.

"Yeah, but that's the surface. Let's get deeper, here. Pick one, and tell us what's holding you back from him, then we'll do the other," Nell suggests.

"Start with Beckett. I love those suits," Cammie says with a dreamy sigh.

"Beckett . . . is complicated. He's made it very clear that he's committed to a match between us, which is good. He's been interested in me, and what I have to say. He's been attentive on dates, and not complained about all the self-defense exercises I've been making them do."

"But?" Nell prods.

"But . . . he's really rich, and from an important family. While he's been respectful and attentive, he has also made it very clear at every opportunity that he has expectations for how I'll behave and dress as his wife. I was running late for a date once, and ran out of here literally barefoot." I squint at Nell, the one who made me late, and she cracks a grin. "He didn't take it too well, and made someone come and get shoes for me while we stood awkwardly on the porch. He wasn't mean about it, but he wasn't flexible, either. I'm human. I'm going to make mistakes anyways, but add in the fact that we come from *completely opposite* social stratospheres . . . it feels like I'll live the rest of my life with him as a disappointment that he has to cover for."

"Ouch." Cammie clutches her chest like she's been stabbed. "Have you told him that? Because I can't imagine he's trying to make you feel like a disappointment. You said he's been respectful. Maybe that's just your interpretation, and he doesn't know you'd feel that way? I mean, have you *shared* your background? There's no shame in being broke, Demy. You can learn how to use the right fork and swipe his credit card for all the right clothes. Heck, I'd be *happy* to teach you that part." She winks, and I appreciate the touch of humor.

"I haven't told him, no. But, I'm going to go on one last date with both of them tomorrow, and get out any last questions and conversations."

"That's smart," Nell interjects. "Get your thoughts and questions straight, and then lay it all on the table tomorrow. You can't hold back, as hard as that is. And listen . . . you know I came from a similar background as you. We were dirt poor, and my uncle was an abusive drunk. But Atlas accepts me for who I am, warts and all. If either one of them can't do that for you? He's not the one. That's it. If he really cares about you and wants you to thrive in his circles, he'll link arms with you and *help you* fit in. He won't leave you to the side like some sort of wife-erella. But you have to want that. Do you want to join the upper echelons of society and swan around to parties with a security detail and wear ball gowns for the rest of your life, while he runs a multi-billion dollar business empire?"

I swallow hard, feeling a little dead inside at the life she's out-lined. "Is that all you think my life would be? Meaningless parties and hours spent getting dressed up?"

"It doesn't have to be, but you need to know what you want. Some people would freaking *love* to worry about nothing while a rich man handles everything. Other people would feel like it was a cage. Only you can decide what you want." She flicks her eyes to Cammie briefly before adding, "I imagine he'd also have you with a security detail at all times, since he's an important man."

"Being a wealthy wife doesn't *have* to be all frivolous, though. Even if you don't want to work a job or in the business yourself, there are plenty of charities out there that need people. With so much focused on survival these days, someone with a hundred percent free time could do a lot of good in the world. You could become the face of change for this program. You could lobby to change the interview process, to make sure that people like Vince can't—" She chokes on a sob. I lean forward to hug her, but she holds up a shaking hand. "I'm okay. Really. I'm just saying, marrying Beckett would give you a chance to make a real change in this world. You don't have to be frivolous if you don't want to be."

"That is true," Nell agrees. "I didn't mean to paint it as all negative; big money means big opportunity. It just . . . seems like he *does* expect you to play trophy wife. That doesn't mean he wouldn't be open to anything else, like Cammie suggested. I'm comparing him to Atlas, and he's not your typical billionaire."

Cammie rolls her eyes. "That's an oxymoron. But tell us about Fletcher. What's holding you back from him?"

"Well, he's the polar opposite. He's lived a life of privilege, but chosen to walk away from it due to personal issues with his father. He's still the heir, but he's not actively involved. He's completely relaxed, and we fit together like old friends. There are a lot of sparks between us, and he makes me feel alive." I look down, feeling my cheeks heat as I remember our stolen kisses, and climbing on the roof just for the heck of it.

"Sparks are good, and he definitely seems more down to earth. So, what's the problem? Maybe it's him?" Cammie presses. "You are trying to make a baby, after all. Sparks are gonna grease the skids a heck of a lot."

"Well . . . I feel like I never know where I stand with him. If Beckett's clear and direct, Fletcher is vague, and noncommittal. He's only once actually said anything that made me feel he was all in, and then he pulled back again. What if he doesn't want to marry *me*? He was good-looking enough that you picked him as a secondary match—and he'd probably get matched again if I released him."

"That is a problem," Nell murmurs. "You need to be sure that he's in it for you, because it's a bumpy ride." She raises one eyebrow pointedly.

It's going to be even bumpier, since I'm being targeted by the Cabal.

"Maybe he's just a reserved guy, Demy. I mean, we only went on one date alone, and he was reserved with me, too. It's not like he was all over me and he's holding back from you, so I hope I haven't given you that impression. I think with a guy like that, you just have to put it all out there, and see what he says. I'm not saying an ultimatum, but if you lay it out that you think he's not that into you, and he doesn't tell you otherwise . . . well, he's proven that he isn't. And that's okay, but you need to hear that from the horse's mouth. You can't guess what's in somebody else's heart."

"Yeah," I say, dread pooling in my stomach. "Thanks, guys. I think I know what I need to say tomorrow. And I know how I want it to go, but if it doesn't, I can deal with that."

"Anytime, girl. You're family now, and we have to stick together." Nell rises from the couch and gives me a quick squeeze. "Get some sleep, and you'll be ready to face the day tomorrow."

"We're here if you need us, Demy." She hugs me too, twining both arms around my neck and pulling me in close to whisper. "You were there for me when I needed you, and I'm here for you, too."

Tears prickle my eyes, and I blink quickly as I pull back, not wanting to start crying. That won't fix anything, and it won't help me make the biggest decision of my life. I take a few deep breaths, and head up to my room. It's going to be a long night of staring at the ceiling.

CHAPTER TWENTY-SIX

ELECTRIC

DEMY

My date with Beckett is first, starting mid-morning. I was feeling like a chicken when I picked the times and decided to save the awful "Are you actually into me?" conversation with Fletcher for last. We are meeting on the porch, but Nell intercepts me in the foyer as I'm walking out.

"Demy! Hey, listen. Atlas messaged me this morning. I know this is a big day for you, and we don't want to impinge on that. But, he's also worried that the Cabal might try something at any time, and we don't want to leave you alone with just one man at any point. So, we're going to double on both of your dates today, so Atlas can be there in case anything goes sideways. I promise we'll give you a wide berth, so you have privacy for the conversations you need."

I meet her worried gaze and nod. "It's okay, Nell, that's probably smart. So, you're coming to the lake with us?"

"Yep, we already told the kitchen we need to double up on the picnic lunch."

"Perfect. Well, then, let's go. Beckett doesn't like it when I'm late."

She shoots me a sideways glance but doesn't comment. We walk out onto the porch one minute before our scheduled meeting time, and find Beckett already waiting, and Atlas coming down the path. They're a stark juxtaposition, Atlas is a towering menace, wearing all black and covered in tattoos, his blond hair shaved on the sides. Beckett is the picture of gentility, wearing khaki slacks, a soft-looking blue button-down, and perfectly styled dark hair. His jaw is freshly shaved, and I wonder what it would feel like to run my fingers over his skin there.

"Demy, you look exquisite as always. Good morning, Nell. You look lovely also."

We meet at the bottom of the stairs, and he extends his hand, twining his fingers with mine when I accept it and squeezing softly.

"Thanks, you look spiffy yourself." Nell shoots finger guns at him before parting ways and heading for Atlas, arms open wide.

"She's something else, isn't she?" he asks in an amused tone.

"Yeah, she's great."

"I see you wore your earrings. I'm glad you like them." He looks down at me quizzically when I don't respond right away. "Are you okay? You seem nervous today."

"Oh. Yeah, I'm fine. I think it's time to make a decision, though. So, nerves. Yes. I've got them." I look down at my feet.

His fingertips are firm but gentle on my chin as he pulls me up to look in my eyes. "Don't be nervous. You know what the right decision is. You just have to be honest with yourself."

I nod, unable to form words. He sounds so *sure*. Does he think he's the right decision? Or that he's not? I can't tell.

We walk hand in hand down a meandering path lined with soft white and pink flowers for fifteen minutes, until we leave the manicured lawn, and walk under a canopy of oak trees, the fallen leaves squishing softly underfoot. I can smell the water before I can see it, the soft, earthy smell of fresh water making me happy as the trees open up to reveal a medium-sized lake, with a dock off to the right side, and several different types of boats just big enough for two tied off in a neat row.

We take our time strolling around the lake, with Nell and Atlas ahead of us chatting quietly. They're already choosing a boat when Beckett suddenly stops under the last oak tree before the grounds open up to a grassy meadow bordering the right side of the lake.

"You're making a decision today, but there's an important piece of the puzzle you don't have yet."

"Okay . . ." I trail off, confused. But he doesn't answer me with words. He steps forward, closing the distance between us, and disentangling his fingers from mine. His fingertips leave a trail of fire behind as he runs them lightly up my arm, across my collar bone, and finally up my neck to cup my cheek in his. His touch is feather light and scalding at once, and I find myself leaning into his touch, waiting to see what's next.

He doesn't make me wait long. Beckett is as dominant physically as he is with every other aspect of his life, and within a heartbeat, his lips are on mine, firm and unyielding. He tangles both hands in my hair, urging me to turn my head to the side. When I do his lips slant across mine, deepening the kiss, and pulling me closer against his chest. My hands fly up, one resting on his waist, the other on his chest, and I can feel the flex of his muscles underneath my palms as he worships my lips.

When he pulls back, I'm breathless, and it feels like he's branded me as *his*. Whatever doubts I had about his feelings on the right choice, they've flown from my head. Beckett is all in, and he's not holding back.

"You're incredible, Demelza. I hope you know that." He runs a finger through my hair, playing with the end of a lock, twisting the black strands between his fingers. Pulling me gently forward again, he brushes a gentle kiss against my lips, this one the polar opposite, but no less scorching than the first. "Come on, let's get out there, and then you can ask me all of your questions." He gives me a cocky grin and twines our fingers back together for the rest of the distance to the small dock.

Butterflies are still swarming in my stomach as we choose our boat. It was so unexpected, not to mention unexpectedly *good*, that I'm finding myself more confused. I need to lay out my worries for him and see what he says. Maybe I've built too much up regarding his expectations, like Cammie thought, and I'm putting words in his mouth. I blow out a breath slowly to steady myself.

"How's this one? Word on the street is you like rowing at the gym," Beckett teases as he points out a small wooden boat with two oars resting in cradles. A simple cushioned wooden seat bisecting the keel is the only other thing in it.

"It's perfect, and I *do* love rowing. Not as much as archery, though, now that I've tried it."

"Well then, let's do it. I can't wait to see your skills in action." His smile is warm, and for the first time, it's like the pressure between us vanishes. We're just two people, having fun and doing a casual activity. No expectations, no tension.

He climbs in first, and then offers me a hand to steady me as I step into the boat. Unlike rowing in the gym, the boat wobbles un-nervingly when you're standing up, and I hurry to take my seat on the bench next to him. It takes us a couple minutes to get in synch with rowing, but when it clicks, we're gliding across the water with ease. We row around enjoying the quiet for a few moments, and I realize he's waiting on me to start the conversation.

"I'm worried you'll be disappointed, having me as a wife." I blurt the words, unable to hold back and still say what I need to say.

"I was . . . not expecting that. Can I ask why?" He's still looking ahead, focusing on steering the boat, but his voice is calm, placid as the lake water underneath us.

"I don't know. It just feels like we come from such different backgrounds. I'm broke, Beckett. I had ten bucks to my name when the bus picked me up. I only joined the program because I had run out of money to keep running, and I was exhausted. I don't know which fork to use if they put out more than two. I don't feel comfortable wearing giant, glittery ball gowns. And heels? Well, they're beautiful for a special evening, but that's not who I am every day. You—you're so put together, always. Even now, we're outside doing a physical activity, and there's not a hair out of place. You're always dressed to the nines, always perfect, and I feel . . ." I trail off, unsure how to describe it without the word *inferior*, and that burns the back of my throat. I can't bring myself to admit it, even with the rest.

"Demelza, stop for a second. Look at me. Please?" he adds, when I don't immediately do as he says.

Shame and embarrassment must be written all over my face, because he shakes his head at me when I look up.

"I don't care if you're poor. Not one bit. What is the point of me having money, if I can't share it with someone? You might not have wealth of your own, but do you understand how important it is to me to build a family? I can have all the money in the world, but you can't buy a child, a wife, and a happy home. You can't buy love, or devotion. And yes, I care about respectability, and getting the small details right. It was drilled into me from an early age. But we can find tutors for you—it doesn't have to be a source of embarrassment. Nobody is born knowing which one is the lobster fork. You can learn. I won't be disappointed, as long as you do your best."

He wraps me in a hug, and I accept it. But a little part of me, deep down, feels withered, like a dandelion on a hot sidewalk. *You can learn. Try your best.* There's nothing wrong with that, per se, but he didn't disagree. The way I am now? That would disappoint him. All that lovely sentimentality can't cover the fact that he wants a wife like him. Proper. Genteel. Perfect.

"See, Beckett, that's part of what I'm trying to explain. Ever since our very first date—"

"Atlas! Atlas!" We spring apart at the yell, and I spot one of the security guards racing across the open meadow towards the small dock, waving to get Atlas's attention.

He immediately starts rowing toward shore, and we follow. Nell and Atlas are closer to the dock, so we're still in the middle of the lake when he and Nell climb out to meet the security guard. The man is running hard, arms pumping hard, and when he skids to a stop on the dock, he leans over and braces both hands on his knees. We're rowing hard to see what's up, and his words chill me to the bone as they carry across the water.

"We found the mole!"

Atlas looks confused. "What are you talking about?"

"Sorry I'm so short of breath. Your radio isn't working, so I ran to get you the news right away." The man shoves himself upright, resting a hand on Atlas's shoulder, and I recognize him. It's Lars. My blood feels like ice, and I grip the oar harder as we paddle.

"Atlas, Cabal!" Nell calls out, pointing towards the treeline, and everything seems to happen at once. Atlas turns halfway towards the tree line where black SUVs are rolling to a stop, and Lars is suddenly in motion—there's something in his hand, and Atlas yelps, grabbing his neck before falling to the dock like a sack of bricks.

Nell screams and tries to lunge for him, but Lars grabs her. He wraps a thick arm around her neck and jerks her against his chest, and horror washes over me as he pulls out his pistol and presses the muzzle against her temple. She stills when she feels the bite of the cold metal, but doesn't take her eyes off Atlas.

"What did you do to him?!" Her voice is shaking. "If you've hurt him, I swear—"

"Shut up! Do you want me to shoot you? Shut your mouth, and you two, get over here and out of the boat. If you try anything, I'll kill her, and leave her dead body right here for him to find when he wakes up."

We'd frozen when he attacked Atlas, but we both start rowing again, more slowly than we were. I'm terrified, but I can't take chances with Nell's life. It doesn't take long for us to reach the dock, and Lars gestures impatiently with the barrel of the gun for us to climb out.

"Hurry it up, we've got somewhere to be."

"Why are you doing this? You're a guard here. They know who you are. Your life is *over* if you don't stop this right now," Beckett threatens.

He tightens his grip on Nell's windpipe, and she scratches desperately at his arm as her airway is cut off, and levels the pistol straight at Beckett's forehead. "My orders only state that the women have to be brought in alive. Would you like to be the carcass he wakes up to?"

249

His orders. Oh God, he's been working for the Cabal the entire time. I trusted him, and he was planning to betray me all along. Was anything he told me even true?

"Beckett, just do what he says, please." I grip his arm so hard, my fingernails are probably digging into his flesh.

He falls silent with a jerk of his head. And Lars gestures for us to walk ahead of him. "Hang a left at the end of the dock and walk straight towards the tree line. It's easier to haul in one woman than three of you, so by all means, make my job easier and do something stupid. No? Shame."

He sounds half-crazed but we follow his directions to a T. I can't risk Nell or Beckett, even though I know this isn't going to end well. Not unless there's some kind of miracle, where somebody realizes what's happened to Atlas before we're taken off the NLC's property. As we enter the thin smattering of trees, my hopes of rescue start to sink. A quick glance over my shoulder shows that he's loosened the death grip on Nell's neck, but the pistol is still firmly locked against her temple.

Tears are trailing non-stop down her cheeks, and I want to scream. I stumble over a downed branch, but Beckett catches me before I can fall.

"Pay attention, and keep your eyes forward. We don't have all day."

A few more minutes of walking, and my chest tightens at the sight of a cluster of black-cloaked men standing behind a perimeter fence, on what looks like an unpaved service road. The fence is at least ten feet high, and has signs tacked every fifteen feet with electricity bolts and "Hazard" in neon yellow. They've all got weapons in their hands, save for one with a huge pair of bolt cutters and thick rubber gloves that go up to his elbows.

My taser is still in my pocket! I just need an opening, and maybe I can cause a distraction.

They hear us coming, and every one of them turns to stare as we approach. When we're only fifteen feet away, one of them barks an order into a comm wristband, and an explosion rocks the ground under our feet.

I freeze and duck on instinct, but the explosion isn't here. When I spin towards the sound, it's across the property, at the opposite end of the grounds. The man with the bolt cutters doesn't waste any time, and by the time we've recovered from the explosion, he's got a sizable hole cut out of the fence, and is peeling it open like a tin can. He holds it open with the rubber gloves, and the men on the other side surge through, weapons raised.

Instinct kicks in, and I turn to bolt to the side, grabbing for my taser but one of them crashes into me, tackling me into the dirt and kicking up leaf litter. Wrenching hard under the man's weight on my back, I manage to free the taser. Out of nowhere, a black boot descends, crushing my hand and the taser down into the dirt. A scream tears from my throat at the pain, and it feels like several of the little bones in my hand and fingers have broken under the vicious boot. When he removes his boot, the taser is crunched and broken on the ground, and one of my fingers won't straighten.

I clutch it to my chest as he pulls me roughly to my feet. My ears are ringing, but whether it's from anxiety or getting tackled, I can't tell. Glancing around frantically, I see that Nell and Beckett are on their feet and already through the hole in the fence, being shoved towards the closest SUV with blacked out windows and lights. One of our captors opens the back hatch, and Nell is manhandled into the back, despite a solid kick to the groin she lands on one of the men. She's spitting a string of curses as the one she kicked reaches in after her, and she abruptly falls silent.

My breath comes in short, quick gasps, as I'm forced through the fence by the painful grip on my upper arms. Beckett is forced into the SUV next, and I see them jab him in the neck with a syringe as he abruptly collapses against the SUV's carpeted floor. I drag my feet and try to sweep my leg out to dislodge my guard, but he sees the move coming and shoves me forward, into Lars's waiting arms.

He sneers at me as he puts me in the same headlock he used on Nell, tightening it to the point where I can't breathe. My lungs burn and I thrash as the seconds tick by, but he chuckles darkly in my ear, enjoying the struggle. *This man would enjoy killing me.*

I scratch at his face and ears, but all too soon my limbs start to grow weak, and I make one last-ditch effort to donkey kick him in the kneecap—anything to get him to let me get the lungful of air I so desperately crave—but I miss. My vision is swimming and just as my arms start to fall away, limp, the pressure disappears from my windpipe. I gasp, eager for sweet, sweet oxygen, when his hand clamps over my nose and mouth, smothering me with a foul-smelling cloth. I suck the fumes down deep, no more able to stop the reflex than I could stop my own heart beating.

I thrash again, but his arm is tight and immovable around my chest, like a steel band. I blink once, twice, and then I'm moving through air thick as soup, and being shoved into the back of the SUV. I land next to Nell's limp form and fixate on the pulse thumping steadily in her neck. The sound of slamming doors is the last thing I hear as my world fades to black.

Thank you so much for reading Marked! Whether this is your first book of mine or you're already a Populations Crumble fan, I hope you enjoyed the ride. This book was really fun to write, and I enjoyed being back in this world, seeing the changes and also some familiar faces. I'm already working on book two, Captive!

The second book is available for pre-order now (or, you can add it to your reading list if you're a Kindle Unlimited reader):

Pre-Order Captive Now!

While you're waiting . . .

Download a free bonus map of the NAA Tri-States here

Wondering how it all began? Catch up on the Populations Crumble trilogy here!

CHAPTER TWENTY-SEVEN

PLAYLIST

Pompeii—Bastille

The Sound of Silence—Disturbed

I'm Not Alright—Shinedown

Fire—Sara Bareilles

Paper Rings—Taylor Swift

Stitches—Shawn Mendes

The Other Girl—Kelsea Ballerini & Halsey

I'll Follow You—Shinedown

Dancing in the Moonlight—King Harvest

If You Love Her—Forest Blakk

Wrecking Ball—Miley Cyrus

Sound of Madness—Shinedown

BEFORE YOU GO . . .

Thank you for spending your free time with me, in my world and following my characters—it is a true honor. Demy is the reason this book was written; she came to me one day, exactly as the first scene is written. Wearing tatty clothes, and running for all she was worth, straight towards the NLC's bus of doom. Basically, she was the complete opposite of all the characters in the first trilogy. Her story wanted to be told, and I hope you enjoyed reading it as much as I enjoyed writing it and delving back into this familiar world.

I absolutely love to see your reviews and read your kind words, so if you have the time to drop some stars for Marked, I would appreciate it so much! Your reviews and good ratings help new readers find my books, and that's priceless! It also shows publishers and agents that my books are well-received, and thanks to all of your kind words on Dwindle, I was picked up by a literary agent this year. That's all you, guys. All your kindness and love, and it's opening doors that I never dreamed would be opened.

I'm not supposed to cry writing end notes, am I? Sorry. Back to business!

As a newsletter sign up bonus, I have created a map of the NAA's tri-states, because I know you were just all *dying* for all the hairy details, right? Download it here:

If you want updates on my latest releases and publishing process, as always you can follow me on Facebook here @kagandyauthor, **join my super awesome (and brand new!) reader group YA Dystopian Romance Book Lovers here,** find me on Instagram @kagandyauthor, or email me any time at kagandyauthor@gmail.com. I'd love to hear from you. :)

About the Author

K. A. Gandy was born and raised in Jacksonville, Florida, and is married with two kids. She has worked as a restaurant hostess, library book shelver, ranch hand, tour guide, Realtor, tech whiz, landlord, and small business consultant, all in addition to pursuing her passion for writing. She likes to write late in the evenings and thinks drinking hot tea and baking great cookies fuels hopes and dreams. If you would like to find more of her works, you can sign up for her newsletter here. You can also get updates on Facebook here.

MORE BY K. A. GANDY

Reign (Populations Crumble, Book 3)

Kidnapped from their honeymoon resort, nothing is as it seems. Betrayal, intrigue, and secrets abound as Sadie works to free the captive women. But will she end up the savior, or the next captive?

Marked (Populations Crumble: Resurgence, Book 1)

She doesn't want to get married, but with her would-be captors on her heels, she's got no choice but to hope the NLC's strict security protocols will be a safe haven. Marriage is a small price to pay for her life, after all.

Captive (Populations Crumble: Resurgence, Book 2)

When things go from bad to worse, Demy and Nell's very survival is on the line.

Fantasy

Aerthen Sight (An'Loran Chronicles, FREE Prequel Short)

The Lost Talisman(An'Loran Chronicles, Book 1)

The Hatchling – Pre-order now!(An'Loran Chronicles, Book 2)

www.ingramcontent.com/pod-product-compliance
Lightning Source LLC
Chambersburg PA
CBHW031217020726
47499CB00002B/618